D1444223

MICHAEL Z. LEWIN

THE ENEMIES WITHIN

THE MYSTERIOUS PRESS

New York • Tokyo • Sweden • Milan

Published by Warner Books

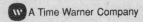 A Time Warner Company

MYSTERIOUS PRESS EDITION

Copyright © 1974 by Michael Z. Lewin
All rights reserved.

This Mysterious Press Edition is published by arrangement with
the author.

Cover design by Andrew Newman
Cover illustration by Mike Fisher

The Mysterious Press name and logo are trademarks of Warner
Books, Inc.

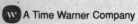 Mysterious Press books are published by
Warner Books, Inc.
666 Fifth Avenue
New York, New York 10103

A Time Warner Company

Printed in the United States of America

First Mysterious Press Printing: June, 1991

10 9 8 7 6 5 4 3 2 1

to
MOM
and
POP

THE
ENEMIES WITHIN

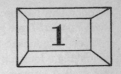

1

I spent the day at the races. Tropical Park, it was. In Florida, where the going was good and the weather a balm. I turned a profit of eighty-two cents, before expenses, and only missed making my fortune because a three-year-old making its first start—this was December no less—had an abnormally long nose at fifty to one. My animal was at elevens and I'd been so sure and so right he'd run the favorites off the map that I didn't cover him to place.

The slushy snow was ankle deep. It was a quarter past five and the dead of night when I got home. One thing about where I live these days, it's a lot shorter walk to my bookie's.

By five thirty I was well into relieving the if-only's with a quart of beer. Feet on the windowsill like a winner. I have a southern exposure now. Though it only exposes the six-story building across the street.

At five forty-five I heard someone fumbling at the office door. I was stilled with surprise. But there was no mistaking the sound.

I roused myself and put in the nine strides from my living room window to my office door. Proper leverage on the knob —lift, then pull. Open my sesame.

A man, on the hefty side and of average height, was deciding whether or not to leave. From the safety of his open overcoat, jacket and tie, he looked me up and down. "You are Albert Samson, then?"

"I am."

"May I come in?" Sarcastic.

"Sorry about that," I said as I made way for him. "You see, until June I had my office in another building, but I got evicted because they're tearing it down to put up the Pacers' new stadium so I had to move. To save some money I brought my old door, only it doesn't quite fit whereas in my last place it was always open." I get garrulous halfway through a quart.

"I see." He looked me over, then the office, and seemed to be making a long job of it. Which gave me time to notice he had grayed temples. Artificially gray. I'm not refined about such things. His streaks had to be pretty crude for me to notice.

I gestured him to a chair. Then went to post behind my desk.

"Excellent," he said with surprising conviction.

"Oh yeah?"

"I have an errand needs doing, Mr. Samson. I hope you will consider it."

I had time to listen. I pulled out the notebook, leafed through, pretending some of the pages weren't blank, and said, "Shoot."

"I am in a difficult position." He sniffled. "I write plays, you see. Now a man, a Mr. Bartholomew, has come to town from Chicago for the purpose of reading one of my plays to decide whether he will put up the money to produce it. You see?"

"I see." More accurately, I saw and I didn't see.

"He is staying at the Kings and Queens Motel. 2002 West Washington Street. Do you know it?"

"No. But I can find it."

"Room 17. Now, the problem is this. I gave him my play a week ago. Eight days. November twenty-fifth."

"Yes?"

"Now he refuses to give it back to me."

"What?"

"He won't give it back." Sounded kind of pitiful. "And it's the only copy I have."

"You didn't keep a carbon?"

He seemed surprised I should ask. He would be even more surprised, no doubt, to find a dusty old play of mine in my bottom dresser drawer.

"Why no. I never expected to have a problem like this."

"And what exactly do you mean, won't give it back?"

He hesitated. My asking questions was not how things should be. "Well, I saw him this afternoon and he laughed at me. He said he had it and he was going to keep it. More than that. He threatened me if I tried to get it back. He carries a gun, Mr. Samson."

"This must be some play."

"Well," he said modestly, "I like it."

Stay alive long enough and you get all kinds. "I have a friend at police headquarters," I said, "who should be just about right for helping you with this problem."

"Oh, I don't want the police."

And here I'd hoped to give Miller something important to work on for a change. "Why not?"

"A lot of reasons," he said as he tried to think of some. "The play, it isn't too generous to the police, for one thing. And all I want is my manuscript back. Having Bartholomew put in jail wouldn't please me. I mean, if I can get it back from him then maybe he'll still want it badly enough and he'll pay me for it."

"Well, I'll go and ask the man for your play if you want me to. But you'll be paying forty dollars per eight-hour day plus expenses, with a ten-buck minimum."

"Shall I pay you now?" He pulled a ten-dollar bill from an old leather wallet. It was a new ten, and he seemed positively pleased to be handing it to me. But he wasn't making ready to leave.

"You're sure this guy's still in town?" I asked.

"Oh yes. He said he'd be staying for at least a couple more days."

"I'll go tonight, just in case."

"Fine. Excellent."

"I'll need your name and address."

"M. Bennett Willson." He spelled it for me. "I'll give you my shop address. I own an antique shop. The House of Antiquity." It was an East 10th address; a 636 phone.

"And what is the name of the play?"

"Oh. Why will you need that?"

"So when I go to Bartholomew I can tell him what I want."

"I've been thinking about that," he said. "He'll know exactly what you mean if you tell him to 'stop messing with Bennett Willson's property.' "

Come on. " 'Stop messing with Bennett Willson's property'?"

"Yes. I think that's vernacular he'll understand. Exactly."

"You *don't* want me to pick up this play for you then?"

"Oh no. There's no need for you actually to get the manuscript. I want you more to show that I am willing to take action if he continues to act badly." Maybe I looked confused. "I'm worried about keeping his good will, you see, if there is a chance."

"In case he finally does decide to produce this play you won't tell me the title of?"

"It's not that I won't tell you. It's just you won't need it."

"What's the title?"

"The Kokomo Case."

"The Kokomo Case?"

"That's right. But as I've said, I've given considerable thought about the best way to approach Bartholomew. And I'm sure if you kind of burst in on him . . . dramatically, burst in on his consciousness, as it were."

"Surprise him?"

"That's right. I'm sure that being a kind of tough customer he's used to bullying people and that sort of person usually breaks right down under a strong, forceful attack."

"You have things figured out, don't you?"

"I think so," he said with a glimmer of puffed pride. Then, "I hope so."

"So you want me to burst in on Bartholomew's consciousness and tell him to stop messing with Bennett Willson's property?"

"That's right. Forcefully."

"Threateningly?"

"Oh yes. Please." He hesitated a minute. "That's a good idea," he added. As if to convince me that it had been my idea and not his intention all along.

I just sat for a while. If it's true that it doesn't take much beer to get me tipsy, it's also true that it doesn't take much absurdity to sober me up.

"I'll take your case for you," I said. You only live once.

It shocked him just a little. "Gee, I already thought you had."

After the funny man left, I had quite a chuckle thinking about what Miller would have done with him if I'd been able to steer him police way. I also had another quart of beer.

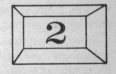

2002 worth of West Washington Street is most of the way to the airport, but not one of the classier areas of town.

Nor was the Kings and Queens one of the classier motels on West Washington Street. It was the kind of place I might stay at. A peculiar choice for a man supposed to have enough money to produce a play he'd stolen. But I am a trusting soul; and it was certain that I didn't have anything better to do.

A kid was behind the desk. "What can I do you for, mister?"

"The guy Bartholomew in Room 17, is he in?"

"How the hell do I know?"

"I just thought you might have noticed. How long has he been registered?"

The body was young but the mind was old. "What's it worth to you?"

"Not much, considering that I know he checked in on the twenty-fifth. I was just trying to crosscheck. Be a buddy and look it up for me. Next time my girl friend's husband is out of town we'll come here." He snorted, but seemed inclined to tell me his hourly rates. "Promise," I said, and crossed my liver. "The next two times."

"You were close," he said. "Seventeen checked in November twenty-second. He's there now if you want to see him. But you better hurry."

"All services laid on?"

"We get a lot of traveling men."

"Can I have a card?" I said, to show sincerity. He got one from under the counter and I left him. To wander in the wet December darkness looking for number 17.

Two rows of motel rooms ran straight in from the road. They looked like the rails on a race course, horse's-eye view. The shuttered windows the eyes of wishing watchers. Watching wishers. Room 17 was second from the end on the right. Just short of the winning post.

I knocked on the door.

Someone inside called, "It's O.K., Sugar." I can be excused for thinking he didn't mean me.

I knocked again.

"Come on in!"

Well, why not? I opened the door and found the room lit only by a blue light. A man was in bed, the covers pulled up to his chin.

"You're a little early," he said, "but I'm ready."

Promises, promises. "Not for me you're not."

"What the fuck!" Bartholomew sat up sharply in bed. His top half, at least, was big. "Who the hell are you?" he said, and he dived for a stack of possessions laid out on a bed table pulled out from the wall to stand next to the middle of the bed.

"Hey! Hey! I'm not here to cause you any trouble," I said quickly, remembering my client's magic word, "gun," and keeping my hands high and visible. "It's not my fault you don't answer the door when people knock."

But he wasn't going for a weapon. He was shoveling private things off the table onto the floor. He wasn't fibbing when he said he was ready.

"Look, buster," he said, his mind back on me, "just what do you want?"

As long as he was unarmed and still in bed—probably too modest to get up—I had what we call the upper hand. I let it hover a bit. "Is there a grown-up light in here?"

He gestured to a desk lamp by the window. I turned it on. Then went to the door and turned off the blue overhead. On the desk there was a lightbulb; no doubt the blue one was part of his overnight kit.

From the door I came over to the bed, pulled up a chair and put my slushy feet up on the bedspread. "So, what is this little thing between you and Bennett Willson?"

"So that's it!" said Bartholomew. Whatever property he was messing with, he had enough other sins to be relieved by this turn in the conversation. "What are you, a little local muscle? Ha! Ha! Little queer like him? This is really funny. Haw! Haw!"

I was glad I had decided to avoid any reference to a play, much less a play called *The Kokomo Case*. It hadn't pushed even my deductive powers to lay odds against there being such a play or this guy being a potential angel.

When Bartholomew had nearly subsided, I leaned a little closer. "I *am* a little local muscle, *buster*. And I *do* want to know why you're doing what you think you're trying to do." It didn't make much sense, but it sounded tough.

Bartholomew wasn't impressed. He no longer even sounded under duress. "Look, I told the little poof what I want. I'm a private dick out of Chicago. I got a guy who wants me to find a girl Willson knew when he was in Kokomo. Early sixties. Your Willson got upset when I found his house out Monrovia way. But all he is doing by sending you in here is telling me he knows something about the lady I'm trying to find."

"What's her name?"

"He knows. Shit, I told him. Melanie Baer. But what she calls herself now I don't know. Where she is now I don't know. Look, you move along now and tell this Willson you scared me good, and all he has to do is give me a convincing lead and I'll go away for a while. Come on, man. Play a little ball."

"What's the name of the man you're working for?"

"You don't listen, do you?" he said less genially.

"You're going to be around town for a while?"

"I'm not exactly packing to go. My client is keen and I'm pacing him like a pro. He's so nutty to get a lead on this broad he'll believe almost anything."

I felt like slugging the guy. It's people like him who give seedy detectives a bad name. I've never done anything like that. I wouldn't even consider it unless I got the chance.

"Look, friend," I said, bringing my feet off his bed harder than I had to, "if you leave town I want to know about it. You keep me informed." I put my hand under my jacket lapel. Boom-boom. My best voice of menace, and all for naught. He seemed much more comfortable—certainly more familiar—with threatening situations than I was. I was surprised he was so easygoing about it all.

"Sure. Sure. Why don't you leave me your card." I brought my wallet out of its holster inside my jacket. Gave him a card. It was fresh and impressive with the new office-apartment address. "Great," he said without looking at it. "Now would you kind of mosey along, because I'm expecting someone."

So I moseyed. And sure enough, I was just letting the door slam when the sensuous woman herself hailed me from the dark, nonstreet end of the motel row.

"Hey, baby. You aren't going to leave me out in the cold just 'cause Sugar's a few minutes late, are you?"

She came up close. A lot closer than my ten dollars could buy.

"No, sweets. I'm just the first shift. You can have him now."

Without dropping an eyelash, she stepped away and knocked on the door. The desk light in the window went out.

The last thing I heard was Bartholomew calling, "Just a minute. Not quite ready."

Lucky Sugar.

Nine thirty, and I drove back to city center. It was a quiet, self-contained world I took with me. Just before I got evicted from my previous office-home of eight years I had sold my car. I have a little panel truck now, and the windowlessness behind me closes in sometimes. On wet winter nights. It's a black Chevy, '65. The car was a Plymouth. I have no brand loyalty.

Moving house disquiets. My new quarters are over a carpet store, still downtown. I didn't find them till the end of September, which meant two months bunking at my mother's. September, not a good time to come to a new place when place is important to you. Funnily it didn't hurt business much. The changes just tore again at my scarry roots.

I didn't really want to go home that night. There was nothing for me there. Just a report to write up. Six boring days' worth of an abortive divorce surveillance. Six days best presented to the lawyer's client as "Nothing," but which I would have to spin out, minute by minute, to prove I was present and awake at the scene.

I didn't go home to work. Instead, I drove to the House of Antiquity on East 10th. Biggish. I was surprised when I saw a bright light on in the office. I wondered if my client was still hard at work at this hour. What could there be to do so late? Hell, no need to patronize.

I pulled up across the street and debated whether to do a little window shopping. But there are limits to the ways of killing even my time and the rain was changing to snow.

It wasn't as if I was following anything as strong as a hunch or enjoying myself enough to feel self-indulgent. I was just upset at the very notion of a man who had walked into my office expecting me—*me*—to do his intimidating for him. The balls! And with a cock-and-bull story like *The Kokomo Case.* "Kace," no doubt. It would be a hot day in a Hoosier winter before we saw that title in lights.

I twiddled my thumbs for two full minutes by the watch, and smiled at myself in the rearview mirror the whole time.

I suppose I couldn't fault the guy completely. Why do people come to someone like me? Mostly they don't, of course. I work for lawyers, or for other detectives who need an extra detector, but not for "people." Once there was a kid, but presumably too young to know better. And I do have the advantage of being the cheapest PI in town. Now I suppose I'd had a guy pick me out *because* I am superficially the least desirable op he could find. What he hadn't had the perspicacity to appreciate was that gloss is cheap and that to appear as grubby as you really are takes a measure of virtue, wisdom and urbanity which your average doltish pri . . .

M. Bennett Willson left the House of Antiquity and locked the door at 10:16. His car, a dark Renault, was parked almost directly in front of the store.

I had to U-turn to follow him. It was already more action than I'd had in my six previous workdays. Twelve-hour shifts at that.

Sure enough, we headed southwest. Through Maywood and Valley Mills, past the turn to West Newton.

Bartholomew had said it upset the man to have his house in Monrovia found out. So maybe it would upset him when he knew I had found it too. I could show him what intimidation is like, that it's not a step to indulge in lightly.

I was curious about other things Bartholomew said. He'd

called Willson queer, for one thing. It was not a fact that had been immediately evident to me. Grayed temples, talk of writing plays, and unfamiliarity with the potboiler sides of life are not the acid tests.

I was also curious about Willson's connection with Bartholomew's subject, Melanie Baer. The original link was in the past, but Bartholomew was right to suspect something current from Willson's behavior.

On the other hand, maybe Willson just didn't like anyone making inquiries in his general vicinity. If he was homosexual, for instance. Indiana ain't the friendliest place. Farm animals or close relations we understand. But never perversion.

Or maybe Willson lived out in the country because he made his own antiques. There are lots of reasons people don't like other people sniffing round.

Willson drove fast and the roads were pretty empty. The only trouble was that outside the city the temperature was lower, the snow higher. We made good time to Monrovia. That is, to near Monrovia. My client didn't drive into town, but turned off Indiana 42 about two miles the Indianapolis side. Onto a straight and narrow country road, and as I turned after him I wondered whether I was going to have trouble avoiding being spotted. But about a quarter of a mile ahead of me I saw Willson turning again and it looked like we were home. I killed my lights and moved up slowly. It was a house. Lights in the windows, twinkling for the antiquarian's return.

The house was surrounded by trees, as if he had made a clearing in the forest to find the room to build. Except all the trees were small and on both sides of the residential site flat fields made even the young trees look like a grove of redwoods.

Through the leafless forest I saw the Renault disappear into a garage. Simultaneously I saw the front door of the house open. I pulled up as close as I dared and stopped to watch.

Willson walked slowly from the garage across the front of the house toward the full silhouette of a thin man standing hands on hips in the doorway.

They stood face to face and talked, neither moving. But when messages were exchanged, Willson trotted up the two steps to the door, and they made up differences with a long embrace.

Then retreated into the house, leaving me parked lightless on a country road outside a farmhouse near Monrovia, Indiana. What was weird was I had the feeling I'd been there before. Part of it was coming off that six-day watch when I would have given my hamburger for a scene like I had just witnessed. But it was also the knowledge I had followed in perhaps the precise footsteps of the Chicago detective, Bartholomew, who was at this moment undoubtedly a good deal more contented with the world than I was.

He must have followed Willson home one night in the two weeks he'd been in town. Seen the scene I had. There was a ring of routine about it all.

It upset me to think that if I drove away now I would know exactly what Bartholomew knew and nothing more. So I slipped out of the truck. I walked slowly, carefully through the tree stalks. I approached the house from its right front corner. One-story frame, not recently built. It looked big close up; it stretched farther in both directions than I'd thought from the road. Originally the house of a small farmer with a big family.

I made my way slowly. All of the windows I came to were dark, but no blinds or curtains were drawn. I passed five windows before I came to the back. I crossed over and turned the corner to start working my way up the other side.

I was six inches from the first window when it lit up like a beacon. I dropped to a crouch and brought an eye up slowly into the nearest corner.

The room's occupant was Willson's friend. He was pointing his bottom at me, bending over an oven's open door. Poking at something. Warmed-over dinner, perhaps. The friend was slightly built, not much over five and a half feet. His hair was cut in what I called a D.A. in my young manhood. Jeans, flannel shirt not tucked in.

He took a casserole dish out of the oven in óven-gloved hands. He set it on a tray. Got utensils from a drawer, condiments from a shelf and carried the trayful out of the room, turning the light out behind him. The friend looked younger than Willson, but not a lot. A little careworn, perhaps. Certainly—well what do you expect—certainly effeminate, with lashy dark eyes.

I continued on my trek to the front of the house. The living room was long and narrow. And in contrast to the other rooms I'd passed it was fully lit. Willson sat with the tray on his knees. His friend wasn't to be seen in the room.

I watched Willson eat. Whatever it was, he ate it with relish. It was full of different colors. I wished I'd brought a plate.

The friend startled me, passing very close to my window. He carried a bottle of beer. Foreign label, but I couldn't make out which. Willson drank from it without benefit of a glass.

Quite a delivery boy this friend, because having paused to deliver the beer and a few words he went out of the room again. I couldn't hear what was said. Double glazing. I turned toward the back of the house, to watch for the kitchen light. But instead the light in the room next to the kitchen came on. I made my way back along the house, curious to see what Friend was bringing Client now.

What I saw was Friend slipping out of his clothes into something more comfortable. Friend took the clothes off carefully, folding them on the bed, back to me. Friend wore ladies' underpants, and frilly at that. They were the only distinguishingly feminine article he wore. But after the panties were off, Friend paused to have a good long look at himself in the mirrored closet door. I had to duck down to avoid being seen in the reflection because the mirror faced the window I was peeping through. I counted a slow ten before I slipped up for another look. Friend was still looking in the mirror. I went down again for twenty. It was when I came up the second time that I got my shock.

Friend was hanging the folded clothes up in the closet. Then he turned to come out of the closet. And that was the shock. Friend was not a boy friend. Friend was a lady.

It was a long drive back to Indianapolis. The temperature had dropped; the road was visibly icy. I was confused, but headed back to my new home with a decisiveness which surprised me. At least it was a home and it was mine and it would not trick me. It was also warm. The simplicity of writing my overdue divorce report appealed to me for the first time and I drove faster than I should have.

When is a queer not a queer? When he decides to live with a woman. Unless Willson was a woman too; that would be the long shot of the day. By following Willson around all night I had moved into unknown territory without thinking about it. It would be hard to tell him what I'd done, what I'd seen. No medals for "beyond the call of duty" in my line.

Maybe it went further back than that. Willson had come to my office and for whatever reason—catching me bored—he had got me to do something bad. I am not in the intimidation side of this business. I'm just not good enough at it. I hired out to collect some bills in my second year—I have no principles against debt work, *any* work—but I just didn't do justice to them; I couldn't collect them. The details are boring—the argument flawed by special circumstances—but by my age you begin to learn the things you can get yourself into with safety and the things you should avoid. Willson's project was one I should have avoided.

Snow was sticking. Even downtown. I hadn't checked the forecast. I didn't know whether we were in for a big one. Early in the year for a big one, but I parked on the street. If it did snow deep, I'd be more likely to get out from a meter than from the open parking lot I rent regular space in. No meter problems till Monday morning. A long time from now.

The office was exactly as I remembered leaving it. Alas. So was the living room–kitchen. So was the cubbyhole with a door I am now pleased to single out as my bedroom. It has very little else in it.

I undressed and lay down. Why would a man attempt, if feebly, to appear homosexual in Indianapolis?

It was some sort of cover. But what could M. Bennett Willson be covering?

The lady friend, unsung and unnamed.

The lady friend: one Melanie Baer?

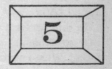

Ordinarily I sleep late Sundays when my woman's not on the agenda. Not so much from depression as from lack of stimulation.

But Sunday, December 3, though she had three more days out of town, I got up early. And was rewarded. White paint would make even downtown Indianapolis look fresh. Snow made it beautiful. I put on my rubbers and walked around for an hour. Bought a paper. When I got back, I put on a pot of coffee. A big one, all for me, me, me. Comfortable chair by window. No artificial light.

As the cuckoo clock finished chirping nine, someone started banging ten. The first few bangs were in time with my clock. I was lulled. But instead of fading away, the banger became more insistent. I realized his efforts were meant for me.

As I jerked the door open I was undecided who could be so eager to see me on a Sunday morning.

M. Bennett Willson, red-faced and determined, stood before me, puffing. "I want to talk to you," he said, and he strode past me. "Why didn't you go to see Bartholomew last night like you said you would?" The man was angry.

"What makes you think I didn't?"

"I paid you to see him last night. You said you'd see him last night. I want to know why you didn't." He took a step toward me as we stood on my rugless wooden floor. His shoes were dripping with melting snow.

"I did see him last night."

"The hell you did."

Which annoyed me under the circumstances. Gently—that is, with fingertips—I pushed him by the chest back into a chair. "If I were lying, which I'm not, I wouldn't be the first of the two of us." I mean, who's supposed to be the intimidator around here?

He shut up for a minute. Nothing like class.

Or so I thought until he pulled a stubby pistol out of his pocket. What I need is a battery of personality evaluation tests before I take two-bit clients.

He just held it and pointed it at me. I expected him to hiss some threat and squint and then betray himself as an amateur at killing by developing a tic in his left ear lobe.

But he just looked at me; I sat down on the edge of my desk. The little gun looked like it'd come out of a riverboat gambler's garter. "Lost my house, lost my gold, could lose my wife but the luck can't hold. . . ."

He thought he was reading what I was thinking when he said, "It's old but it works." I nearly killed myself laughing.

I said, "I could make a good job of redirecting that thing, but I'm thinking what a pain in the ass your blood would be on floorboards like these. I'd never get it out of the cracks. To make it look right you've got to have someone bleed uniformly over the whole area."

He just sat there. I considered it progress, because his passion was cooling.

"I'm going into my back room. There's coffee on the stove. I'll pour you a cup and then we'll talk about whatever you think we should. You can come with me if you like, or you can sit there. How do you take your coffee?" I walked slowly past him, through to my coffeepot.

It gave me a breather. Apart from breathing and pouring coffee, all that occurred to me was that Willson was a man who needed help. And who wasn't likely to trust anyone to help him.

From the front room I heard him say, "Cream and sugar." I like a little milk in mine. Which is what he got with his sugar.

The gut gat was out of sight when I got back. I never saw it again.

I sat down behind my desk and got out my notebook. Wherein I keep the whole of my detecting life. "What makes you think I didn't see Bartholomew last night, Mr. Willson?" Well, doctor . . .

"Because he was there. I mean . . ." It was crunch time for him. "What I mean is Bartholomew was prowling around my house last night." He said it with resolve and resignation.

"How do you know that?"

"Because when I got up this morning there were footprints in the snow. They came in from the road. They went all around the house with obvious stops at the windows. At one place he went back to my—to one of the windows he'd already looked through. My bedroom window. And then he walked back to the road. That's where he must have left his car."

"I see," I said. I sipped my coffee. "Mr. Willson," I said. "It's time for us to start being more economical in what we say to one another. Not necessarily tell the whole truth, but make what we do say wholly true. Do you understand me?"

"I—I think—"

"Let me give you an example. Yesterday you came to my office in order to get me to intimidate Bartholomew. He's put pressure on you; you decided to fight him back. I realized that. But I don't believe there is any play called *The Kokomo Case* and if there is, Bartholomew probably couldn't read all the words in it."

"There is such a play," he said. But in such a way that he conceded the drift of what I said.

I shrugged by way of acknowledgment. We were communicating. "I took your job because you are entitled to hire a private detective to convey a message. You should know that last night at . . ."—I checked my notebook—"at eight twenty-five I talked to Bartholomew at his motel. I told him in a firm way that he should lay off you. You should know that he was not very impressed. He told me that he is looking for a woman called Melanie Baer you knew from Kokomo. He also told me that the way you responded when he approached you about Melanie Baer made him suspect you have up-to-date information on the woman. And that is the substance of my conversation with him. You did not hire me to guard your house and keep people from walking on your snow. You did not hire me to follow Bartholomew around on his midnight rambles"—I remembered how I'd left him—"if he takes them."

Willson slouched in my chair.

"If there is something more you want me to do, ask me directly. My confidence concerning anything you may tell me is defined by law. You did not pick me from the city's detectives because you expected me to be particularly trustworthy. We both know that. But you were lucky. If you want to hire me to help you I'm available after about four o'clock this afternoon. But only you know your problem, and only you know whether I can help. Take my card. If you want me, give me a call and we'll chat."

Which made two cards handed out in two days. Fantastic advertising. At this rate I'd have to order more before the end of the decade.

Willson left me to my Sunday. I found the urge to idleness had passed. Summoning all that deft articulateness—treading between truths without exactly lying—had taken some adrenalin. I felt pretty rotten about selling him the "it's time to be honest and get down to cases" stuff and then not telling him it was me who'd peeped around his country place. But you can learn to live with feeling rotten, particularly about a man who points guns.

The funny thing was I thought that, given the chance, I might be able to help the man. His real interest seemed to be to hide his lady friend from Bartholomew's client. Like a game; it appealed to me.

I finished the pot of coffee and started on the surveillance report I'd been putting off for two days. I worked hard on it, with the kind of intensity that April the fifteenth brings for tax returns. I got it done before two thirty, addressed and ready to go. Then I turned on the TV, cracked a beer and settled in to wait.

6

Willson called later than expected. My right pocket lost seventy-two cents to my left pocket: the pool on time of call by thirty-six minutes at two cents a minute. It's just as well, because my left pocket wouldn't have been able to pay. It doesn't have any money to call its own. Willson called at 5:17.

"Mr. Samson, I would like to meet you this evening. Would that be possible?"

"Of course."

"There is another party involved."

"The other party is coming?"

"The other party is coming," said Willson, playing it close to the chest.

"When and where?" I asked.

"Would eight o'clock tonight, at my store, be possible?"

"It's fine for me," I said.

"All right. If you get there early, please wait. I—we'll be on time, early, if possible."

I was the one who was late. Snowplows had built a wall with my truck inside and it took a while to dig out. I didn't have a shovel. If I'd been living in my old office, I'd just have walked. But being on the southwest of downtown instead of the northeast makes all the difference.

Willson looked worried when he answered his door. "Are you alone?" he asked, and looked up and down the street.

"With my conscience," I said. "Are you alone?"

"Of course not." He double-locked us in, and switched on the burglar alarm. He looked out the window again. There could have been a hundred shadows hiding undetectable in the darknesses across the street, but Willson seemed satisfied. "This way," he said finally, and he led me the only logical way I could be led. To the lighted room, his office.

The person waiting there stood holding a glass. Stood despite a plethora of wooden chairs which lined the walls. I waited to be introduced. Willson waited before introducing me. First he pottled past me, behind his desk, behind the person, and pushed out a chair. "Please sit down, Mels," he said, more forceful than polite. She complied. The ice in her drink clinked in the glass as she made abrupt contact with the seat.

It was, of course, my Godiva lady of the windows. Dressed like a man. Jacket, tie and a big rodeo buckle on her belt. "This is Mr. Samson. Oh, sit down, Samson. This is Melanie. Melanie Kee. Can I get you a drink?"

"Sure. Whatever's going." Price was right. "How do you do, Miss Kee."

"Mrs. Kee," she said. "Top mine up, Mars." He did, from a bottle behind a potted tree on the desk. I got the same. Gin. Ice came from below.

Melanie was tall for a lady, or seemed it, because she was slim. But after hearing her voice, how anybody could take her for a man was beyond me. No it wasn't. I could see devotees of TV medical dramas whispering behind her back, "Poor boy." She had black hair; looked a good thirty.

"This business must be quite a strain for you," I said, making conversation.

"This is a departure for us, you know," she snapped. "We've never confided in anybody before. I don't know what makes you so special." Within a few words I knew that while she made a very feminine man, she wasn't the most feminine of women. And that about some things she was none too content to leave the decision-making to Mars.

But then she smiled. My specialness must have come through, or she remembered why we'd all come together. "I look better in my casual clothes. More convincing, I mean. More like a tall jockey."

"Do you go to the races often?" I asked hopefully.

"Mars and I drive down to Cincinnati sometimes."

"Mars?"

"Bennett, then. Him." She pointed to the tired-looking antique dealer. "His real first name is Martin. So I call him Mars. For various reasons." She laughed. She might have thought it flightily. I began to believe she'd seen a lot in her life.

"I think it's time we started talking about serious things," said Willson.

"Oh I take the races very seriously, Mars," said the lady gaily. "Don't you, Mr. Samson?"

"When I'm not working, Mrs. Kee."

Willson said, "We do have a problem. And we'd like to know what you think we should do about it."

"Shoot," I said. Gaily.

"Melanie, as you will already have gathered, is not my wife," said Willson. "She is an . . . an old friend from Kokomo. We both grew up there. We went our separate ways and then, six years ago, quite by chance, we met again in Chicago and . . ."

"Rekindled old friendships?"

"And decided," he said gravely, "all things considered, we were happier together than we had been apart."

"That sounds a little ominous," I said.

He shot a glance at Melanie. She was already shooting at him. "We had been separated for three years before we remet. In the meanwhile Melanie had gotten herself married—"

"May I ask why you didn't stay together in the first place?"

"There was . . . a . . . misunderstanding," he said, picking his words carefully. Answering the question he'd asked himself again and again for a long time. Perhaps. "For reasons which are now historical it seemed the appropriate thing to do. I went to Chicago. Melanie went to St. Louis. While she was there—"

"I'll tell this part, Mars," said Mels quietly. "I went to St. Louis because I argued with my father because he didn't like Mars, Mr. Samson. Mars, you see, was a bastard." She emptied her glass.

"Pardon?"

"Illegitimate, if you prefer. My father was against me having anything to do with him. The problem is that we weren't just nobody, my father and me. For Kokomo we were 'important.' People cared what we did and kept track of what we did. And my father cared what people thought. It was all a mess. But I couldn't have Mars, so I left home too. On the rebound, as they say, I married Edmund Kee, which was a mistake I have been paying for ever since. He is our problem."

She leaned back to reflect for a moment. Then to recite, "Edmund was the seventh child of nine. The fourth boy of five in a Scottish Catholic family that had lived in St. Louis for four generations." She said it as if it meant something and I dutifully took notes. "I don't really know a lot about his childhood. We were never close that way, but I don't think Edmund was ever quite right, if you know what I mean. But when I met him he desperately wanted . . . to get married. And I wanted someone to marry me. So we did." Ironic smile. There had been time for a few drinks before this ordeal. Mars wasn't hurrying to fill her empty glass again. "What with one thing and another I began to realize I'd made a mistake. Then I began to realize what kind of mistake I had made. So I ran away from him."

"That was the spring of 1965," said Bennett Willson. "They were married in August 1962. The last time I'd seen her was in Kokomo in June 1962." The dates were gravestones in his life, well flowered.

She continued, "The problem is that Edmund is Catholic, as I said. More than that. He's kind of maniacal about it. The rules and regulations part. For instance he would never, *ever* give me a divorce. But the problem is he couldn't just settle for that. I mean *I* would settle for that—I mean *we* would." More exchange with Willson. "I mean for my not being divorced. That's perfectly all right with us, if only he would leave us alone."

"He doesn't leave you alone?"

"No," they said together.

"He's known you're here for a long time then?"

"No," they said together.

"Edmund's idea would be he and I should live together and I should get his meals for him and breed for him *because* we are married, and for no other reason. No matter how horribly unhappy we were. No matter how much more we had learned since the time we married him."

I turned to Willson. "Does that mean that Bartholomew has been hired by Edmund Kee? That what he is trying to do is locate Mrs. Kee here?"

"Yes," said Willson, "but that is just a little ahead of ourselves. We've been through this before, you see. Kee located Mels in Chicago and he quit his job and sold his house and moved up there just to make trouble for her."

"He found her with you?"

"No. He hired another detective, from St. Louis, who found her working in a department store. Kee came to where she was living and made a scene. Then we moved away. It was all quite complicated. It involved selling a house I owned there."

"What kind of business is Kee in?"

"He's a statistician," spat Melanie. "A computer statistician, which really describes the kind of flexible personality he has."

The way she'd been holding her empty glass had been bothering me. Her too, I guess, because she stretched herself to the bottle and brought it home to momma.

"You were able to move here without leaving tracks?"

Willson said, "We spent some time in Florida trying to decide what to do, where to go and how to do it. It was a matter of not leaving tracks and of making plans the right way round. It was a matter of disguise too. I guess you've gathered how that part of it works."

I said, "Bartholomew was pretty emphatic to me that you, at least, are queer."

Another smile, exchange of understanding looks.

"You didn't tell me that before."

"You hadn't told me very much before."

"When Bartholomew made himself known to me, that was just about the end. We were so sure we had covered ourselves this time. Willson's not my real name, for instance. It would have taken real work to track us down. I would have thought."

"Is your husband a wealthy man, Mrs.—Melanie?"

"Shit," she said. Sounding like a real jockey at last.

"No," said Willson.

"The description of his work. Sounds like some income with it."

"He may have saved up for another run at her," suggested Willson.

"And the problem now is how to get rid of Bartholomew, and presumably his employer?"

"That's it exactly."

"Do you have any ideas about what you might want me to do?"

With passion Melanie said, "We don't want to have to move again. You have no idea what living, day by day, under a cloud which may rain destruction is like. It destroys part of you. You worry and frown even when you're most relaxed and happy. It's always there. And that's the life we want back."

"To have to run again," said Willson, "it would take too much out of us. If we can possibly help it. It's why we decided to confide in you. When you turned out to be—"

"Not as stupid as I look?"

"It's the critical time for us. We can always run, I suppose."

"And run," said Melanie to her newly emptied glass. "And run."

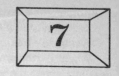

7

Before I left the House of Antiquity I extracted two additional privacies from Mars and Mels. Their real home address, which I already knew. And M. Bennett Willson's real name. If Bartholomew used it, I shouldn't be surprised: Martin Willetson.

A check also changed hands.

The prospect of conversation with Bartholomew was not iffy. We agreed the next move was for me to see the man again. Use the tool Bartholomew had given us: belief in Willson's homosexuality. Why concede any information about Mels? Couldn't hurt to try.

As we parted, I said, "We're agreed then. We've never heard of Melanie Baer."

"Right," said Mars.

"Right," said Mels.

I didn't follow them after the meeting. I didn't do anything dramatic. I just went home, read a bit. My thinking about them was strictly miscellaneous and on my own recognizance; the check was predated for the morrow.

But I did decide that Bartholomew was a funny egg. I'd burst in on him, yet before long we were having conversation. Either he didn't hold grudges or he'd spent a lot of time around people with bad manners.

Mars and Mels? Less bemusing. I could believe the dates they gave me. But the editorial details about people they'd known and loved? Just one duo's opinion. Nothing to quibble about at the moment. You go on what they give you in this racket.

My real reservation was whether constructing a false trail might not be the wrong line altogether. Mightn't they have some legal redress? A husband's interpretation of religious scruples has no enforceability in law that I know about. If Kee was intimidating them . . . After all the woman left him years ago.

Messy though. But messier than delay and deception? I wrote myself a note to ask Clinton Grillo about the legal options. A note keeping open my options in case Bartholomew didn't go for the first option we threw his way. Grillo's my lawyer for matters that don't take energy or celibacy.

Then I wrote down Bartholomew's name. He had said, about his employer, "He's so nutty to get a lead on this broad he'd believe almost anything." If we did set up a snark hunt, it would be with the cooperation of the hunter.

Then I wrote down Edmund Kee. The statistical man.

Then I wrote Mars and Mels.

And then I wrote down my woman's name. About a hundred times.

I haven't had much practice at intimidation, but I read a magazine article once which helped me work out a philosophy. People are least secure either away from their own ground or when they're surprised. Why else do the cops take a fella "downtown"? At three A.M.

So because it seemed like a good idea at the time, I set the clock for very early that Monday morning. Tail early: five thirty.

I was parking on Washington Street near the Kings and Queens by six fifteen. Slipping the lock to room 17 by twenty-five past.

Bartholomew was alone, snoring gently. I wondered if I would ever talk to him when he wasn't in bed.

There was a glass of water on the night table. Next to his wallet, his watch and his change. I waited till he finished an exhalation. Then I emptied the glass on his upper lip. He sucked it up his nose and his mouth too. He jumped all around. It made me feel like I was doing him a violence. I wrung my hands with glee.

"Wakie wakie."

He spluttered and spat and sat up. Even then his eyes stayed closed for a minute. It must have been a very pleasant dream.

"What the shit? . . ."

It was his fault. He had accepted my role as local muscle on our first acquaintance, despite my scholarly demeanor, and then he had refused to let me muscle him. How would I like that if I really was muscle?

"You were snoring, Bartholomew," I said. "You disturbed me and I couldn't sleep."

Some people have no sense of humor.

"You," he said. He was a slow awakener, but he remembered me. I was flattered, but I didn't want him too awake or I would lose the initiative I'd prepared so carefully. I think that magazine article was by Bobby Fischer.

"My employer has been thinking about you, Bartholomew, and the more he thinks the less he likes you. He sent me over to see if I couldn't make an arrangement which would keep you from provoking him."

"You begin to provoke me," Bartholomew said quietly.

"I hope I didn't disturb you. But you're a hard man to catch in, and alone."

He did a lot more rubbing and scratching. "What the hell is all this about?"

It was time for my big move. "My employer and I had a little chat. You remember him. Bennett Willson, the queer." I added the description harshly, to suggest if Bartholomew called Willson names, I might take them personally. "My employer," I continued, "is devilishly annoyed that you're snooping around about some broad he knew when he was a kid. I don't know if you've ever been a queer, but it's not the easiest thing in the world around this town. And he doesn't want to move. That means you got to move." There it was, my big move.

Bartholomew yawned and stretched. "So he tells you Melanie Baer was just a broad he knew as a kid. Shit."

I felt it slipping already.

"And did he tell you that this Melanie Baer he just knew as a kid"—sarcastic—"was also a broad he knocked up when he was a kid? And that it was only nine years ago and he was twenty-six?"

"Knocked up? You mean—"

"I mean exactly what I mean. He neglected to tell you that, did he? Shit."

I'll never make a proper bully. "So?"

"So according to my client, he was going to marry the broad, only she skedaddled and married my client in St. Louis instead. Only then she skedaddled on my client. Went to Chicago; he caught up with her there and she took off again. Five years now." He shifted position in bed. I remembered now, he was very tall. I felt like a damn fool to have tried to intimidate him a second time. It was worse this round. I'd volunteered.

"Shit," he said, as if reading my mind. "You're lucky I'm a gentle person."

"I'm more intelligent than I act," I said hopefully. "But Willson's connection with the lady is still nine years out of date."

"Well, how would you track down a guy's wife that's been gone for five and a half years?"

"Family?"

"None. Only child. Mother dead a long time ago. Father committed suicide. None of the relatives in the hometown, Kokomo, have heard from her since she left nine years ago.

And they say it in the way that means they didn't hear from her even when she lived there."

"Friends?"

"Only she didn't have any in St. Louis. My client, well, he has enough family to take care of any new member."

"So you tried to find out if she kept up with any friends from Kokomo."

"And the only name I came up with in Kokomo?"

"Martin Willetson?"

"Right, little fella. Bang on. A word of advice. You ever want to get some gossip in a town, go to the librarian. Librarians know everything."

Must be sublimation. "I'll try and remember that," I said falsely. I was trying not to interrupt his narrative flow. I'd have said go to the local private detective.

"So Willetson," he continued, oblivious to my thoughts, "was her only boy friend. Now, he is illegitimate. Not that bastardy is a new book in Kokomo, but it doesn't make life easy. He grew up with his mother and they say the father was a traveler with money and a conscience, because when the baby came along so did a house."

"His mother still lives there?"

"Yes, not that she'd tell me about the boy. I tracked him down by chumming up with her mailman. First I got the Indianapolis postmark; then the address off a letter she wrote him."

"Must have taken quite a while," I said.

"And a dollar or two." He smiled. He could. "Now we know she arrived in St. Louis pregnant and we know who her only boy friend was. And we know where the boy friend lives now."

"Which doesn't prove a damn thing," I said.

"No," he agreed. "Not until he goes through the roof when I mention her name." He mimicked a nightclub comic mimicking a queer: "Get out of here! Go away!"

The best I could do for my client was shrug. You make your bed . . .

"Look at it my way," said Bartholomew. "I come to Indianapolis to talk to the guy on the off chance. I expect him to rub his chin and try to place the name. Instead, he explodes. So I invest some more time doing background on him. I find he has a nice little business, a nice little friend stashed in Monrovia. It just makes me wonder all the more. So what, I walk in? Why should that bother him? Why isn't it just water under the bridge?"

"I give up. Why?"

"All I can think of is that it means Melanie Baer just isn't ancient history." He sat quiet for a few seconds. "So here I am. I don't know what Willetson knows, but I want it. This carrying on has got my client excited. I've got to come up with something. I don't really see what Willetson thinks he owes her. Considering his present arrangements."

I couldn't offer an answer off the cuff.

"Anyway, she ran; he stayed put. It's possible he never knew she was pregnant. All the locals seemed to think she was going to go to college and be a genius. So now they just figure she got bit by whatever's been biting kids and making them hippies. Now funny thing is, they say the neighbors never heard of him having a girl friend before either. His mother kept him close. My theory is her running away kind of set him off. Freaked him out, like they say, and made him the way he is, you see."

It was a long sad story; gave me time to work up a lie. "He told me you came in aggressive. You frightened him. He's had some close calls with his boy friend in Monrovia, you see. That's on a knife edge and can't take trouble of any kind now."

He shook his head slowly. "I won't buy it, friend. He knows something. All I want is whatever he knows. I'll go away. I'm on a good thing here. This guy, the lady's husband, has kept me fully employed for five months now. I'm not in a hurry, but I need to make some sort of progress. Slow but steady."

"I'll talk to him about it. But it may take him a few days to figure out what he wants to do."

Bartholomew sighed. "What did I just say, friend? Slow but steady, right?"

I nodded. He got up out of bed, a massive figure in his jockey shorts. I turned to go.

A giant hand grabbed me hard by the remaining hair on my head. It bent me over a giant knee. It hurt. I looked up, shocked at the frowning face. Bigger than ever. He brought a .38 revolver up like the moon till its barrel was lined up with my nostrils. I could see the big lead bullets, all pointing my way. "And, little buddy," Bartholomew said, "don't try any more games with me. The third time will break your luck. I'm a pretty nice fella. Easy to talk to. Affable, you might say. I'm on an easy case and I talk to you because you might see sense and get Willson to help me. But don't get me angry again, friend. I need my rest."

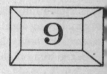

I am really stupid sometimes. So stupid that even someone as stupid as I am knows how stupid I am. You'd think, by my age . . .

It was too early to go anywhere. Too dark to see anything. I stopped at one of the West Washington diners. Had a cheeseburger for breakfast.

. . . I'd know enough to know what I can do and what I can't. To know what I am and what I'm not. You don't get any saner as you grow older, but you should get better at . . .

I had a stack of raw onion on it. And French fries with raw onion. I was off people. Anybody I came across better watch out.

. . . avoiding situations that bring out your little peculiarities. That's what maturation is—improved skill at avoiding difficult situations. I mean, I know I am not a violent type of person. And knowing that means that I never . . .

Two cups of coffee. Bowl of cereal. Ask for garlic to put on it.

. . . play at pushing people around. Pouring water on them. Never! I know better, damn it. It's not just that I don't believe in it. By now I should know full well that I'm not good at it.

It wasn't the most relaxing meal I've ever eaten. I caught myself in the breakfast rush. When I came in I had slung myself into a booth of capacity six, and as the rush progressed the rest of my breakfast world was filling up. The waitress was less than charmed when I kept ordering strange things. Little did she know I am a professional grouch, hired by the management to make a stress situation. To measure her waitressing good humor. Next I would tell her there was a fly in the maple syrup.

I was joined for breakfast by three sanitation men who ordered three stacks. "I'll have a stack too," I said.

Only by the time the flapjacks came, I was too bored with my own company to play games. The four of us ate in the kind of bad-humored silence which Monday mornings provide so well.

I was irritable, aggressive. Not pleasant to my fellow man. Quite unlike my jovial self. It was only eight and I'd already done enough stupid things to fill a day.

My co-breakfasters left. I called for more coffee. Finally, I worked on my notes. Brought myself up-to-date with my Bartholomew encounter. Already felt a long time ago. How soon we forget, when we try.

I stayed upset. It was more than disquiet with my own behavior. It was because, I realized at last, my clients had not seen fit to inform me about trivia like Melanie's pregnancy.

What's the point of my having Willson's real name—in case Bartholomew knows it—if Bartholomew knows Mels was pregnant when she bailed out of Kokomo, and I don't?

Ah phooey. Screw them all. I hate people who keep silly secrets.

I paid the bill, left a worthy tip and went out to freeze in the truck for a few minutes. It cooled me off. Work, I thought. Busy beeness. It was my only chance.

I don't ordinarily let things get to me this way. I professional it out. Stay aloof.

Loneliness can make even a good fella bad, a happy fella sad. Activity. Go back to fundamentals. What is the job you were hired for, my son? Oh yeah. Untracking the giant detective.

I thought about it. How do you convince someone to go look in San Francisco for a lady who lives in Monrovia?

A lady who left home pregnant. What happened to the kid?

Suppose I went back to Bartholomew and said I'd only just asked Willson about Melanie Baer. And then spun a story that grew from there?

It wouldn't work. Bartholomew would want to know how Mars had come across the information. Why he'd been so upset when first approached.

And more important, it would be better to start a false trail at a point besides Willson. Because when Bartholomew finally played the false trail out, he'd come back to where the trail went bad. And the idea was to get him permanently away from Willson & Co., not just away for a while.

So . . . take away Mars.

Which left Kokomo. It was the only other nearby point associated with Melanie Baer.

Suppose I could get one of Mels's relatives to volunteer to missteer Bartholomew. Perhaps get a letter from Melanie, from—from anywhere. As long as it appeared to have no connection with Mars.

So, find a relative. Or perhaps someone to play at being a relative. Hmmmm.

I started the motor. I wanted to do something. Action! I wanted to go to Kokomo! Live big!

I pulled out of the diner's parking lot. First, a detail. Then the world!

It was nearly nine by the time I got to the House of Antiquity. No parking problem on East 10th. Except for one. There was no Renault in sight.

The store was open. I didn't know whether and how to wait. Go home and come back?

I wasn't in the mood. I went into the store. Maybe I'd buy a present to welcome my lady home. A betrothal offering. Maybe something she needed, to counterbalance me.

In the store I found a young woman and a middle-aged man. I approached the woman. I nearly said, "I'm looking for something cheap," but I remembered, just in time, what I was really shopping for. "Is Mr. Willson around?"

"No, he's not," she said courteously. "May I help you?"

"I've really come to speak to Mr. Willson. Do you expect him soon?"

"I'm most awfully afraid that I must disappoint you, because John"—she gestured to the man—"John just took a call from Mr. Willson, who said he was buying today and wouldn't be in. Can I take a message for you? Have him call you or something?" She smiled sweetly. A little courtesy goes a long way in my world. I didn't have the least inclination to pour water up her nose.

"Do you expect him to be in tomorrow?"

"I believe so. He's supposed to meet a distributor for lunch. He almost never breaks that kind of date."

"I'll try to stop in then," I said. "And thank you very, very much." If my overprofusion confused her, it didn't confuse me.

It did leave me a problem. Discretion said that I should postpone my Kokomo follies until I had had a chance to discuss the play with Willson. He could give me leads. Melanie could pick likely relatives to enlist.

The only problem with discretion was that it left me with

nothing to do until I could talk to Willson. And the one thing I didn't need was a day with nothing to do.

Kokomo it was. If nothing came to nothing, I wouldn't tell them about it.

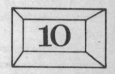

About a mile south of Kokomo there is a steak house. They gave me creamed cheese for my baked potato once, when I ordered sour cream. The steak house has stuck in my mind like the creamed cheese did in my mouth, but this time when I pulled into the parking lot it was to use the phone book. I passed on the food. In the book I looked for Kokomo Baers. There were eight. Then Willetsons. There was only one. I got good directions with some gas. I was there by eleven thirty.

The idea was Willson's mother might help me more than she had helped Bartholomew.

It was a well-kept white frame house, picket fence. A picture postcard of "where grandma lives." I walked up the walk. Knocked on the door. And there we were.

"Yes?"

"Mrs. Willetson?"

"Miss Willetson, yes."

"My name is Albert Samson. I'm working on a project for your son which you might be able to assist."

"And what might that be?"

"It's a little complicated. Could I come in and talk to you about it?"

She thought it over. And not quickly. I was startled that she looked so young. Mars was thirty-five and had a haggard manner, which suggested he hadn't kept too well. If this was his mother, it looked like Mars hadn't kept at all. She didn't look over forty-five herself.

"Samson, you say," she said finally. "Martin has never written about you."

"I'm not a regular employee. I don't work at the store. I'm a private detective and the project concerns some bother being stirred up by another private detective. I believe he tried to see you not long ago. A very tall man?"

Acidly she asked, "Is there any reason I should believe you are working for Martin?"

I got out my wallet and showed her first the check Willson had given me. Then my ID card, to confirm that I was in fact the payee. She studied them very carefully. I got nervous. Willson would not like to be presented with the *fait accompli* of my contact with his mother. Or to hear I'd tried to *accompli* the *fait*, and failed.

Then I remembered Willson was out today. "If you want to check on me," I said, "you might try calling your son at the store."

She said, "Come in."

I followed her from the doorway to a couch placed, peculiarly, facing the window instead of the room. She showed me where she wanted me to sit on it while she drew the curtains back. It was as if we would need an unobstructed view of the street.

She sat down.

"The problem," I said, "concerns that other man who was in Kokomo about two months ago. He tried to talk to you, I believe."

"That's right," she said. "He was mannerly, but he wanted to know things which was none of his business." One of the lace undercurtains slipped over half of the window. She got up and refixed it at the side of the frame. I began to wonder if we were there to watch anything. Whether the arrangements weren't more consistent with people watching us. It agitated me. I kinda forgot what I'd come about.

"The problem is," I said slowly, regrouping, "he has pushed the things he is interested in, whether they were legitimately his concern or not. He has come to your son because he thinks Martin has heard recently from a girl he used to know. Melanie Baer."

In a fraction of a minute Miss Willetson aged visibly.

"My son Martin never knew any girls while he lived with me," she said emphatically. Even proudly.

"Pardon?"

"And he certainly did not know anyone called Melanie Baer."

I had realized I would have to speak carefully with Willson's mother. I didn't know, for instance, whether she thought his housemate was male or female, or whether she knew there was a housemate at all. But some simple things I expected to be matters of fact.

"I understood while he lived here, Martin—"

"No," she interrupted with warmth.

I tried a different tack. "The point is this other detective seems to think your son knew this girl and he is annoying your son about the subject."

"It's not so. He couldn't."

"But he is."

"I mean Martin. It was just not, not possible he should know that girl."

I couldn't think of anything more to say. My rationale for being there at all was too flimsy to survive adversity. I made a few more noises, and, to our mutual relief, left.

"If I can be of any more help . . ." the lady said as I backed to the door.

As I got into the panel truck, I saw the curtains fall back across the front window.

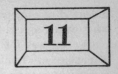

11

Which left me in Kokomo at eleven forty-five on a Monday morning.

Not the worst of fates, but it felt like it was. I despised myself, briefly. Everything I'd tried in the long morning: a catalogue of how not to.

Information from Bartholomew, yes, but only through his grace. I'd done my best to make it hard. A man without certain refinements, perhaps, but basically gentle. To have kept from killing me already.

And my client's mother.

Excuse me, Mr. Samson. Do you always begin work for somebody by going to visit his mother?

Poor lady. Not exactly on top of world events. Concerned with securing idiosyncratic social forms. *Her* boy never had girl friends. *Her* boy never knew a Melanie Baer. In any sense. And *she* was beyond reproach, which any interested neighbor could attest to by bothering to look out of the neighborly window into hers. The strange man who'd gone inside the house could be seen clearly, erect in his chair at all times.

Ah well.

Wonder how she'd come to mother a bastard in the first place. A question I'd neglected to ask.

Take Your Winter Vacation in Kokomo.

I drove from Miss Willetson's house to town center. Kokomo is the Howard County seat. And County Hall is in the middle of a square in the middle of town. Trains still run through Buckeye Street on the west edge of the square. I angle-parked on the south, so I would have a good view of a train from the truck. If one came by.

I've come to Kokomo several times since I moved back to

Indiana. I remember the first one best because I came across a bar with a sign in the window: No Mexicans.

1963 that was, the year I opened my detective store in Indianapolis. As I reminisced my feet got cold. I decided to be constructive. Accept my fate. I got out of the truck and went to a phone booth. And called my own number.

Dorrie, my answering servicer, sadly reported that there had been no calls in my absence that Monday morning.

Then I called the House of Antiquity. Was Mr. Willson there? He was not.

I didn't have his home phone number, so two down. I called the Indianapolis office of Clinton Grillo, Attorney, father of a former school chum. He's one of the few people in this world even older than me.

"May I speak to Mr. Grillo, please? This is Albert Samson."

"One moment please. I'll see if he's free."

Free as a bird.

"Yes, Albert. What can I do for you?"

"I'm glad I caught you, sir. I'm on a case and I have a couple of questions about what has arisen."

"Something immoral, I hope." Though his beard is gray, there's life in Clinton yet.

We talked about injunctions against molestation, but it was messy and full of ifs which only Martin Mars M. Bennett Poof Willson Willetson could answer.

"Now if you could prove this Bartholomew was something like, say, a Peeping Tom," he said, at one juncture. I moved the subject along.

"Something completely different now. Can you tell me how I can find out who owned a house before its present owner?"

"That's a local title matter." He gave me the name of a Kokomo acquaintance who might be inclined to assist me. Nice guy, Clinton Junior's dad. Nicer than his son turned out to be.

I looked up the lawyer I'd been given, Robert Goger. I dropped Clinton's name and it got me an interview at three.

I tried to think of other people to call. If there'd only been three Baers in town I'd have tried them all. But eight? All I could think of was my woman, the off chance that she had come home two days early. But that was silly. It was past noon and I'd had a silly morning.

I wasn't about to have a silly afternoon. I left the shelter of the phone booth, fed up the parking meter and had a walk around.

I was in Kokomo, all right.

Having accepted that fact, what could I do to make the best of it? Why, find out things about people I knew. Knowledge doesn't hurt a fella. It keeps a fella young.

The first place I spent some time was at the Howard County Probate Records Office. It took a while, but I found the will of Melanie's father, Freeman Baer. His estate was left in its entirety to Melanie. The entirety was valued at $140,000. Which is enough to finance a detective's Kokomo vacation any day. Freeman Baer's death had occurred January 15, 1963. Cause was not listed. There were no probate records for Mrs. Baer, at least that the young lady in charge of finding such records could find.

"You know," she said, "you're the second person since I've been working in this office who's asked to see these files."

"I am? Who was the other person?"

She laughed condescendingly. "Now, how would I know that? I don't take names." It was true, I still had mine.

"Was it a man?" I asked innocently.

"Oh yes," she said.

"Was it a very tall man?"

"That's him," she said cheerfully. Quickly, as if the memory was so well engraved that it required no recall time.

I said, "Well, you be careful when you go to bed with him."

"I was," she said.

There were limits past which I would not follow Bartholomew's footprints. Or whatever marks he left.

At one o'clock I was definitely not hungry. I invested a few blocks to have a crack at the Kokomo Tribune Building. Perchance to find some obliging crusty reporter who would reminisce about local gossip. Why Freeman Baer had committed suicide for one thing. But all the reporters were out scooping.

I spent a little time in the *Tribune*'s tombs. But I was too restless to give the old copies a good search. I did locate Freeman Baer's obit. It was lengthy but discreet. Apart from a short bit about an accident cleaning a gun. I did find that Baer first came to Kokomo as a young man. Whatever that was worth. And I also noted that at the funeral there were no mourners named Baer.

The obit led me to a notice on the subject of Elvira Baer in February 1955. She had died after hospitalization. And was much mourned by seemingly innumerable relatives. Along with all the local people, several attended the funeral from as far away as Cleveland and Owosso, Michigan. It suggested a life as a family member of importance. She was thirty-six when she died, though she had been married sixteen years. Melanie, the only child, was eleven.

It was not a cheerful way to pass time. So I quit about ten to two and went looking for the library. Somebody told me once that if I wanted to find something out in a town I should ask the librarian. So I did.

"Excuse me. I'm a visitor in town and I'm trying to find out about some people who used to live here. I wonder if you could help me?"

The girl behind the desk gave me a long searching look. "I dunno," she said. "Sorry." By that time I'd realized she was too young to be a real librarian.

I called it a day until three o'clock. By trial and error I found the most comfortable chair in the library and then had a whack at its thinnest volume. It was called *Gothic Architecture and Scholasticism* and from what I could gather in three quarters of an hour it was as much about how habits of thought pervade all manner of human activity as it was about either Scholasticism or Gothic architecture. Like, James Joyce didn't have to see a cubic Picasso and say, "Shit, man, I can do that with books." It was enough for them to share the general milieu. Each came out of the contemporary cultural pool. Doing his own version of the common thing, to coin a habit of thought.

I wondered how I was reflected in art.

At three o'clock sharp I was with Robert Goger. A keen-eyed, well-dressed gentleman in his midsixties. Sharp but cheerful.

"So you're a friend of Clint Grillo's," he said, after shaking my hand and seating my . . .

"I appreciate your seeing me at short notice."

"No problem. I'm on half time these days. It's a good part of maturity. You have more friends and better ones. And you have more excuse not to bother with people who aren't friends—or friends of friends."

"My main interest is finding who owned a house here before its current owner."

"That's not hard. You do it by giving me the address and waiting till I call you tomorrow. Unless you're in some great hurry."

I wasn't. I gave him the address. He was obviously in no hurry. He seemed to invite conversation. So I tried him on my other subject. "I'm also trying to get a little background on the family of a man called Freeman Baer."

Somberly he said, "I knew Freeman Baer very well."

I was pleased, but didn't know whether to show it. What to say? So I said, "Did you know his daughter?"

"Yes. Let's see, she would be twenty-six, twenty-seven now. Wherever she is."

"She's not in Kokomo then?"

"Left in 1962. She graduated from high school. And a week later she was gone."

"Why?"

The question was too unadorned to leave the conversation conversational. I felt a wave of anxiety thinking Bartholomew had been here before me. But he couldn't have. Could he?

Goger didn't know just what to say. But curious to see where I would lead, said, "She had a falling out with her father concerning her future."

"Something irreconcilable?"

"It must have been. She didn't even come back for his funeral."

"I understand Mr. Baer took his own life."

"Yes."

"Do you know why? Was it related to the quarrel with his daughter?"

I could feel him measure how much credit Clinton Grillo's name alone should provide. "Freeman Baer was prone to swift attachments and swift disenchantments. Emotional. But he killed himself seven months after Melanie left home. That doesn't suggest she was what was on his mind at the time."

"You say Melanie didn't come back for the funeral. Did she know her father died?"

"It's quite possible she didn't."

"I've had a look at Mr. Baer's will. Melanie remained beneficiary, which suggests he wasn't completely disenchanted with her as a daughter. But did she ever find out she was beneficiary?"

"She did."

"So she's reasonably well off wherever she is."

"That I don't know about. She refused to take her father's money."

"What?"

He smiled briefly. "I was executor of Freeman Baer's will and I located Melanie in St. Louis about a year after he died. She had married. I wrote to her informing her of her father's death and of his bequest. She replied saying she didn't want anything to do with it. I wrote back emphatically asking her to reconsider. She replied in the negative."

I shook my head. "She wouldn't do anything with it?"

"She wrote me one line. She said, 'Give it to my father's bastards.' "

"Wow. So what did you do?"

"It seemed to me that considering Melanie's youth—she was still under twenty-one—and other factors, we shouldn't act on her reaction too abruptly. The money is in trust for Melanie and her children. I think that is the closest we could get to intent."

"But she still hasn't claimed it."

"No. I do know she and her husband moved from St. Louis, but at the moment I have lost track of her. I have been rather free with you, Mr. Samson. Quite apart from having confidence in Clinton's assessment of men." We exchanged smiles. Both knowing Clinton Grillo's eye for the ladies. "But your line of questioning suggests you may have up-to-date information about Melanie Kee."

"I do," I said. I fully appreciated his confidences. "She is separated from her husband, on rather vitriolic terms. She's living near Indianapolis."

"She's well?"

"Reasonably well. I've only met her once. I would expect I'll be meeting her again."

"Would you consider asking whether she would agree to hear from me again on this subject?"

"If I can I will."

He sat back. "Good," he said. "Thank you." He seemed to relax. "This is one of the few outstanding problems I've got left in this legal practice of mine."

"You seem to have done quite well." Indeed, the office, the man, as I got used to them, both had the textures of quality.

"We are the biggest in town. That must speak for something."

"Your good name. Good names become a habit."

"Thank you. I would hate to have to pass this situation on to someone else, though. I'd very much like to get it wrapped up."

I understood what he meant. I changed the subject. "Would

you be willing to tell me whether Freeman Baer left a lot of bastards?"

"Freeman sowed his wild oats. It's surprising how many he did leave. Six."

"Six! And did none of them make a claim for part of the inheritance?"

"I don't think any of them ever knew Freeman was their father."

"Might I ask how you know with such precision?"

He laughed. Then he laughed again. "Read it in a book."

"What?"

"Read it in a goddamn book. Would you believe it?"

"I don't think I would."

"It's true though." He let me dangle.

I dangled. I squirmed. I said, "I . . . but would there . . . I."

"It's funny. It comes from I.U., this book. You know those sexual books that guy Kinsey turned out?"

"Yeah."

"Well, they kept a sex research unit down there. I guess graduate students and people like that. They made Kokomo a 'study area.' "

"No kidding. When was this?"

"Well, I don't remember exactly when they started, but I remember they came to Freeman about three, four months after Elvira died. Let's see, that would be . . ."

"She died February 1955."

"So it was summer of fifty-five. He mentioned it to me. He said he was going to give them an earful. Right. That's when it was. I remember I talked to their people August that year. Hot as hell."

"I would think that telling people secrets for them to put in a book wouldn't be conducive for getting real secrets."

"Ah, but you see that's how they work. They tell you that you're going to be just one of thousands. That the book isn't going to be published for maybe ten years, that they aren't going to say what state you're in, much less the particular city and your name. And that it will only be read by scientists. You ask, can you get a copy when it's done and they say sure, but you never hear about them again. It was finally published end of 1961. I saw a notice of it. Cost ten bucks. I know Freeman ordered one too because I told him about getting mine. But I'd be surprised if there were more than four or five copies bought in all Kokomo."

"So you had a read about yourself."

"That I did. Course you couldn't really pin anything on anybody just by reading it. For one thing they don't give complete life stories. They broke it all up. They take what you did when you were a kid and put it one place. What you did before you were married, another. You have to know most of it already to tell who's who from what they put. I got mentioned in two chapters, myself. But nobody had more bastards than Freeman."

I stayed quite a while with Goger. Quite long enough for me to leave him and drive back to Indianapolis without feeling I should do more work that day.

When I got home I did try to get ahold of Willson-Willetson again. First at the store. Then I tried to get his home number from information. It wasn't listed.

So how could I feel bad about going to the movies? I couldn't. I did stop at the Indianapolis Library to request the 1961 sex study. A poor second, perhaps, to 1971 sex.

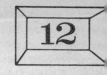

12

I slept like a baby log. Until the phone went. The phone is in the office. The floor felt very cold to my feet. The air felt very cold to my nose. The phone felt very cold to my ear.

Willson's icy voice said, "Samson, I must see you as soon as possible."

Possible was in about fifty minutes at the House of Antiquity. He volunteered to come to my office, but that would only have taken him fifteen minutes. I told him it would be quicker for me to come to him. Willson met me near the door and marched me darkly to his office. I dropped into a wooden captain's chair. He said, "That man, Bartholomew, he came out to the house yesterday afternoon."

I absorbed it only slowly. "What house?"

"My house. Our house. Where Melanie and I live."

Hide, more like. "I never did get your phone number there," I said.

He was annoyed, but gave it to me. "Bartholomew came out there yesterday?"

"That's right. It was dumb luck I was there. Melanie was sleeping in the bedroom. I stayed home yesterday because she wasn't feeling well."

"Did he see her?"

"No. Thank God!"

"So he doesn't suspect the person you live with is Melanie."

"No. Not as far as I know. I'm sure he believes—"

"So what did he want?"

I was waking up to the fact that the man was upset. His eyes slashed back and forth across the walls in front of him. He was defensive, frightened that some ear would project itself Aymé-like through the wall. "I don't know what to do. I don't know who to turn to."

I waited. Feeling sympathy for the man. He was turning to me. A man who makes his life a secret doesn't have the pick of the barrel.

"Bartholomew says Melanie had a child and killed it."

"Oh?"

"He said her husband was trying to find her because she had killed their child."

"What does Melanie say?"

He said nothing at first. "She was napping. She didn't hear the man come. She never knew he was there."

"And you didn't tell her?"

"How? What could I have said, Mr. Samson?" He was wringing his hands and my heart. "Melanie is everything to me. I have done . . . given . . . done more than you can ever know. For her, to be with her. To have her. I've never loved another woman. When she left me the first time, I just didn't know . . . how to proceed. The one day, the next. When I found her again in Chicago it was like getting out of jail and back into the world. We believed in each other, sacrificed for each other. Put ourselves"—he chose words carefully—"in jeopardy for each other."

"You're afraid it's true then?"

"No," he said sharply. "Not that it's true that she killed her child, or that she killed any child." He hesitated.

"But . . ." I led.

"But it's possible she had a child and didn't tell me."

I nodded to gain time. Not because I understood. Surely, when you purport to be honest with someone, an omission of important fact is tantamount to a lie. Which left them very close, except she might lie to him. But why? "Why shouldn't she tell you if she had had a child?"

"It's possible."

"You think it's more than just possible then?"

"I can hardly think Bartholomew would be accusing her of killing a child if she never had one."

"If she'll agree to be examined, it's easy enough to tell."

He snapped back, "If I ask her it's easy enough to tell."

At last I saw what he wanted. "You have a kind of understanding. You would be breaking confidence just by asking."

"That's it," he said.

He wanted to use me. His confidences and hand wringings were in part exchange.

I drew back a little. "So," I said, "what can we do?" Make him ask for it.

"It's hard."

"Did Bartholomew say what he wanted?"

"He wants Mels. He's sure I know where to find her. That I wouldn't be wasting time with . . ." He smiled, not altogether friendly. There was an underlying arrogance about the man. "Well, he wasn't too flattering about you, Mr. Samson. He said he'd expected to hear from you again yesterday."

"I saw him yesterday morning and said I'd talk to you. But you weren't at the store."

"I called you right after he left, but your service said you were out. I left a message."

"I must have missed it." Or consciously decided not to ask for messages when I got back from Kokomo.

We had progressed to a rather intimate state of affairs. But unable to manipulate me into volunteering, he finally said, "I wondered if you might talk to Melanie. Without me there."

"Ahhh," I said.

"If you say that Bartholomew came to you, maybe not saying that he accuses her of killing, but that he says she had a child. Something like that."

"You want me to find out the things you don't want to ask her yourself?"

"I guess so, yes."

I shrugged. Call me minion, but call me. "When do you want me to go?"

"This afternoon I think. I wouldn't go this morning. I'll call her about eleven to say you want to see her. That will give you time to prepare. Get there, say, about two. Unless I call you back."

"Whatever you say," I said. I felt chastened. I keep feeling that feelings are important. I should know better. My prime function is to deliver a job of work. To report. Personal reportage. I flirted with journalism before I settled on this line of work. Would that journalism had flirted with me. "May I ask a personal question?"

"Go ahead," he said.

"Does Melanie have a drinking problem?"

"Not really," he said, then paused. "But we've been under pressure unusual even for us recently. It's hard for her out there, alone so much."

"Might it be better not to warn her I am coming?"

He got angry at that. "No. She is no alcoholic, Samson. She is in full control of herself and will be fully articulate when you arrive."

I enjoyed his getting angry. Revenge for his trying to pull my strings, have my mouth say his words. I've never really liked being told what to do. It's a temperamental deficiency in this occupation.

I left Willson a few minutes before ten. He was not an imposing presence, but I was beginning to appreciate his confidence in himself. If he thought a seedy private detective would intimidate someone who was a nuisance, he had the balls to go get himself a seedy private detective.

Then if the seedy private detective grew into a better class of plant, he could set aside preconceptions and use him, me, for more delicate work. I felt like a $2000 claimer who'd been entered in a stakes. But I wasn't happy. I guess I'm just not psychologically suited to advancement.

I drove home. My parking lot was clear enough of snow that I could reclaim my prepaid parking place. I did and went upstairs. It was about ten thirty. The phone was ringing. It stopped before I got to it.

I called Dorrie. "Yes, there was a message, Mr. Samson. Please call Miss Howell at Goger and Rule in Kokomo."

I thanked Dorrie profusely and, before I forgot, I made out her December check. Whipped curs respond to kind voices. It's true. We do.

I called Kokomo but the number was busy. Ten minutes later, I got a secretary who said Miss Howell was busy. Could she call back? Sure, baby.

Miss Howell called back at a quarter past one, just as I was getting nervous about leaving for Monrovia. She sounded about six years old, but she had, she said, traced ownership of the house I asked about. Mr. Goger hadn't been specific; would back to 1900 be sufficient?

Sure, baby.

In 1910 the house was sold by Elias Pugh to Matthew Walters. Matthew Walters sold the house to John Bean in 1927. In 1932 the house had been repossessed for back mortgage and then sold at auction to Sherman Cook. Cook sold the house in 1939 to Freeman Baer who sold it in 1940 to the present owner, Mildred Willetson.

I thanked Miss Howell profusely.

Whether you should think when you drive is a matter of what you have to think about. I nearly killed myself as I turned left into the Monrovia house's driveway. It was the other guy's fault, of course. There shouldn't be any traffic on a country road.

The house looked different, in daylight, with most of the snow melted away. There were well-defined flower beds across the front. And I noticed that the grass was unusually fine —narrow swarded—and the lawn very level. There was a lot of work there. I'd found one of the things Mels did to pass the time.

Melanie Baer Kee looked different too. Younger, firmer, brighter. Or maybe it was just that now I knew she was probably only 27 as we neared 1972, if she'd graduated from high school in 1962.

Sober, she had the very presence, bearing, that Willson lacked. "Come in," she said. "Mars tells me there are some things you want to talk about."

He wouldn't lie to you.

I followed her into the living room. We shared a pair of chairs facing each other and an open fire. Only inside did I appreciate how much work, style, the furnishings of the room showed. I don't usually like designed rooms. They feel academic. This one only felt comfortable. It was a shame to interrupt the pleasure of it. Maybe it was the fire. I felt sharply, and for the first time in quite a while, the various pleasures I miss living the way I do.

"I'm afraid this conversation will not be as easy as I would like it to be, Mrs. Kee."

"Mars told me on the phone that Bartholomew had been making threats about me to you. He didn't say what."

I sucked my lips. Where to begin. "In the last two days a surprising number of questions have come up."

"That sounds ominous."

I agreed.

"Shall we do the dirty deed over a cup of coffee, or do you want to do it straight?"

"I'd like a cup of coffee, if it isn't too much trouble."

"I have it ready. I expected you would be punctual. I won't be a minute. Then we'll get down to dirty linen. How do you take it?"

"Milk, cream, or nondairy product, but no sugar."

She left the room unhurriedly for the kitchen. I could visualize exactly what she would do there. My visual impressions from three nights before were sharp.

What was also sharp in my mind was the contrast between Mels today and Mels when I'd met her, nervous, tipsy, at the House of Antiquity. The lady showed no nerves today and seemed to have complete self-control.

She brought the coffee with cream. Hers was black and if it was from the same pot as mine it was strong. The kind of stuff you'd think would put hair on the chest, if you didn't know better.

Sip. Sip. "Mrs. Kee, have you had any children?"

She smiled. "Does Mr. Bartholomew say I have?"

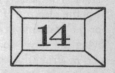

The conversation took a long and pretty complicated course. It was a matter of who said what, who wants to know, whose side are you on, boy. An owl's worth of whos.

I think chemistry was the deciding factor. We came to an understanding by about three thirty and I, at least, felt it was because we liked each other. Maybe with my woman away I was starved for someone to feel me special. But I'd like to think we acknowledged each other, Melanie Kee and me.

She had had a child in St. Louis. Her pregnancy was the reason she married there, in haste. The child was a boy but before it was a year old it had died. He had sickened quickly, then died one afternoon in her arms. She did not talk easily about it.

Eventually, because I had to, I told her Bartholomew said that her husband said she had killed the child.

No surprise, startle or shock. She said, "That's what Edmund would say. I'm not surprised he would say that to some detective he hired. Why shouldn't he?"

Which had to do, she said, with her husband's attitude toward children. As an overlooked child himself, he had a fixation about having children of his own, her words, her cause and effect. Children he would do for, lavish attention on. In the ways he had been neglected himself.

She painted an isolated, inward man, who had latched on to a lonely pregnant girl with fantasy-fed passion. She had run away from home, but, "independent" for the first time and without preparation, had accepted Kee, had allowed him to care for her, marry her. Without asking questions about his motives. And without his asking questions about hers. At the time.

"I've read a lot of psychology books since we came here. I understand it better. Then I was just glad to have found someone," she said. The way she said it meant a lot. The someone was a thirty-year-old St. Louis civil service computer programmer.

Kee had never had sex with a woman, and he didn't "have" his wife until well after the child was born. "He took the Catholic point of view seriously," she said. "The bit about sex being for making children. You would be surprised how seriously he took it. Everything was kids, kids. I kept telling him, things can happen to kids. That maybe something would happen to little—little Edmund."

"Did you expect something to happen to the child?" I asked, beginning to pave the way to my other question *du jour*.

"I think I always knew," she said. "Always. That's why I let him be called Edmund Junior instead of Martin."

It was a showstopper. I asked if we might have some more coffee. She left the room with an emotional smile to reheat what she'd already made. That was at three.

About three ten we started again.

"This is good coffee," I said. Though I am more gourmand with coffee than gourmet.

"I grind it myself. I have time to do a lot of that sort of thing."

We paused.

"I spent yesterday in Kokomo," I began.

"Oh?"

"I spent a few minutes talking to Martin's mother—I didn't tell him. And then I initiated some inquiries about where, that is, who she got her house from."

She put her coffee on the floor, and rubbed her eyes. No apparent reason.

"I found that she got it from your father."

She still didn't help.

"So I have to ask, are you and Martin brother and sister?"

"Half brother and half sister," she said quietly. Quick intake of breath, and she looked me in the eyes again. Wry smile. "That fact must explain a lot to you."

"Yes," I said, "I guess it does."

"Why we live this way." She pulled at her trouser leg. "I used to have the longest, prettiest hair. You're not shocked?" she said.

"No. I was surprised when I first got the idea, but it seemed to fit with certain things. If you were just hiding from a husband, even a fanatical one, there seemed no special reason for you to pretend you were a homosexual couple."

"It was to help explain why we would live so isolatedly," remembering decisions from long ago.

"Lots of people like to live isolatedly," I said. "But it worked. Bartholomew thinks Martin is living with a man."

"I know. Bartholomew was here yesterday. I heard him talking to Martin."

"You know? Martin said you didn't know."

"I pretended I was asleep."

I shook my head. "For two people trying to fight the world together, you seem to have a lot of secrets from each other."

She shrugged. "I can't explain. But we know each other. We decided we were better off together than separated. We decided to live this way, and if we aren't honest all the time, then it's intended well. To lie to someone you love can show you love them, don't you think? There are things the person you love doesn't want to know."

"Is that why you never told Martin you had a child?"

"It was such a shock when he found out he was my half brother. He was very strictly brought up, you know."

"He didn't know why you ran away?"

"No and he didn't know I was pregnant when I left. I only just suspected it. His mother"—there was no love lost—"never told him who his father was. I don't know whether his mother remembers who Martin's father was. It was something nobody talked about."

I frowned. "How exactly did you find out?"

She drained her coffee cup. "I was a protected—sheltered they call it—child. Because my mother died when I was eleven and my father took care of me to make up. So I didn't know any better than to study and read a lot and I never went out with boys or had a job or anything like that. The ironic thing is Martin's mother was the same way with him." Mels studied the past in her coffee grounds. It made her hard. "How my father ever got in there I do not know.

"Well, Martin went to work in this antique business. Then when I was seventeen and he was twenty-five we met in the library one day." She threw her hands up. Poof! Behold the magic.

"Since neither of us was supposed to go out, we saw each other at the library. His mother didn't want him to go out with girls. And, well, everybody knew he was illegitimate. We fell in love. Worked out ways to see each other in other places." Worldly-wise. "We had it all worked out. I would graduate from high school. Then we would tell our respective parents. Get married. Live happily ever after.

"Well, the afternoon I graduated I came back to the house with my father. He had a graduation present for me. I knew what it was, a car, but I didn't tell him I already knew. We got into the house and he was about to take me into the garage where he had it locked up. I said I wanted to talk to him. I told him I had something to tell him and it concerned my future. He was amazed. He thought, I don't know what he thought, maybe I didn't want to go to college after all. Something like that. Then I said to him, 'Daddy, I have a boy friend and we want to get married.' I was all set to tell him how I would still be able to go to college—though I wasn't so sure because I had a suspicion I was pregnant. But he didn't say anything. He just sat down. Then he said to me 'Who? Who is it?' And I told him it was Martin. He jumped up and said 'No! No!' He said it six or seven times. I cried and said to him, 'He's kind and he's good and he's hardworking and I love him. I know what you're going to say, Daddy,' I told him. 'You're going to say you don't like him because he's illegitimate.' Daddy just sat down again and he said, all quiet, 'It's not because he's a bastard, Melanie. It's because he is *my* bastard.' "

It was my turn to hide behind the bottom of a cup of coffee. There was little need to ask what effect the news had had on her. The actions I knew about explained that.

She honored my pause and, I think, understood I was offering her a stopping point. But she said, "When you are a kid and you are sneaking out to meet an older man, to make love to him without anybody else in the world knowing, the last worry that crosses your mind is the possibility he's going to turn out to be your brother."

She paused, for me to say something. But what can you say? I said, "It must have knocked you for a complete loop."

"Daddy and I just sat there. And then he ran out of the house. My first impulse was to wait for Mars." She laughed, recapturing a good deal of the innocence she remembered. "I would have had to wait, because he was at work. He didn't see me graduate. We were very careful about people connecting us. But I sat there in that house. You were in Kokomo, you say. Did you see the big house my daddy had?"

"No, I didn't."

"I sat there for, oh, a long time. Alone. I remember cleaning house. I remember deciding to do fifty things, fifty cleaning acts. And I did them. And at the end I sat down again and it was then I realized I was waiting for Martin, but what for? What could he do? I hate that moment. When I realized what had happened. It took more than an hour for it to sink in." A laugh, more forced. "But when it sunk, it really sunk. I went upstairs and I packed some clothes and I opened up my piggy bank and I left."

"Why did you go to St. Louis?"

"It just happened. I wasn't really upset or confused. I'd been preparing for a change in my life, with graduating, and getting married. I took a bus to Indianapolis and there were buses that night to St. Louis and New York. St. Louis just didn't sound as sinful as New York." She smiled again. Not weakly. The woman was not weak.

"May I ask about your father?"

She wrinkled her brow. "I never saw him again."

"Did you write to him?"

"I never communicated with him again. I never really had the chance, you know." Then, abstractedly, "Martin sees his mother. His mother was why we chose Indianapolis. That, and because Martin's business contacts in Chicago would be useful here, where they wouldn't, say, in Tahiti or South America. But my father didn't live long enough for me to be able to contact him again. About the time he died I was going into labor."

"Do you know why he took his own life?"

"Me, I presume. My inglorious fate. We were pretty close. I think he was proud of me too. I did very well in school and he was really impressed about that. I think he thought that meant he would have done well himself if he'd gone."

"I asked only because he did, well, wait, for—what—seven, seven and a half months."

"I don't know, Mr. Samson. All I can tell you is that my graduation day isn't the kind of thing that fades from the mind in seven months. Or seven years."

It struck me as a little harsh; people, even fathers, can overcome first reactions to upsetting news, can get down to solving problems. But it was her business; she was entitled.

Goger had obliged me to ask a question on his behalf. I got to it clumsily. "Your father didn't disinherit you, you know."

"Why should he?" she said heatedly, and again showed the stern core. "Nothing I did 'wrong' was my fault. How am I supposed to know Martin Willetson is my half brother if nobody tells me he's my half brother? He's a man like any other man. I can tell you that."

"That's not what I was trying to get at. You see, I talked to Robert Goger yesterday and he asked me to ask you to make arrangements about your father's estate."

"Oh."

"That's all."

She snorted delicately while I thought. Her father killed himself about the same time little Edmund was born. Maybe he'd just found out there was going to be a little Edmund. Whose grandfather he would be on both sides. Melanie had run away, but not hidden; if Goger could find her after Freeman's death, surely Freeman could have found her earlier. Early enough to figure out whose the child must have been.

"When was little Edmund born?"

"January 26, 1963. Eleven P.M. The poor darling. He was so lively and lovely. And he looked so much like Martin it was embarrassing." She spent several seconds here, but I didn't know whether she was laughing or crying. Finally laughing won. "Edmund, that is my husband, Edmund, his family tried to find a family resemblance. Edmund never told them it wasn't his child, you see. His family just thought he'd been keeping me on the side and didn't tell them until he had to." Deep breath. "That was one of the functions I served for Edmund. I masculinized him in the eyes of that horrible family of his. They were so persistent about who in my family little Edmund looked like that I almost told them."

We shared the day's Wishful Sadistic Thinking Minute. Then I said, "But did you know that your father's inheritance was still owing to you?"

"I haven't thought about it for years."

"It's a lot of bread," I said chummily.

"Well, I suppose we could have used it in times past. But Mars does pretty well, you know. We go off for vacations twice a year and we don't lack comforts."

"Except peace of mind—and freedom from people like me."

She smiled with some warmth. "In ordinary times, when we have no private detectives in our day-to-day lives, we are really very happy. I like vacations," she said. "I buy new *dresses,* and then throw them away at the end. It's very exciting."

I didn't quite have the nerve to tell her she was very lucky. Nor did I stay for more coffee. Though we chatted pleasantly for a good fair few more minutes. She felt better having talked about her historical things. A lady masquerading as a man is likely to lack close friends.

When I left Melanie I asked her to discuss with Martin what to do next. I made some suggestions, which was part of why we stood near the door for so long. I thought we could mislead Bartholomew, even though to do so would concede Martin knew something about Melanie Baer's whereabouts. Since Bartholomew was already sure of that, any deception which didn't include the admission would look phony. I also suggested Martin tell Bartholomew I was their official representative; he should bother me, not them.

"And you also ought to consider getting in touch with Mr. Goger in Kokomo," I told her. "It can hardly hurt you."

"Maybe I will. Just to tell him to give it all away." She'd done that once.

"Well, perhaps a worthy charity. Say, the Samson Home for Hoosier Gumshoes."

But I didn't believe it would happen. We were chummy, but you've got to be *really* chummy with someone for them to give you that kind of money.

15

Home is where the heart is. My home was burning. It came from TV dinners. Never mix two different kinds.

Debilitations notwithstanding, I found it pleasant to have an evening on my own while elsewhere my employers got straight with each other. I sat back in front of the Pacers on TV and felt catalytic. And there are times when catalysis can be cathartic.

It's nice to be in the middle of an employment. To have the satisfaction of progress without the threat of completion. With any luck it was now a simple matter of deciding which course best fit the requirements. Whether we went for an attrition policy, sending Bartholomew chasing wild fowl until Kee's money ran out. Or whether we went for a settlement. Find exactly what Kee thought he wanted. Why, after five odd years and a fair degree of agony, Kee was still in search of our Melanie.

She, of course, impugned his rationality. There is disinclination in these modern times to trust either computer devotees or fine points in religion. In "now," we shy from future and past, we the slobs with heartburn.

There was, however, no direct information about Kee. Without it the choice had to be attrition. Bartholomew, amenably, had said, don't bother me with the truth, just give me a plausible lead I can follow for a while. Bartholomew was a most reasonable fellow. I felt ashamed to have abused him. Willson had manipulated me into an aggressive stance and I had mindlessly taken my cue from that stance ever since. I resolved to apologize to the man.

Then there was the accusation that Melanie killed this child we only recently discovered she'd had. Convincing me it was an overheated notion Kee had used to spur Bartholomew with hadn't been hard for Melanie. In fact, easy. I presumed she could convince Mars too, though how he liked to discover facts she'd deliberately kept from him, I didn't know. They played a lot of cloak-and-dagger. Presumably he would understand and forgive where someone else might not.

But how seriously Bartholomew took Kee's accusation? I wondered whether Melanie could convince Bartholomew. In a pinch we could go to St. Louis and check the death certificate, certifying physician, that sort of thing.

St. Louis. Who did I know in St. Louis?

Of course, if there were significant chances that she had actually killed a child then it would become a police situation.

Ah well. Tomorrow. Make note. See Willson; decide course to take. See Bartholomew; apologize. See if he really is human or just an overcompensation.

16

Dreams are private things, but my last one took a disturbing turn at the end. Bucolic gambols interrupted by thunderclaps, rain, chasms, insects and gas. My sleeping mind was trying to tell me something. I woke up with a start.

"We do sleep deeply, don't we?" said a thunderclap, very nearby.

I don't always sleep deeply, actually.

I sat up and hit something in the dark with my chin. I swam out with my arms, to clear the air. To clear whatever it was away from my face, from my nose. It stung. It hurt. It choked. All the breaststroking in the world couldn't get it away. I coughed and gasped.

It had spoken. So it was a who.

"You were so soundly asleep I was afraid there for a minute I wasn't going to revive you."

I was still choking. Still burning. I didn't feel revived.

Whoever it was switched my bedroom light on. Which blinded me on top of everything else.

"Baby having trouble breathing?" A hand took me by the hair and pulled my head over the edge of the bed. It was a firmer hold than I'd have thought anyone could get. I couldn't resist being tipped over the edge. My forehead hit the floor and was pinned there. "Let me help," said the voice, and hit me hurtfully on the back.

I tried to figure where my assailant was. Which side. If I was upside down then I must have some kind of shot at his shootables. I made my best guess and clenched my fist. I hit out as hard as I could. I cracked my knuckles excruciatingly on the metal crotch made by the underside of my bed springs and one of its legs.

That just about did it, considering I was running out of breath as well.

"Phew. It stinks in here," said whomsoever. "I'll be in your office when you're decent." My eyes were focused enough to see a big foot abandon its position near my nose. He left me wrong half out of bed, supported now by a shoulder and an ear. I'd rotated somewhat in my attempt to counterattack.

I left my bedroom armed with a baseball bat, a Little League souvenir. I was going to rush my office and take it by storm.

But instead of waiting there like he said, he was lurking beside the bedroom doorway. I came out and he got me around the neck with one arm. I dropped the bat to try to pull the arm away.

"You see," he said, "water is a schoolboy's toy. If you really want to surprise someone you use ammonia." He held a little bottle under my nose. I knew the smell was familiar. I'd smelled it in my dream. I squirmed like a fish on a line. It seemed interminable. It must seem endless to the fish too.

But in the end he let me go. Threw me back. I was too small.

While I was coughing, he guided me through to my office. And sat me down in my client's chair. He sat behind the desk.

"I could go on making your morning difficult for you," said Bartholomew. He drew his extremely large revolving bullet thrower from under his arm and fondled it. "But I'll let it go at that. We'll have a little chat, shall we?"

I didn't defer. I didn't anything.

"Not feeling talkative yet? And I thought you were an early riser." He started looking through my desk drawers.

I didn't like that. It was invasion of privacy.

"What do you want?" It was the cleverest thing I could come up with.

"I'm tired of being stalled. I want a little action." He continued through my drawers. I tried to get up to stop him, but my knees exercised their veto.

In the top left he found my notebook and took it out. "You see, I get the impression you and Willson are trying to give me the run-around. Now I'm a reasonable fella. I don't mind a run-around within limits, but my employer begins to think I am giving him the run-around, and that just isn't fair, is it? Is it?"

I declined to opine.

"And there were those nasty little visits you made to my motel room. Now, I don't really like that sort of thing, you know."

I didn't answer, but my senses were beginning to right themselves. Not that I would be smelling or tasting soon. But I began to hope I would think again.

"I can't help believing you and your cute friend know things I want to know." Then mock expansive: "You should sympathize. A man wants to find his wife. That's a legitimate inquiry. A man's entitled to know where his wife is. So why all the fucking around, huh?"

I said, "I was going to come and see you tomorrow."

"Today?"

"Today."

"Well, isn't that nice. And now I've saved you the trouble of coming all the way out to visit me again. And what stunt did you have in mind this time?"

"None."

He looked at me.

"I wouldn't have come till I'd talked to Willson," I continued. "But I also wanted to apologize."

He just shook his head. Disbelieving. I got up. In the circumstances that might have been threatening. You'd have thought he would brandish his gun again.

But he could see I was a threat more to my person than his. He put the gun on the desk and watched me totter forward. "On the last page of my notebook. It says, 'See Bartholomew. Apologize.'"

"Where?"

"There."

"You don't expect me to read those chicken scrawls."

"Well, that's what it says. Look at it."

He did. I inched back to my chair. When I had landed safely, I spoke. I didn't even waste time looking for a seat belt. I said, "I was thinking about the unjustifiable way I've intruded on you. I'd like to apologize."

At least I'd taken the initiative away from him. I felt it. Maybe I should get up early more often.

"So maybe you're not just a dumb turd after all," he growled grudgingly. "Now what did you want to talk to me about?"

"I've had a long talk with Willson. I've finally got wired in on the background of this case."

"So?"

I hesitated, trying to remember just what Bartholomew had told me. Whatever story I laid on, I didn't want to tell him anything he didn't know. If I could help it.

"So Willson has finally told me about his connection with Melanie Baer."

"So where is she?"

"I mean his connection when he was a kid. Or at least when he was in Kokomo, because he wasn't exactly a kid then."

"Next you're going to tell me it's the twentieth century."

"No, look. Look at me, that's why I want to apologize to you. Willson didn't come to me because he trusted me, but just because you had put some pressure on him and he's sensitive to pressure. For reasons you know."

"So?"

"So he set me up to pressure you, like made you a real villain. It's taken me time to straighten it all out, get his confidence. So finally, he's telling me about this Melanie. So I was going to go to him today and put it on the line. He tells me what he knows, like where she is, or where she was not too long ago, or somebody who knows where she is. Whatever, and then I was going to say that we should concentrate on making a deal with you."

"What the fuck kind of deal?" He was showing remarkable patience, I thought. While I groped my way around my mind.

"What Willson wants is to be left alone, right? In his situation, attention makes him nervous. So when I find out what he knows and what he thinks he owes this broad, then it can't be hard for us to figure something out. It really depends on you."

"In what way, do you figure?"

"Well"—deep breath—"it depends how much your interests overlap with your client's. And just what this jazz about the broad having killed someone is all about."

"All I know is what my client tells me." The common cold among practitioners of our trade.

"Which is?"

"Which is that while they were living in St. Louis this Melanie kills the kid. My client says she kept talking about killing the kid, and then one day he comes back and the kid is dead."

"Police?"

"He says he didn't want to jail his wife, but even the coroner said the circumstances were unusual."

"How?"

"Don't know. Look, I'm not God. I admit I don't trust him completely. But he has a right to hire me. . . ." Shrug. "He says he didn't talk to the police because he didn't want to alienate her. Because he figured he was the only one who could help her. Only she cut out on him. But my job is to find her; what he intends, I know not. He talks about going to the police soon if I don't find her."

I raised an eyebrow, but didn't say anything.

Bartholomew continued, "I've told him your client knows something; now he is getting impatient with me. Most I can wait is this afternoon, or maybe over the weekend."

"So suppose I talk to Willson and get back to you?"

"So suppose you do."

Which was what I'd been intending to do all along. I suppose the gain for the morning's efforts was letting Bartholomew know my plans.

He stayed around for a while. I made a pot of coffee, and we talked about things. He used to be a cop in Chicago. That's where he learned the ammonia trick. "Not that we ever did that there," he said, "but the fellas talk, you know, around the dressing rooms. About what they'd do if Mayor Daley ever let them take the kid gloves off."

17

Bartholomew—Artie—left on the stroke of seven cuckoos. I tried to go back to sleep. It was hard work, and I failed. But I wasted a good hour trying, which put me into a civilized time of day. Civilized to begin a day with. I had a few thoughts about what to do, but decided to play safe and get a little explicit authorization before moving this time. I decided to see Willson.

About eight thirty I was breakfasted and ready to leave the house. I called Monrovia, to make sure Willson was coming into town. If he'd already left then Mels would probably be up.

She was. "Last night I told him everything I told you."

If only we could be sure that was everything there was to tell. "How did he take it?"

"He's having a little trouble understanding that I kept it from him because I love him."

"If he loves you then it will work out."

"Yes."

"Is he coming into work today?"

"He's not here. But I can't swear he's coming to the store."

"It'll work out. You've survived hard times together before."

"That we have, Mr. Samson, that we have." Considering my knowledge of her affairs, you'd have thought she'd call me Albert.

I brought her up-to-date.

"You talk to Mars," she said, "and do what you think is best."

So I left home for the House.

As usual I arrived before Mars Willson. The girl assistant was dusting antiques to get ready for the clamoring hordes. I appreciate familiar faces even when they aren't exactly family. I said, "Boss not in?"

"Not yet. Still looking for him?" She remembered me! A clean-looking girl, but not glamorous.

"Looking for him again."

"A salesman?" She said it doubtfully.

"You can tell by my smooth line of patter."

"It's just most salesman's order books are . . . a little more formal than that notebook."

"Needless formality is the hobgoblin of little minds."

"What?"

"I said, does the boss ever take liberties with you or do you find him well behaved?"

"You got to be kidding," she said. She showed no signs of

human sympathy for the man. It meant he never let down. Even when he was tired he kept everyone at a distance.

We were dusting a real leather upholstered couch when Willson did come in. That was about nine fifteen and Amanda and I were just getting pally. Strictly platonic, in deference to her brother-in-law the wrestler. Brick the Bruiser.

I followed Willson back to his office. He looked none too well. Glamorous, but not clean.

"You keep stirring things up," he said uncharitably.

"It's what you pay me for."

"Yes and no."

"You need to know as much as the opposition knows to have a chance."

"Yeah, yeah."

I respond to the mood *du jour*. "Look, friend, life is what it is. It's too short to careen around bitching about what you can't change. And it's too short to go around fighting with the few people you really care about. We've all got problems. That yours are up for discussion now is something that can't be prevented any more than a tax audit."

"All right, all right," he said, still irritable. "I'm sorry if I'm sliding my own troubles onto you. What did you want to talk to me about?"

It concerned this little stratagem I had for salting two birds with one cellar.

Maybe I just had tails on my mind. I pulled the panel truck away from its parking meter and a car five lengths behind me pulled out at the same time. I spotted it right away and sure enough it turned south on College behind me and then west on Washington. I was puzzled. Partly because I was sure Artie Bartholomew and I were solid enough to keep him from putting new pressure on me for at least a day. And partly because the following driver was a lady.

Women are reasonably common in our business, but there

are certain jobs they just aren't normally used on. Tailing is one. Which still left the question of who she was and who she represented.

We headed straight out west for several blocks. Numerous opportunities for her to turn toward some place more interesting than West Washington.

I got a little nervous.

When we passed West Street still in tandem I tried going very slowly and keeping close to the right so she would have reason and space to pass me. She didn't. She just pulled up close behind and matched my 25. My 20. My 18.

No real person goes 18 miles an hour on West Washington Street. Which clinched it.

It was time for evasive action. A new experience. I'd never in my life been tailed before. As far as I knew.

I hit a red light at just the right time. I was stopped first in line in the left-hand lane. She pulled up behind me. I had the full duration of the light to study her face in my rearview mirror. It was a beaut for unsuspectability. She looked like a young grandmother with a droopy nose.

I timed the light, picked up the yellow and gunned across the path of a bread truck in the right lane.

She never had a chance. Steve McQueen couldn't have followed me around that truck. She had to go straight out Washington. She had no choice.

I squealed into the first side street and pulled up in front of the biggest car on the street. I waited watchfully for twenty minutes. No Granny. No McQueen. And I began to relax.

I did the remaining distance on side streets. Roughly parallel to Washington, running mostly on Ohio, until I got to about 2000 West. I turned onto Traub and parked close to the corner of Washington. I walked to the Kings and Queens Motel.

I tapped on the door of 17 gently but firmly.

A voice said, "Yeah?"

I said, "Albert Samson. I'd like to come in with my hands up."

"Wait a sec."

It was a long sec. His watch must have been slow.

Artie Bartholomew opened the door expansively, considering the tenor of our past visits. I raised my hands, and he waved me in.

"Been catching up on some lost dreams," he said.

"I disturb you only because I said I'd get back to you. I've talked to Willson."

"And?"

"And he's told me where Melanie Baer lives. I'm on my way to see her now." I said it loud and clear, cards on the table.

"Where does she live?"

"I can't tell you that, Artie. Willson made me promise. I go to talk to her and find out what she has to say about things. Then we see where we are."

"That's not exactly being helpful, you know."

"It's the best we can do. You can wait it out a day or so, can't you?"

"I don't like it. I'm getting bored here."

"Learn to live with it. I do. Willson also said if you get nervous about things, like if your client gets nervous, we can cover loss of income within reasonable limits."

"Which are?"

"Which means, hang loose. Go down to Lockerbie Street and look at some home-grown hippies."

"I cannot promise anything, Albert."

"So don't promise anything. I said I'd keep you up-to-date. It's December 6, 1971. Now that's settled, I'm going for a bite to eat up the road. Want to come?"

"No."

I walked, slowly, back to the truck. To give him time to change his mind. I got in and shifted it up the road to a particularly poor diner in the airport direction. I read the paper and downed a couple of doughnuts with a cup of coffee. I wasn't hungry at all; it was the best I could do.

═══════

From 2000-odd West it's not a bad run to Weir Cook. I checked the truck in the overnight lot and walked leisurely to the main information center.

A bleary-eyed man who'd become too heavy to fly asked me what I wanted.

"What time is your next plane?" I asked.

"Where to?"

"Oh it doesn't much matter."

I'd hoped to bring a little dash to his life. But all I got was dots. Systematically he pinned me down. In fewer than twenty questions.

The next plane staying in the Midwest but not to Chicago, for which there was frequent service, left in twenty-eight minutes for Milwaukee.

From Ozark Airlines I got a round-trip ticket, which I charged. These days there are credit cards undiscriminating enough even for me to have some.

From a concessionaire I bought an Air Wisconsin travel bag, and a paperback: *1001 Small Businesses You Can Run from Home.* I trotted to the boarding gate. On the way I passed a droopy-nosed grandma embracing three droopy-nosed grandchildren. I boarded the plane.

In less time than it takes to eliminate 783 small businesses I was in Milwaukee. I went to a phone booth and booked a hotel room. I charged a rental car, giving my local address as the hotel. When they gave me the keys I drove directly to the Milwaukee overnight parking lot and walked back to the air terminal.

Where I went to the local Ozark desk and turned in my Milwaukee-Indianapolis trip on a Milwaukee-Chicago, Chicago-Indianapolis ticket which I bought under an assumed name. Flintlock O'Halloran. The first name that came to mind.

By one forty-five I was a plane flight closer to Chicago center and by two forty-five I had rented a bright blue '72 Ford and was somewhere in the Loop.

It was research time. I got a parking spot in the State Street parking facility, bought a quality city map, and walked to the library.

Kee is not the least common surname in Chicago, but a surfeit of Edmund Kees there ain't. He was a little farther out of town center than I would have expected of a computer statistician living on his own. We all have prejudices. He lived on Franklin Boulevard.

Then I had a shot at getting him at work. Which was not so easy. Registers of government employees exist, but the more you already know about what you want to find out, the quicker you can find it. There are a lot of governments in a city the size of Chicago, and a lot of employees.

It took me nearly an hour. But I finally got him: E. Kee, Programming Administrator of the Chicago Area Census and Ethnology Committee.

I wrote down the office address. If it had been earlier in the day, I might have tried to find the guy at work.

The address on Franklin Boulevard was an apartment. My prejudices would have been thrown for a touchback if I had found Kee in a frame house with a garden full of flowers.

Even the apartment was a little residential for my notions. Franklin Boulevard is a divided road with a grassy kiddy haven in the middle. It looked like quite a reasonable place for kids but it was hard to see it as a locale for the man alone.

But parking was easy. And a rented car's heater is a lot better than a privately owned panel truck's.

18

Before the guy in the '68 Dodge turned off the motor and looked at himself in the rearview mirror, I guessed who he was. The time was right. The dark suit was right. Then when he got out he carried a black attaché case. He was also tall and round-shouldered. He wore a tweed overcoat.

I followed him up to the building and as he opened the downstairs door with his key I said, "Mr. Kee?"

I hadn't seen the steely eyes, but they didn't make me doubt. "Yes?"

"The name is Albert Samson. I'd like to talk to you."

"Indeed."

"Melanie Baer? Arthur Bartholomew?"

"Come in."

It was a walkup; he lived on the third floor. A long thin apartment with rooms side by side by side. The door was in the middle of the pod and a corridor ran inside the apartment parallel to the corridor outside it. On entering I saw six doors altogether, counting the living room he took me to. The place demanded to be lived in by a family. Even the decoration was bright.

He didn't speak until we were seated.

"Where do you come from, Mr. Samson?"

"Indianapolis. I'm a private detective and I work for a man who used to know your former wife."

"She is my wife."

"Legally."

"Morally."

I shrugged to indicate I didn't think we had started well. But I hadn't come to quibble; I'd come to let him know he was in no position to make trouble.

"I understand not all people see things as I do," he said,

showing more flexibility than I had been led to expect. I began to wonder if anyone ever leads me to expect what I end up getting.

"There are facts we will agree on," I said. "You are not living with the woman, and haven't for a considerable time. And you have hired a private detective to find her."

"And she has hired you to protect her." He put poison in the "protect" but the venom was aimed at Mels, not me.

"No."

"No?"

"I have been hired by a man your private detective has been harassing."

"Martin Willetson."

"Yes."

"But you don't deny that Martin Willetson knows where Melanie is."

"He knows where she is."

"So that makes him an accomplice."

"Hardly an accomplice. If a woman wants to leave her husband, that is not a crime."

He paused and the eyes twinkled. I wondered if he knew something I didn't. Then he said, "If she steals a child it's a crime."

"What?"

"Melanie has my child. Surely you've met Melanie?"

Grope. "Yes, I did. But she didn't mention any child; I didn't ask. Except the child who died."

"The child she killed."

"Look, let me get this straight. The child who is no longer alive, who was born in 1963 . . . you're talking about another kid now. Is that right?"

"I am talking about *my* son," he said. "The child Melanie took with her when she left Chicago."

Oh, *that* child. . . . "Bartholomew didn't mention a kid Melanie Baer was supposed to have with her," I said.

He stood up. "That is because I didn't tell him. His job is to find Melanie; it's my job to regain the child when Melanie is found."

The idea that knowing about a child would have helped Bartholomew trace the mother—that didn't occur to him. Children leave tracks. Doesn't anybody tell the whole truth to his private detective?

"You see, I've never seen my son," he said sadly. He walked to some drawers, part of a shelf unit. He rummaged, and brought back a handful of papers. "These are as close to my boy as I have gotten," he said.

One at a time he handed the papers to me. "Doctor's report in St. Louis of a positive pregnancy test. Prenatal records of a normal pregnancy. Birth certificate."

I looked for the date. November 17, 1965. Definitely not the kid who died. Who this man said was "killed."

Kee was saying, "She had the boy at home, Mr. Samson. I don't know why she didn't go to a hospital. If she was hard up for money, I would have paid. She must have known that." The documents kept coming. "Postnatal examinations. Vaccination records."

It was quite a collection.

He said, "These"—the vaccination records—"are the last trace I have of the boy. They cover the first seven months of his life. Then stop in June 1966. So that's when she must have taken him and left Chicago." He added darkly, "I hope, I pray, she took him when she left Chicago."

He was asking questions I could not answer.

He talked quietly, sympathetically, to himself. "She called him Freeman, after her father. Not a name I would have chosen."

The kid would be six now. "Can I make copies of these papers?"

"They are copies, Mr. Samson. Keep them. By the way," he said, still somber, "I've checked the Chicago education records to see if a Freeman Kee, or a Freeman Baer, started school this year. He didn't. There is also no record of any child under either name having died in Chicago."

What can you say to that?

I said, "You understand all this is new to me?"

"Yes."

"I came up here to find out what you wanted from your wife if you did find her."

"And now you know," with dignity.

"So it's the child. You're not suggesting your wife would come back to you?"

He chose his words carefully. "When I locate Melanie I will ... offer to make a home for her, as well as the boy. I can't say I really ... want her, but I accept my moral responsibility to house the mother of my children. I can't believe, after the immoral road she has chosen, she would appreciate ... me. But I would, will offer." Over the summit, his tongue rolled more quickly down the other side of the question. "But she is not an appreciative person, Mr. Samson. She is not, never was, capable of feeling appropriate gratitude. I would accept her back, but I can't say I expect her back, despite my being her husband."

So after all this jazz, it wasn't Melanie Baer he was looking for at all.

Back to work. "And to keep you from harassing my client?"

"Just tell me where Melanie is. Why not, if Bartholomew is such a nuisance?"

"My client," I said, "feels some vague responsibility to her. He doesn't know anything about you; he certainly doesn't know anything about a child she is supposed to have made off with"—too true—"and his opinion is if she wants to hide from you, that's her business."

"He is keeping a father from his child," said Kee warmly. "That makes him an accomplice. He deserves whatever he gets."

"There are legal steps that can be taken," I said.

He smiled. "It took me a long time to save enough money

to go about this properly. But you can be sure I have sought legal advice. I have also hired a bonded, recommended, private investigator. Melanie got away from me once before, after I tracked her down with a detective. She isn't going to get away this time. I'm going to gain custody of my child, or she's going to know the reason why."

"Look," I said, "I know where Melanie is. Why don't you harrass me instead of messing with my employer?"

"If it seems appropriate, I'll keep after you both, Mr. Samson. And don't threaten me with the law. I am the last person to deny the protection of the law to every citizen of this country. But my wife will find no refuge in legal maneuvers. Moral force is stronger than legal force. And as I understand it"—he smiled—"your client seems to lack on the moral side more than enough to compensate for any strengths he may seem to have in the letter of the law."

Yet another interview in which I had lost all initiative, aggression, control. Because I didn't have complete information. I was getting used to it though. I knew what to do.

I left.

19

I didn't know what to do next as I walked down the sidewalk to the car. I didn't even recognize it at first, the car. It looked much too fancy to be the one I was responsible for.

At least I now understood Kee's residential situation. He had picked the apartment not for himself, but for him and his son to live in, with an optional room for the wife.

Then I thought about Artie Bartholomew. "Bonded and recommended." Yet the guy was hardly different from me. If anything, less "moral." Maybe I'll be a success yet.

All periphery.

I started the car and pulled into traffic. It was dark and cold. I was in a strange part of a none-too-familiar city. I had nowhere special to go. I didn't know whether I should be pleased I was finding out new things rapidly, or annoyed because nobody ever told me the whole truth.

That *was* annoying. I couldn't recall a circumstance when so many people had told so many half-truths to each other in the guise of confidence. Willson had come to me trying to recover his play. *The Kokomo Case*, no less. Kee had neglected to tell his very own private detective the real reason he was looking for his wife. Melanie had kept from her sole soulmate the trivia that she had once had a child by him, and now was omitting the detail about a second child by somebody else. Wherever that child was.

It was bald truth that the only virtuous good guys in the whole world were two honest, hardworking, brave, private detectives. And what had they spent their time doing? Assaulting each other.

I came to a park with a lake; to keep in the park a little longer—once around would have suited me fine—I took a right when it seemed appropriate. That was a mistake. When you don't know where you are, go straight. That way you can always go back.

I've read about Oak Park. . . . What wonderful surprises life pulls out in the draw. I stopped at a bar and grill willing to utilize either, and ended using them both.

It had an old but well-tuned pinny and after five games I was on the brink of replays. The food came. I quit to eat.

Replays, a recurring dream.

When I got around to the realities of life's raffle, I had to decide whether to stay overnight. For what? Certainly not more converse with Kee.

But? I could try to reconstruct Melanie's Chicago history. Or Willson-Willetson's. Or I could cross-check the documents I'd been given. I took them out of my jacket pocket. Not much I could tell from them. Freeman Kee. November 17, 1965. Freeman. Melanie's tribute to her father's memory. Yet she'd seemed hostile talking about him to me. One's allowed ambitendency of feeling, I suppose. I'd bet she would take the money before long. That was all right with me. I don't feel bad dawdling on rich clients' time. Maybe I could take a few leaves out of Artie's book. Be a success. I wondered what Sugar was doing tonight.

By my last French fry I knew I was Indianapolis bound. The most important outstanding questions on the agenda concerned the newly unearthed kid. And the place to find out about a kid is his mother.

I found out where the airport was. It was past eleven when I gave back my car and confirmed that the next plane to the biggest small town in the country was at ten to midnight.

At eleven thirty I got a brainstorm. Why not call my woman? My beloved, long-missing, now-home, gorgeous, sweet-tempered, wise, virtuous and clean woman. She was home tonight after three weeks away. Huzzah! Huzzah!

"Well," she said when I finally got through. "Where have you been?"

I was well into my third minute of a literal answer before she suggested, delicately, that literality was not what she had in mind. In my letters I had apparently made reference to the fiesta atmosphere which would be waiting for her when she returned. She'd got her hopes up, had an extra bath. For a cold, dark, empty house. Even before she hung up I got the gist: she wasn't pleased.

But it wasn't really my fault, was it? I mean, work and all that.

I got change from a nearby news vender and called her back. I'd been so distraught without her, you see. And too bored to write notes to myself about times and dates, about promises made. Then this job came along. Please forgive me. Please marry me.

"Just like a man," she said, the ultimate liberated putdown. And hung up again.

A fella can't do anything right.

It left me just enough time to snatch my Air-Wisconsin bag and run to the boarding gate, where there was a big window. Through it I watched my plane taxi to the runway. Please come back for me, I cried. But it didn't. With the same inevitability as trouble with women, it lofted itself, banked left and flew away.

I looked at the ticket in my hot sweaty little hand. Well, screw it.

On my way back to the ticketeers I eliminated sensible options like going to a hotel or taking a bus. I would wait it out for the next plane.

Which was at five thirty. Excellent. A good penance. Everybody should spend the night in an airport waiting room now and then. It would make them appreciate the privacy of a house, the comfort of a bed. However cold, however empty.

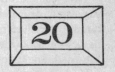

As I slipped into bed about breakfast time I did the only constructive thinking I'd done in hours. Airport waiting rooms not being conducive.

I could write to the doctor on whose letterhead confirmation of Mrs. Kee's pregnancy had come and ask him about Melanie's first kid.

It pleased me to have an idea. It felt so long since I'd done anything but get buffeted by the winds of forked tongues.

I got out of bed and tiptoed to my notebook. Anyone who could forget his woman was capable of anything. I wrote down my idea. Compulsive protection against myself.

I decided to call her. The first step on the road to rehabilitation. But I got into bed on the way. Where I fell asleep.

I woke up before noon and felt much too good. The real me has to conserve his energy, go to bed early, avoid excesses. But I felt good anyway. Not fresh enough for deep thinking, but good in the way of having some of the restraints off. A little fatigue acts like a little alcohol.

My notebook reminded me of the St. Louis doctor. But it didn't look so good. No doctor would be likely to tell me everything I wanted to know just being asked. And there was no guarantee the doctor involved with pregnancy testing would have had anything to do with the death of a previous kid.

But I still wanted to find out the circumstances of the first kid's death. You weren't going to catch me jumping onto new ground—the second kid—before I was sure of my footing on the old ground. A new day, a new me.

I walked over to the City-County Building and took the elevator to the fourth floor. The Homicide and Robbery with Violence people.

Every time I come there, I expect hundreds of people homiciding and violencing each other. It's what the sign promises. Alas, just another business office. Reception desk, other desks. Cubbyholes along the walls. Not even an excess of uniforms, because this is a detective branch and plainly clothed.

I have reasonably close acquaintance with two violence men, a sergeant and a lieutenant. That day I got the lieutenant, which was nice because I've known him longer.

Miller hadn't been a lieutenant very long, a little more than six months. But he had moved in to stay. His cubbyhole wasn't big, but it was full. Books, paper piles, cardboard boxes.

I watched him erasing a mistake on the report he was typing. You would have thought the prevention of a crime depended on the obliteration of that typo.

"Yeah?" he said without looking up.

"Your six months are up. I've come for your soul."

"It's over there in the wastebasket." Click-clack, "g" and "h." "You'll probably find it while you're fishing around for your lunch."

"Gee, you're pretty good. Do you do home typing on your off days?"

Et cetera. A certain competitive style has crept into our badinage. Miller got elevated from sergeant after he made the arrests which one of my cases turned out to warrant. It was one of the flashy but irrelevant cases which involve no substantial menace to the public's weal but which the papers catch onto like millionaire uncles. It pushed Miller into the limelight, not to mention a little alkaline glare for me. Shortly afterward, Miller got kicked upstairs. And I got solicited, briefly, by a better class of client. As time passes I remember my part in his promotion as more than just bringing him to the brass's notice. I've begun to presume he would never have been promoted if I hadn't brought that case to him.

He, on the other hand, recalls having been on the top of the hill already. My case was just a big blow when a little puff would have been enough.

His version is nearer to the truth, of course. But I don't like to admit it. I refuse to admit it. A fella likes to have been good for something to his friends. So they can pay back the favor.

"What's the matter, Al? Wanna borrow a quarter?"

"Merely come to collect a little of the great debt I am owed," I said pretentiously.

"Be happy to give you a dime. Got change for a five spot?"

"It's nothing hard, Jerry. One tiny letter, one tiny question. I'll type it for you myself."

"What is it?"

"A query concerning a cause of death. Any peculiar circumstances. That's all."

"So why don't you do it yourself? You purport to have some clout with death certificates, as I recall."

"It's in St. Louis. My stick is big, but not that long."

"St. Louis!" He thought about it for a minute. "You're not . . ."

I smiled. My track record has been uppish lately, last year or so. I'm like a seven-year-old sprinter who's just found the speed to win cheap claimers. A late bloomer, like.

"I just want to check out a nasty accusation I've heard about how somebody died, that's all."

He picked up a pencil and drew a fresh sheet of paper. "What's his name?"

"Whose?"

"The nasty accuser."

"Krist," I said.

"Spell it."

I did. "K—r—i—s—t, Jesus H."

A couple of seconds elapsed before he set his pencil down and gave me that you're-not-cooperating-do-you-want-to-take-this-rap-all-by-yourself stare.

"Look," I said. "Somebody else has said the nasty accuser is a psycho. I'm trying to confirm the death was natural. I'm sure it was. I just want to check it, that's all."

More elapsed time. "And if the Missouri death certificate says 'heart attack' what then? You presume natural or unnatural?"

"Uh, well, that would be a little surprising. I mean heart attack."

"Why?"

"Because the death I had in mind concerned a kid about a year old."

"Nothing's easy with you, is it?"

"What am I supposed to do? I applied to join the police force, but they wouldn't make me a lieutenant. I have to take what comes."

"It always has to be your way, doesn't it? You can't put yourself under anybody else's authority, can you?"

"There's no need to go serious, Miller. I would appreciate your help, both as an old friend and a responsible public protector, in learning whether Edmund Kee, Junior, of St. Louis, Missouri, born January 26, 1963, died about eleven months later of natural causes or unnatural causes or something in between."

He wrote as I spoke. His speed writing is better than his typing.

"Why not?" he said.

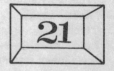

On my way down I decided to go back up. On the first floor I changed elevators and went to the top of the City-County Building to have a look at the city in winter. It was a lovely clear day. I stayed up there for quite a while, identifying all the landmarks I could. Restaurants I knew. The site of my former building.

I felt the tourist and I liked it. Why not? I could still be in Chicago today as far as the paying client knew. What's an afternoon among friends?

Why does everybody pick on me, all at once. What have they got in common?

After I'd had my panoramic views for the day I de-elevated to ground level. I walked through Monument Circle on the way to my truck. After I got the truck I drove to my mother's, but via Tenth Street. Another of the many sights of Indianapolis, the House of Antiquity.

Willson's Renault was outside it. He was no doubt inside and thinking, occasionally about me. When would I be back? What news would I bring?

I was confused about the job. I was in deep water and didn't know which way the current ran. It was difficult. I had plotted with Willson. Go see Kee to find out exactly what he wants, what he will take. On the way, lay a dummy trail for Kee's sleuth. Rather nice, too. Drop in on Bartholomew and say you are going to see Melanie, then give him time to follow you. And lead him a trail to anywhere, Milwaukee as it happened. Bartholomew should think you are friendly enough and stupid enough to trust him. It was all very tidy. Except when I actually got to the man who was the real trouble.

The angular Kee. Just what the hell do you want, I had asked him on behalf of my client, Willson, and to some extent on behalf of Willson's . . . what? Girl friend, sister? Buddy? Willson's Melanie. What is it you want? Melanie back? You can't have her, you must know that. Just to cause trouble? Well, we'll get the law on you. Some moral vindication? See previous answers.

"I want my son," he had said.

Son? What son?

Oh, that son! The one I've never heard of, no one's ever told me about. That son.

All of which had left me with decisions.

Plan A: Go directly to client. Do not pass Monrovia.

What do I say? Kee says he wants his son back. What son? See previous . . . I'd been through the surprise child routine already with him, for Christ sake. Melanie's was the knack of having unbeknownst children. She dropped them like flies. Two in less than a week.

And what would Willson do? What could Willson do?

Go to Melanie. Ask her.

Plan B: Go directly to Melanie. Do not pass client.

I hadn't kept very good track of time, so I didn't know whether to expect a full house or just a pair of deuces when I got to Bud's Dugout.

Ma was pretty busy but not too busy to frown at me when I walked in. The frown would be for the cock-up over the return of my lady. I have the reputation, in the family, of not being completely reliable. It's hard to live a reputation down. Especially when your actions live up to it.

Ma waved me to the back room, as she does when things are less than private out front. But I went to the pinball machines instead. I'm a free man. Arrrh. Freeman Kee, where are you?

I don't know whether you have to be brought up on pinnies to appreciate them properly. I think not, but I consider it one of the advantages of my childhood that I had access to good machines. One of the ambitions of my life is to run a pinny championship. Forty different machines. Total points from five plays, each machine. No last-number replays and very sensitive tilts. Scores against other competitors like in duplicate bridge. I'd just like to stand in the middle of the competition hall and listen to the tinsel tinkles of the scoring bells, the thwacks as extra games are slammed on the program. They are the applause of the crowd, the feel of the home run. Respectively.

It was nearly three thirty when I left my mother's luncheonette. Mothers are there to forgive.

And I decided to uncomplicate life a little bit. By the direct thrust of a couple of questions at close quarters.

The isolated house near Monrovia looked particularly alone as I drove up that Thursday. Snow enhances a house, makes it look cozy and like a refuge. Melted snow, taking as it does the color of mud, is more realistic. There are no refuges.

I stood at the door and rang the bell for a good three or four minutes. I couldn't believe my bad luck. Nobody home.

It showed how stupid I can be. There in my notebook is a most excellent and rare phone number, appearing in only a select few notebooks. All I'd had to do was use it. "Mels, baby, you gonna be in this after?"

Real life is too lifelike. I accepted my fate. But decided to look around a bit anyway. Who knows, a woman living alone, terrible things might have happened and she might be lying on the kitchen floor approaching the point of no return at this very minute. It was certainly my duty to check out the possibility.

Melanie was not visible from any of the outside windows. Moreover there was no car in the double garage. I went back to my own vehicle and after some halfhearted scraping to get the mud on my legs down to low ankle level I got in. There was something unsatisfactory about things. I started the motor and the heater but sat and read my notes. I went over my interview with Melanie. I had liked her, felt sympathy for her. A kind of admiration and appreciation for the hard times she had been through.

But I hadn't found the source of my disquiet in my book when Melanie drove up the driveway behind me in a little black Valiant.

That was it, of course. The picture I'd been led to draw of Melanie's day-to-day life was housebound extremity. That for the sake of her grand illicit passion she was utterly isolated and isolationist.

She pulled right up behind my truck. We met by my door.

"Mr. Samson," she said, as if it was not a completely pleasant surprise. "I wasn't expecting you. Is there some trouble?"

She made coffee for us as she had done before. The breath of routine helped me. I knew my stuff, the questions I had come to ask, but I didn't ruminate as I should have done.

Fatigue was catching up with me, fogging my intuition. And by the time she came back, I still hadn't figured how to get past the chaff to the wheat.

So I winnowed. "I didn't realize you went out during the day."

She smiled and sat down opposite me. But she was not relaxed. "After we first moved here I didn't go out of the house alone for thirteen months."

"Wow."

"I spent each day planning my next day. I would call Mars at lunchtime and order the supplies and books I wanted him to bring me. I read a great deal about all sorts of thing. I drew. And I worked on the house. It wasn't in very good condition, you know, when we bought it."

"You wouldn't be able to tell from the way it looks now."

We paused. She didn't make the natural progression—here to respond to the compliment—so I knew we were on less intimate terms than when we had last parted. "What happened after the thirteenth month?"

"We decided to experiment. We divided the area around here into places Mars goes to and places I go to. I tend to go to larger stores, supermarkets, because they're anonymous. I go out like this." She displayed herself, a delicate man. "We've had no trouble."

I said, "I don't quite understand why you decided to live like this."

"We're not like other people." She stated the fact mildly, commonest thing in the world. Yet she was tired, possibly tired of it. "Our relationship . . . is taboo, and prohibited by law. We can never have friends the way other people have friends. We're different from other married couples. We're not married, for one thing. Suppose somebody got interested in us and checked? We're closer to each other than real married people. We aren't having any children."

"But . . . aren't the chances rather remote . . . ?"

"We have to think of the consequences," she said tiredly. "If something happened, then we would be broken up forever. Even jailed. You don't gamble unless you are able to lose. We decided to spend our lives together. We've both put all our apples in this one cart."

She stopped, and I let it rest. The reasons were not the kind which could convince me, which perhaps could not convince Melanie now. But the reasoning was not being done now. It had been done under the duress of discovery five years before. When dangers and enemies were sharper, more visible, over their shoulders. They lived this way today because they'd lived this way yesterday.

"Besides," she said. "Not even what we've done has protected us."

We thought on that one for a moment.

She then said more heatedly, "And it's more honest, to live like this. We *are* different. Not the same."

And you aren't lost to the Kees yet, I thought. Then I said it.

"You came out here to talk about Edmund, didn't you." Resigned statement. Willson had told her of my plans for going to Chicago.

"Well, your husband caught me off guard," I said.

It was me asking to be prodded along. Asking her to grunt "How?" or "Yes?" or to make some attack on Edmund. But she didn't do it. Maybe she didn't want to hear anything I would say after starting like that. Maybe she already knew what I was going to say. She just sat there. The good vibes we'd had before were gone. And that unnerved me. What it did to her I don't know. But all of a sudden—or was it? We were both tense. We sat silent and staring. We are lost now, she was thinking. Maybe. Only she knew if they were.

At last I said, "Your husband doesn't want you back." No response. "He says he wants his son."

"But his son is dead!" she ejaculated. "I didn't beat him, I never hit him, and I never *wanted* him to die. He just did. I don't know where the bruises came from. They just did and he died and there was nothing I could do about it." She cried, dry. Reliving the horror, at a distance. Then pulled herself together while I remembered that this had happened less than two years after her father told her she was pregnant by her brother. "The doctor said it was blood disease," she said savagely. "Would you like to know about blood disease? I did a lot of reading my first year in this house. I know all about it. Its chances are greatly increased by inbreeding. All you have to do is study the Hapsburgs." She positively challenged me to ask for detail.

"That's not the son he's talking about."

"What?"

"It's not Edmund Junior. He wants *his* son, Freeman Kee." I took the documents out of my notebook.

"I . . . I don't know what you're talking about."

"Well, if you don't nobody does," I said uncharitably. I was springing it on her, but, damn it, spring on as you are sprung on. "Your husband gave me these documents. Positive pregnancy test. Birth certificate. Clinic visits. Vaccination record." She looked at them, wide-eyed, one by one. With horror or shock, or with surprise or wonderment? I was beyond distinguishing. I just wanted her to go to a back room and bring out a six-year-old kid and make it all better.

Instead she put them down. She got out of her chair, walked slowly to what looked like a commode. Levers on the flap drew forth a small range of large bottles and a couple of glasses. A liquor cabinet. Of course. She picked up one of the bottles, vodka, and poured half a glass. Drank it down. Replaced the glass and left the commode open, ready to accommodate again.

"You're just like all of them," she said hardly.

"What do you mean?"

But her mind had passed to specifics. "You bring my husband's lies to me and try to twist my guts with them. Well, I'm not going to have it."

The mood passed rapidly from eye to hurricane.

"I'm not against you," I tried to say, without visible audience.

"You're just like them all. Well, you take your damn papers, mister, and you give them back to my husband and you stuff his murdering lies up his ass." I gathered the documents, my notebook, my coat. I didn't want to leave. I wanted to stay and whine "I'm just a pawn in the game." She shouted abuse at me nonstop. Even pawns have to be on one side or the other. I left shattered, but I left. "Up his ass! You hear me? Damn you. DAMN you!"

I was a third of the way back to the city when I finally spotted a phone booth by the road. I veered dangerously to park next to it. I needed it badly. I dialed the House of Antiquity but got a misconnection. I dialed it again and it rang. And rang. And rang.

Rats. Rats and mice. I took a deep breath, and looked at the road. It was a few minutes past five thirty. I began to think about just how I would pick out the Renault in time to flag it down. Christ, the phone was invented for private detectives. Any same who don't use it are nuts. I should have called Willson long ago. He was, after all, my client. I have a legal obligation to him.

Where to catch him. I finally chose the turn from the main road. Too close to the house but the only place I could be certain of singling him out.

I should get there quickly, to make sure to catch him.

I left the phone booth, then went back in. Suppose I were Willson. I would expect to hear from that stupid Samson sometime today. If not from Indianapolis then from Chicago. If I wasn't available at the shop, then mightn't I leave a message with my stupid detective's answering service? To tell him, in words of one syllable, how to contact me.

I dialed my own number. Dorrie, just at the end of her shift. A little luck for a largely luckless day.

"There was a message, Mr. Samson."

"Great."

"It was from a woman who didn't leave her name and said that against her better judgment she would let you into the house between seven and seven thirty—after dinner, she said —as long as you were bearing a king's ransom for Lucy."

I didn't have to ask whether those were the exact words. "There were no other messages?" I asked.

"No, sir. Were you expecting one?"

Well, yes and no.

I went out of the phone booth to the truck. Then back to the phone booth. They are so few and so rare, working phones in booths. You have to make the best of them.

I tightened my belt a notch, like a lifter tackling a record weight. I was doing what was hard for me, stitching in time. I called my woman. To explain that if I didn't arrive—though I appreciated the graciousness of extending the liberty—it wouldn't be because I didn't want to.

"You are a son of a bitch," she cooed. I wish she had cooed.

I did everything I could. I explained how I was in a delicate situation with a possible child murderer. That at the very least there was a six-year-old child missing. Wandering in the countryside, cold and lonely, hungering, thirsting.

"You go where you want to," she said.

I tried a different tack. I proposed marriage.

"You think marriage would legitimize treating us this way?"

The conversation didn't last long. In the end she hung up, leaving me the child in the countryside, cold and lonely and cetera.

I made it at last to the truck, U-turned with discretion and returned to Mars and Mels Road.

I'm not as stupid as I think, I told myself as I stood in the cold trying to warm my hands on the hood fifteen minutes later. There had been adequate reason to see Melanie before contacting Martin. He had used me before to talk to her about things he couldn't, to talk to her about the first child. I was reasonable to want the facts about the second child before I came to him. It hadn't worked out, but I could defend myself in a Court of Responsibility. At least I had my reasons. Now I needed more reasons about why I was standing by the road in the dark in December. I must be nuts. Speaking of nuts, I began to wonder about Melanie.

Speaking of whom . . .

It all happened rather suddenly. I heard a door slam up the road. And since the only doors to slam up the road were Melanie's doors, I stepped onto the road so I could see better. Blurred lighting from the house. Then a burst of light, headlights as her car swung around to face out. Where the hell was she going?

My impulse was to follow her. I did hesitate. Then I got in the truck. I saw her turn at the end of the driveway, not toward the main road but in the other direction. Where to I knew not. I started my motor.

It's a good thing driving is mostly reflex, because my mind was fully on getting after the black Valiant as it sped away. But reflex made me check oncoming traffic. A car turned off the main road, passed in front of me. A Renault. I left the shoulder behind it. Watched it turn ahead into the driveway Melanie had just come out of. Wherever Mels was going it wasn't in response to a call from Mars.

I was on the road and approaching the decision. Follow Melanie or dash in and get Mars to come with me to follow Melanie.

At the driveway turn I accelerated. I had some catching up to do.

Fortunately there isn't much traffic in the Indiana countryside after dark in the Indiana winter. Everyone stays home to make lists to send to Santa. I caught up with the pair of lights in the distance ahead of me, saw the vehicle was a Valiant. The black Valiant. And I passed it.

Speed, speed; slow down, signal right into a field road entrance; turn, kill lights. Melanie passed me. She wasn't traveling fast. I let her go a few seconds, got back on the road and tracked her from pretty far back. In some ways tailing is easier in the dark. You can see car lights ahead at times you couldn't see a car.

It was a long, meandery night. Melanie traveled slow because she didn't know where she was going. Often at a junction she would wait several seconds before deciding which road to take. Twice the wait was so long I had to turn past her in order not to sit, obvious and noticeable, in lane behind her. Once she turned the way I had, once not.

We hit some west Indiana high spots and then drifted a bit north. Waveland, Veedersburg, Attica. I was set to drive to Chicago by ten; I was sure that was where things were heading. I had the mileage, I'd started with a full tank of gas. But when she stopped for gas and a toilet, I took the opportunity to top up since there was another station across the street. Fill'er up. Yessir. Three and a half gallons? I don't like to let it get too low. . . . Yessir. Where are my King Soybean Stamps? Here they are, sir.

We were on our way to Kentland when the pace picked up. I'd been wondering for the third time in the hour whether it would be wise to let her know I was along for the ride. You know, pull up beside her and wave. When she took a right at a sign to Lafayette and pushed her running speed up from twenty-five to fifty.

Destination, it turned out, was Kokomo.

Driving along, my mind indulges by telling itself stories. She stole gold candlesticks from local churches when she was a kid and had buried them. Now she had just remembered where and was going back to pick them up. I've always wanted to unbury a treasure. Of course some folk would say the opportunity to revisit Kokomo was treasure enough.

I was interested who she was going to see at twelve at night. But the answer was nobody. She pulled into the B and B Motel, booked a room, moved her car up to it, and moved in.

I got out of the truck and scouted until my toes got numb. Which with running in place was about twenty minutes. I wanted to know if Melanie was making calls. I didn't see any sign of it from what I could spy through the window of the switchboard.

When I couldn't take much more I took a quick stroll up to the black Valiant. I copied its license number and had a look inside. In the back, on the floor, was a large cardboard box with its top folded shut.

It gave me a start. Threw me into confusion. I dropped into a crouch by the side of the car.

What in hell's name does a woman like Melanie keep with her, no matter where she goes? And then leave out in the cold.

I got an idea, but it was bad.

I blew into my folded hands. I wished I'd been able to get ready for this night pursuit. I'd have routinely brought some handy tools.

I checked my pockets. Not much. You don't open many cars with a dime; with some moldy Popsicle sticks. Damn. I wanted to get into that box.

And at the same time I didn't.

Dilemma.

For the heck of it I tried the car door.

It opened.

Even then I didn't move immediately. What could it be?

There are things worse than finding tiny arms, and tiny legs.

Tiny heads and tiny torsos.

Keeping low I slithered into the back of the car and opened the box. Revealing potato chips, cookies . . .

There were other things. Too terrible to mention. I'd kind of forgotten Melanie had just come back from somewhere when I talked to her. Shopping, it would seem.

I let it go at that. I was satisfied Melanie had settled for the night. I needed some rest.

I thought about booking into the B and B myself. Asking for a room away from the other guests because I was very tired and wouldn't want to be disturbed. It was when I left a call for seven that things would get sticky. I drove around and finally got a room elsewhere.

The night wasn't over though. I sat on the bed in the gorgeously warm room and put through a call. To Monrovia.

Willson answered almost immediately. "Mels, darling, is that you?"

It wasn't, which soon became apparent.

"I got back tonight and nobody was here," Willson told me. "No note. Nothing. I don't know how she could do this to me. I wonder if she knows what real love is. Where could she have gone? Do you know? Is it anything to do with you?"

I hadn't planned to, but I said, "No. I'm calling from Chicago." I can't remember ever having played so cute with a client. "I've been to see Kee," I said.

"You don't have any idea where Melanie is?"

"She's not here with me. Look, would you rather I called you back tomorrow?"

"Yes."

"All right. What time?"

"What's your number there? I'll call you when I get up."

"Better let me call you. I'm going out early. You take a pill and get some rest. Melanie must just have gone off to think.

She's bound to call you before long. You mustn't worry about her."

He wasn't. "I don't know how she can make me suffer like this," he said. "She's supposed to love me." He was worrying about himself.

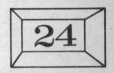

I settled for a seven thirty call. When conscious I called directory assistance; then used the fruit of their labor.

"Is Mr. Goger there, please?" I asked the woman who answered. She was not pleased to hear from me. Don't you remember me, darling, that day under the boardwalk at Indiana Beach . . . ?

"Who is it and what's your business?"

I gave my name. "Tell him it is about Melanie Baer."

"Oh," she said, with morning disgust, and put the phone down on something hard. It was a good couple of minutes before she came back. Not exactly sprinting. "He says can you meet him at the office at eleven."

"I'd much rather see him earlier somewhere else."

"He's a busy man, you know. Just because he's semiretired, don't think he isn't a busy man."

"Tell him, please."

Bang! I would run out of ears unless I got lucky and the phone shattered first. It was the longest phone call, minutes per word, I'd ever made.

"He says, then, at the house before ten. Good-bye!"

"Wait! Where's the house?"

She gave me the address. "Good-bye!"

"Wait! How do I get there?"

I found a diner and very nearly ordered four cups of coffee and a dozen doughnuts to go, just like the man in front of me did. I'm always open to suggestion.

By twenty to nine I had parked across the road from Melanie's motel. Two doughnuts later I realized the Valiant wasn't in sight. Remembered it had been in sight when I left last night. I certainly had all my eggs in Goger's basket now.

He was the only reason for Melanie coming to Kokomo I could think of. No fond relatives or special friends. That I knew of.

I felt sort of bad about Willson. I could have eased his anxieties of the night and I hadn't done it. His attitude had annoyed me. Life perpetrating complications on him, disturbing his cozy little world. I didn't see perturbations of Willson's life as the most important goings-on of the moment.

I finished breakfast and set myself to find Robert Goger's cozy little town house.

It was more like the town itself. I've seen big in my time—from the outside—but this was big!

Nobody answered the door for minutes. Then Goger came himself.

"Nice little place you've got here," I said pettily. "Not enough room for Indianapolis, but maybe if you invite it in two shifts . . ."

He tolerated me nicely and led the way through the catacombs to a room with a huge wooden door. "We'll talk in my office. I presume you prefer privacy."

"Yes."

He took a key out of his jacket. The door opened into a book-lined study the size of my apartment. "None of the servants comes in here. You really need a place to call your own."

"Absolutely. Absolutely."

"Sorry I couldn't come to the phone this morning. But I always swim before breakfast."

"And then you have to regild the gold plate. I have the same problem."

He smiled. "Sorry. Find a comfy chair."

It was my fault really. People are different in different environments. I'd first met Goger in traditional, if well-to-do, lawyer's chambers. I'd concentrated on what he had to say. And I'd missed completely the la-dee-dah. I didn't miss it this time. I'm quick, I am, given enough time.

"You mentioned Melanie Baer," he said.

"Yes. She's in town, and I believe she intends to see you about that money."

"Good. Good! You passed on my message."

"More or less. I told her it was still available."

We sat in silence for a moment. "That's not all you wanted to tell me, though."

"No. I expect her to come to your office today. And I don't want you to give the money to her."

"Oh?"

"At least not quickly. Today is Friday. How long does it take to come up with that kind of bread?"

"It depends. I don't keep it in a box around the office."

"No. But if she rushed in and said she wanted money fast?"

"I would, I suppose, advance her what I could out of my own resources."

"Which would be what? The whole thing?" My eyes swept the room again. His surprisingly luxurious circumstances had startled me. It was showing.

"Of course not," he said quietly. "There's no need to be hostile."

"I know," I confessed. "I am just angry with myself for not seeing a place like this lurking in your background."

"We each have standards we measure ourselves by," he said.

"I suppose this is not a diplomatic juncture to offer you a really fine cigar."

"I don't smoke them. But if you turn your back I'll steal six to give to friends."

The sharp eyes studied me. Even twinkled. "Which would be worse, if I'd inherited this style of life, or if I'd earned and chosen it myself?"

"I'm not sure. I'll form a committee to study the problem."

"How about neither? Though I will inherit it, or part of it; my mother is eighty-nine, still lives on the premises and likes me to live at home. I don't like it much if that's any consolation. But I make do. No, Mr. Samson, I would not be able to advance Melanie Baer the capital sum of her inheritance. And if, for some ill-advised reason, she wanted the sum in cash, it would take several days to realize."

"I don't want you to give her anything at all at least until Monday."

His eyebrows went up. Came down again. "It would be difficult, if she asks, not to advance her, say, a few hundred dollars."

"I'm talking about any big money," I said. "Enough to run away on."

"That's what she is planning to do?" he asked gravely.

"I don't know, but I think so. Last night she ran away from a man she loves because a subject came up she thinks will cause her a lot of problems."

"Will it?"

"She's the only one who knows, and she's the one who ran away. It's easy to say, but she can't pretend it just doesn't exist."

"What is the subject?"

"It's to do with her children."

"There've been more than the one who died?"

"Well, one more that we know about. One died, maybe under questionable circumstances. The other is unaccounted for. His father wants him back and nobody admits knowing where he is."

"I see," he said. He mused. I'd put it harshly, but harsh was the only available way to cover the facts as I knew them. "And now she is running away."

"That's my guess," I said. "And I don't know any reason for her to come to Kokomo except to see you for the money."

"Where is she?"

"I know where she stayed the night, but she was gone when I got there this morning."

"That was careless," he said unforgivingly. I suppose he was used to the best and in this situation two or three ops in shifts would be best and one Albert was not.

"I couldn't come to you and follow her at the same time," I answered shortly.

"Assuming she comes to my office," he said, "where will you be?"

"Outside. I want you to keep her on ice here in Kokomo. Out of harm's ways. So I can push my people in Indianapolis to come up with more information to fill in the picture."

"Well," he said, rising. "Let us hope she does get in touch with me." I got up too. "And if she does I will certainly keep your suggestions in mind." He walked to the door, opened it. "The cigars are in the carved box near the lamp. I'll wait outside for you."

But I didn't take any. It had been what we in the trade call a joke.

25

I wasn't pleased with Goger. Friendly, but only in a professional way. Not committed.

And I still didn't know where Melanie was. It made concrete plans impossible. I should have gotten up earlier. I should have checked into the same motel, gotten the manager to cooperate.

It was because you were tired, I told myself. Because of that night's no-sleep the night before last. That's what I told myself and it was true, but I still wished I knew where the hell Mels was.

Goger's mansion was in the northwest part of town. I drove back to Kokomo center. I wanted to park where I could pick up Melanie if she came to Goger's office. When she came.

Easier said than done. I cruised for ten minutes without getting a shot at any parking at all. Friday, a big shopping day. But shopping means turnover, and eventually I got a meter four spots back on Buckeye. Goger's office was around the corner on Mulberry. I could lurk on the corner, see Melanie come out; run back to my panel truck. Everything comes to he who waits. Everything the other fellas leave, anyway.

I stuffed an hour's worth into the meter's gills and then found a phone. After finding a phone I tried to find more change. After getting a roll of dimes from a bank I tried to wait patiently for the phone again. But it was cold. Not raining, not snowing. Just howling with wind. Wooooooo.

My first call was to the Indianapolis police and the honorable Lieutenant Miller. He wasn't there. Day off.

Undeterred, I called him at home. That's one thing about Miller, he's held his ground. He bought his house on Illinois when he came off probation as a patrolman and he's still there. He even stays home on his off days.

Janie answered the phone. "Who is calling, please?"

Reluctantly I told her. She's never been fond of me. Partly because I'm not a "success" and partly because of some ancient history. But she said, "Oh, hello, Albert. It's been a long time since we've heard from you. How have you been?"

What? "What?"

"I understand you had some injuries in the line of duty not too long ago. I do hope you're feeling better."

"I am. Thank you for asking."

"Oh think nothing of it. I think Jerry is in the basement. I'll go get him."

"Thanks very much."

Well, I must be growing handsome and distinguished in my old age.

"Miller," said Miller.

"We've got an emergency at the waterskiing championships, lieutenant. We need all the hands we can get to help break the ice."

"So what do you want on my day off?"

"Why so surly? Did I interrupt intimate goings-on in the gloom of the loom room?"

"I'm painting the billiard table. What do you want?"

"All right. I want the stuff on cause of death of that kid we talked about."

"Relax. You'll have it Sunday or Monday."

"You mean you'll be back to work Sunday or Monday depending on whether you call in sick to watch the football. I need that information for the natural progression of this case. I need it, I want it. I'll go to the policemen's ball, whatever it takes. I'll even tell Janie about the movie shows at the frat. What will it take to move you?"

"Christ. You sit on your hands for months, then I say I'll give you a little help and you expect me to charter a jet."

"Odds are it's on your desk now and a phone call from you will get it like a five-buck hooker." Quick. "It's important," I said.

"Important?" he asked quietly.

Usually I play down his opportunistic optimism about what I'm up to but I passed this chance to stifle his imagination.

"What do you know, Al?" he said.

"Know? I know I need that information. And if I don't get it today it may be too late to keep the bad guys from suffocating the president by filling up his white house with heroin."

"What's it about? Why's it so important?"

The operator interrupted to ask for money.

"Where are you?" asked Miller. "What the hell's going on?"

I said, "I'll call you back no sooner than an hour from now. Please make an effort to acquire the information requested. That is all. This is a recording."

Miller and I used to have more fun before we started doing important business together. Not money business. I'm not one of his informers; I never have any information. But we scratch backs these days, and it's changed an escapist nostalgic us-against-them type of relationship to . . .

Ah well. *Toute passe* and nothing stays the same either.

It was ten forty-five when I finished my chat with Miller. There were no hordes clamoring to get into the phone booth and it was protection from the wind.

My first impulse was to call poor Willson. "Heard anything from Melanie?" That wasn't a bad question. But I was afraid he'd ask me questions too. Where are you? What are you doing there?

I called Goger's office instead. No luck. I left my name and told them I thought he'd understand why I'd called.

So I left the shelter of my phone booth and walked back toward Mulberry Street. I stopped in a variety store for things to divert me if my loitering outside Goger's took a long time. The demoralizing fear was of waiting there indefinitely with no sign of Mels. Three days later . . .

I picked out a couple of candy bars and a *Tribune*. I could read the want ads. It can't be too late to learn to milk cows. But the store didn't have what I really wanted. A hat or a scarf, a false beard—some degree of disguise. I didn't want Melanie recognizing me at a glance.

They did have pipes; I bought one. And felt foolish. I'd never smoked one and I didn't really feel like starting. Foolish or not, I tucked the receipt for the pipe into my "expenses" pocket. "One pipe for disguise."

I approached the critical area slowly. No Melanie. And no sign of the Valiant. The car would be the key. Find it, stake it, follow it. Melanie was as isolated in Kokomo as I was. She needed her wheels. And when I found them I would find her.

I found them.

As I turned the corner to go to my truck. There, in front of it, was the black Valiant.

Empty, but I could hardly sit in my front seat and trust she wouldn't notice me leering at her as she got into her car.

Now if I lay down in the back of the truck, to read my want ads . . . So I did.

I have things outfitted, to some extent. A long piece of foam, not exactly a mattress, but big enough to sleep on, and insulation against the cold. What with my candy bars and all, I got quite comfortable.

Until twenty-five minutes later, when I heard a rap-rap-rapping on my chamber door.

A cop was banging his stick on my back window. I grabbed my pipe, and clambered to the front and out the passenger door.

"Well, what might you be doing, sir?" asked the cop affably.

"I was just reading the paper while I wait for my wife to finish the shopping."

"Not there to help her with the packages? Not very helpful, are you?"

"No, I'm not," I said, and then I saw he was eyeing my pipe in a curious fashion. "I'm trying to give up smoking," I said, smiling. I fingered the bowl, self-consciously. "See. Nothing in it. Helps to keep something in the old mouth."

"I'm sure it does," he said unconvincingly. "You know why I'm here talking to you, don't you, sir?"

"Not really, no."

He gestured with his baton. I couldn't make out what he was pointing to at first. It looked like Melanie's right rear tire. I peered in the general direction.

"The meter," he said. "You've expired."

"Oh! Oh! Here, let me fix that." I whipped out my roll of dimes. And as I fumbled trying to stuff one into the damn thing's slot I saw Melanie Baer Kee leave the offices of Goger and Rule. My heart dropped. I dropped the dime. Got it up, and finally into the machine. It stuck. "It's stuck," I said pitifully. Then it went in and wheels whirred. I was left standing, facing the Kokomo cop with most of a roll of dimes in my hand.

"Planning to park here quite a while?" he asked. "I think I'd better see your driver's license."

"That would be a good idea, officer. Excellent. But could you just step over here, behind my truck . . ."

I jumped behind the truck and slouched low.

"Look," I whispered, pulling my wallet out of an interior pocket. "I'm a private detective and I'm following the woman who's coming down the street now." He studied the certificates I showed him. Compared my vehicle number with the registration, matched my ID picture with my ID face, gave them all back to me and said, "There's no woman coming down the street."

"What?"

"There's no woman coming down the street. You must have lost her."

"I can't have. I saw her come out of the building she went into and her car is the one parked in front of mine."

"There's no woman. Take a look for yourself."

I did. There wasn't. "That's a relief," I said.

"What's the matter? Would she recognize you?"

"Yes. That's why it's difficult."

"You know," he said almost humbly, "I can retire in about

seven years and I've been thinking maybe I'll take it and go into the detective business. What's it like, I mean really? You meet a lot of women?"

"Yes," I said, "I do."

"I'll only be fifty," he said.

It took a full ten minutes to explain the glories of private detection.

The cop seemed impressed when I told him I work alone and don't do anything else regularly for a living. That doesn't impress me. I just cut back on the living.

In the end he helped me out. I got in the truck again through the back door and he closed it for me. Seven years from retirement and still giving parking tickets. Perfect qualifications for a private detective.

I could use the pension.

My policeman friend ambled on. I had a notion why Melanie hadn't come straight to her car. She might not like to make her way along the street while the cop was present.

Whatever the reason, she certainly appeared shortly after he had turned the corner. Maybe her driver's license had expired or she was uninsured. Or maybe she was just a furtive murderer.

She carried a couple of bags, small purchases, and I liked that. Whatever was up, there were plans enough to buy little things. People in a panic don't buy toothbrushes.

She pulled out carefully, drove slowly. I followed at about three cars. It wasn't exciting. We just went back to her motel. I lurked again where I'd lurked in the night. She went to the desk clerk. He wrote things, turned a couple of circles; she took things out of a little black handbag. She was checking out. Here we go again.

But we didn't. After an unbearably slow pack-up in her room she set off. I couldn't think what she was doing for nearly an hour after paying the bill. Stealing towels doesn't take that long and she hadn't had much in the way of luggage. But some things remain mysteries.

She went to a better class of motel. The Apperson out on U.S. 31. With a restaurant and a swimming pool.

At least there I would have no impulse to check in myself to keep tabs on her. I feel much too uncomfortable in fancy places. I can't skulk properly because I keep running into ice machines and slipping on empty caviar containers.

Melanie Baer Kee checked in without a falter. And I relaxed. Clearly she was on the course I had guessed and charted for her. Goger had advanced her enough money to live in a bit of style, so while she was at it she would.

I left her shadows while she settled in. I had a couple of other things to do.

Like call Miller.

"Jerry!" Janie called. "It's Albert again."

"I got it," he told me. "I wrote it down somewhere here."

"What?"

"Cause of death on that kid, of course. It was natural, no question of that. But I wrote it down."

It cost me seventeen cents before he found where.

"Thrombotic thrombocytopenic purpura," he said.

"What?"

"Purpura of the thrombotic thrombocytopenic variety."

"Spell it for me." Which he did. "O.K., now tell me what it is."

"Cause of death of Edmund Kee, Junior, St. Louis. Died December 10, 1963."

"Yeah, yeah, doctor, but what the hell is it?"

"Dunno, friend. That's your problem."

"You mean that's all you got for me?"

"That is all you asked for. What did you want, 'Shot with poison dart'?"

"All right. Thanks, Jerry."

But my spirit was not at rest. More details to look for.

I called Goger's office. They put me straight through.

"I've been waiting for your call," he said. "She was here."

"I know. I was outside. What did she want?"

"Well, I think ethically I can say the situation is much as you believed. And I did much as you suggested."

"I know she has some money now. She just moved into a fancy motel."

"Uh yes. One that in fact I own. But I have suggested she make herself as comfortable for the next few days as she can."

"Comfortable or cozy, Mr. Goger?" One had to remember I'd been given Goger's name by Clinton Grillo.

"I am acting much as I would have done had I never met you, Mr. Samson."

"Did she tell you anything?"

"You know, I don't think I can really answer that. Yes I can, this time, because she didn't. But should she tell me anything, as you put it—and I intend to give her every opportunity— then I do not think it's realistic for you to expect me to tell you about it."

"How about strictly personal and off the record because I did you a favor and put her back in touch with you."

"It will depend on what there is to tell, and whether Melanie seems willing that you should know it. I'm not being hostile, Mr. Samson. But a lawyer's position with regard to confidences is well defined in the law."

"So is a private detective's."

"I suppose. Yes. But don't concern yourself about one thing. Where Melanie will be for the next few days. I intend to use all my influence to keep her in Kokomo until the details of her inheritance are worked out. I feel I owe her father's memory at least that much." Then he said, "And Melanie strikes me as a much more balanced and mature girl than I had expected."

Mature enough to handle you, I said to myself. But not to him. I'm too mature to say things like that, and there had been more than a few minutes I'd rather fancied Melanie myself.

26

Kokomo with nothing to do. Where had I heard that before? I drove back to Indianapolis.

I didn't go straight home; I stopped at the library. Asked if they'd been plaguing my home address with phone calls and postcards to tell me the Kokomo sex book was in. They hadn't.

I went to the doorway phones and used a dime. Answering service. I should know better.

And then I called my doctor. Doctor Harry, as we refer to him in my circle. A foul-mouthed teetotal flatfooted practitioner who has developed other vices in his old age. Poker, to be precise. He came to the game late—and I must claim credit for the introduction—but was so impressed with the craft and cunning required that he's taken it up seriously. His cantankerous core has developed into a playing style; he bluffs a lot.

But Evvie answered the phone. "Yeah, he's here. This medical, or something you want him to do for you?" Husbands tend to deserve their wives.

"Both," I said.

She called him. He came. "You interrupted my fucking lunch. You know how much time I get for lunch? Not enough time to be fucking interrupted. So what do you want, Al?"

"Thrombotic thrombocytopenic purpura," I read.

"What about it?" As if he had it for dessert every day.

"What is it?"

"Rare. Progressive. Fatal. Blood disease with severe internal bleeding. If you can talk to me on the phone you haven't got it."

"It's not me," I said. "I know of a little kid who died of it and I'm trying to find out what kind of disease it is."

"It's not nice," he said quietly. "Check standard medical sources. I've seen one case, when I was training. It's not pretty."

"Is it a kids' disease?"

"Not especially. No, I don't think so. I saw a girl in her early twenties. The remains of same."

"What causes it?"

"Don't know."

"I mean, is it hereditary or something? Like hemophilia?"

"Christ! Now what did I just say? Cause is unknown. *Unknown*. That means there's no *known* genetic association. Just because I say blood disease doesn't mean it's fucking hemophilia. Anything else you want to know? Brain degeneration in middle-aged private detectives?"

I'd rather not know. "I'll let you get back to lunch," I said.

"About fucking time." Then he said, "Come around sometime, Al. Let us hear from you."

Since I was in the library, part of my master plan, I had a little browse amongst the medical books. Such as they were.

TTP, as we say in the trade, is not exactly your disease in the street. Harry had done pretty well off the cuff. But he missed a few additional charming symptoms: convulsions, coma, fever; anemia and "intermittent neurological symptoms," things like numbness.

I spent an hour.

And became certain Edmund Kee Junior's death was in no way associated with the consanguinity of his biological parents. If his death was a punishment, then God's hand must have been directly involved.

Melanie hadn't understood, but neither had Kee. The medical books acquitted Melanie of any suspicion of beating the child. A progressive disease, with a lot of subcutaneous bleeding. For a couple of months before he died, little Edmund just bruised very easily. At the end, by a touch, much less a slap.

Poor little kid. But at least his suffering was over. The effect on Melanie—who'd already suffered guilt upon guilt—was still being felt.

Pathology books don't make good reading.

But one part of the case was settled. The first—dead—kid had been just one of those things.

The problem with settling one part of a case is that it exposes the unfinished parts. A wall you've started to build looks far less complete than the site before you begin to build at all. My business is wall building. Each stone, each truth I dig up stays there, no matter how long it takes to add another. As long as I'm careful, make sure what I've added *is* stone and won't get washed away in the wash.

On my way out of the library I passed the phone again. And decided to call my client. I'd been putting it off.

He was at the store. "Hello," he said passively.

"I would like to talk to you," I said. "When would be convenient?"

"Anytime. Anytime. It doesn't matter."

"Are you all right?"

"I'm not ecstatically happy, if that's what you mean. My life has been overturned. What am I supposed to be?"

We made an appointment for five thirty. I wanted a little time to wash up, eat.

Mars had not adjusted to bachelor life well. He looked gray all over and weak: I wouldn't have bought a used chair from him. He led me into that woody office where I had first met Melanie. It seemed decades past. It was less than a week.

I said, "You haven't heard from Melanie, then?"

"No. Not a stitch."

"You didn't have any warning? You didn't think she might leave?"

"Not conceivably." It sounded like a blood oath had been taken.

"And she didn't give you any indication of why she left?"

"No."

"Well," I said, beginning to execute my resolve to bring him a little more up-to-date. I told him about Kee and the new missing child. That I had seen Melanie the afternoon before she took flight. That I had asked her about the kid. I said she had gone a bit crazy when I brought it up and had thrown me out. Willson just sat silent. Then I asked him what he knew about the second child.

He wasn't ambiguous. "Nothing. Not a stitch."

"You never heard of her being pregnant, then?"

"No. I'm always the last one to know when she's pregnant. When was this child meant to have been born?"

"I have some documentation, but before I give you details, I want you to do something which might help."

"What?"

"I want you to go through all your records from before you found Melanie in Chicago until you moved here. I want you to make a list of every incident you can date. I need a chronology. Something to pin down where Melanie was and when. Look through your checkbook. Try to remember everything she told you about her husband and when she left him. Do it over and over and try to fill in as much detail as you absolutely can."

"I . . ."

"We need to track down this kid. There's no future until we find out what's become of him and you are the closest thing we have to a source of information."

"But surely we just find Melanie and ask her."

I reminded him quietly, "I asked her the afternoon she left."

He held his head in his hands. There was no doubt today he was concerned about Melanie. Afraid for Melanie.

"She's such a complex person," he said at last.

I didn't ask the limits he thought those complexities might

go to. He considered them without prompting. But the worst he could think of was a worst that hadn't occurred to me. "She might harm herself," he said. "If she's depressed she might harm herself. We have to find her."

Of that anxiety, at least, I could relieve him. I said, "I know where she is."

He jumped up like an old lady hit in the backside with a BB. "What? Where? How? Why didn't you tell me?"

Lie time. "I only found out today. She's contacted her father's lawyer in Kokomo about the money her father left her. I think she's intending to take it and run away."

He sat down again. "Money?" he asked pitifully. Then, "She's going to leave me after all," after it all sank in, or at least settled where it would sink in later.

"She's confused and threatened," I said. "She's on a path which looks like a way out. But what she will do depends on what she has already done, and that's exactly what we don't know." I suppose I didn't have to tell him that.

"I can't see . . . her killing . . ." he said, not convincing either of us. "She never let the subject of children come up."

"You never considered having any?"

"No. God no." He mused. "Of course it all makes sense to me now. Just look what happened to the first one. The child got worse and worse and she knew there was nothing she could do."

"That had nothing to do with your relationship," I said.

"But it's what happens . . . when you . . . have children."

It was Willson's day for learning things. "When all this gets straightened out," I said, "I'll tell you what happened to your child. But it wasn't what Melanie thought it was. It had nothing whatsoever to do with your having the same father."

"Nothing?" he asked weakly.

I left him with a pep talk about reconstructing Melanie's life in Chicago.

Reliable information is the hardest thing in the world to get. Maybe one day, like airplanes, we'll all have little black boxes. Flight recorders. So when one of us crashes we'll have indestructible records to help others figure out why.

I left Willson. Inside, outside: dark and cold. If I wasn't prone to passions, urges to know, it would have been time to say screw them all. Time to go back to selling bananas door to door.

Skeletons of peoples' lives were decaying before my very eyes.

I headed for home. While wall building, I'd let personal fences start to fester. How long since my woman disowned me? A day? Two? Unlike most people I carry a record in my notebook of where I've been and what I've done. I could have pinned down my errings, to the hour. But I didn't have the energy or the spirit. Life was not adequately a continuum for me to believe the past had much to do with the future.

I parked and marveled at how familiar everything looked. The carpet store I live over: "FANTASTIC DECEMBER SALE!!!" There's a sale every month. It's reassuring. He literally changes the month in the window every first. "TERRIFIC JANUARY SALE!!!" Little guy called Slich runs the place. I don't really know him; we both rent from a third party.

I walked up the stairs working on the mechanics of how I would run a sale. Ten percent off the cost of your divorce detective if you act now.

It's my fault for being sentimental about my office door. That carefully preserved relic of my past. If it had glass under the lettering instead of low-grade ply, I would have seen my office light was on. But it doesn't and I didn't. It wasn't until I pried the door open and burst into a fully lit office that I realized the office was, as they say, fully lit.

I don't leave lights on.

Nobody was visible, but the door to my living room was open.

"Yoo hoo!" I criered to the town. Don't shoot. I'm friendly.

"Yoo hoo!" echoed a male voice from my room. I would have pulled my gun, if I'd carried a gun. I would have gotten my gun from the drawer in my desk, if I'd owned a gun and kept it in the drawer in my desk. I clenched my right fist and hid it behind my back.

Artie Bartholomew was just putting my orange juice bottle back in the refrigerator. "I left you a little," he said, and showed me. There was a thin orange film clinging to the inside on the bottom. "I've made myself comfortable; hope you don't mind," he said, still towering over the open door of the fridge. "Can I get you something while I'm here? Some of these de luxe guavas-in-heavy-syrup?"

"Close the door, will you?"

He hesitated, then let it swing shut. The floor is uneven. It took me quite a while to find the orientation that gave the best swing.

And I hate defrosting the damned thing. That's what I was thinking about when he held the door open. Frost building up. So I'm fussy. It was my territory. What the hell was he doing here anyway? "What the hell are you doing here anyway?"

"I've come to give you a little news," he said. "I figured you owed me a little hospitality for that jaunt to Milwaukee you took me on. You set me up, didn't you, you little bastard?" Grin.

Grin. Oh yeah, I'd forgotten that. "It seems like a long time ago."

"Doesn't seem like so long ago to me. I spent a day up there. It never crossed my mind you were suckering me to play for time."

"I'm not as stupid as I look," I said. I liked Bartholomew, personally. It was the company he worked for I didn't like.

"No, I guess not. But I had a fun time when I called Kee to explain why I was in Milwaukee following you. You'd just seen him in Chicago. He wasn't very amused. She was here all the time, wasn't she?"

" 'Was' is the word. She's skipped."

"While you were away? That's funny." He snorted to prove it. "Where was she then? Somewhere near Willetson? In Monrovia?"

Poor old Artie. "Nope. Here in town. Funny thing is, she didn't even know Willetson lived here, what with his changing his name."

He looked at me, then shook his head. "You're shitting me again. If she didn't know where Willetson was, how did you use him to find her.

I smiled condescendingly. "Just lucky I guess."

But he let me off. "Well, I have some good news for you."

"Oh?"

"Kee has called me off."

"What!"

"I said he wasn't pleased when I called him. He just told me to wrap it up and come back to Chi. Caught me with my jock off, I can tell you."

"I don't understand. He's quitting?"

Shrug. "Dunno, little buddy. But he's a funny. He gets ideas in his head and he's on one now. He just wants me to come home. I don't think he's quitting."

"He didn't sound like he was going to pull you off when I talked to him. He sounded like he was going to keep twisting them until we said uncle."

"Well, maybe you scared him, Albert. Frightened him to death."

"Or maybe he thinks he's got another hand with a better grip. I don't like it."

"Neither do I," he said, but his reasons were more self-centered.

"When do you go?"

"Tomorrow morning."

"Don't let me keep you."

"I'll be kinda sorry to leave this old town," he said. He grinned far more lecherously than I could have. Considering my prospects. "I am glad you got back on the early side."

On cue the cuckoo coo-cooed six. "While you're here," I said, "let me ask you something about Kee."

"You've caught me in a garrulous mood." There was a nice camaraderie between us. We had shared a situation which had been hard in various ways, for us both.

"Did he ever tell you about a kid that Melanie Baer had in 1965?"

"You mean the one she killed?" he asked pleasantly.

"No," I said simply, knowing if we ever came up on opposite sides of a court I could prove Melanie hadn't killed the kid. *That* kid.

"Another one?"

Bartholomew left about seven thirty. I dashed to the phone and called my woman. Lucy answered and sounded moderately pleased to hear from me. I asked for her mother.

She left the phone. I strained hard, but I couldn't hear anything.

"Mummy's here," said Lucy when she returned. "But she's just out of the tub and getting dressed. To go out. With a man. She says she's late and doesn't have enough time to tell you the things she wants to tell you."

"I see," I lied. Why does everybody always pick on me? "Lucy, we're still friends, aren't we?" It was not a fair question for a kid.

"Pretty much," she said with difficulty.

"Read any good books lately?"

She hadn't. I let her go. Life, even simple life, is too complicated. The thing I regretted most that cold, dark, friendless evening was the chance to soak in milady's bathtub. There are leg men and there are titty men. There are shower men and there are bath men. I'm a bath man.

I sat in my easiest chair for nearly an hour before I mobilized enough to settle for second best. A shower. It felt pretty good.

Day is day and night is night; fun in one, the next contrite. I passed an easy evening, slept well, and woke up evaluating myself as if I were a doctor following my hospital progress. He's holding his own, I told me.

Why not! A brand-new Saturday, all my very own. Only sixteen days till Christmas, one of which would be a shopping day. If I could win back anybody to buy presents for. I'd neglected my private life. Alienated dear ones; not written letters. A job isn't worth that sort of price.

I cleaned my house. Even ironed a shirt and poked at stains on a pair of pants I knew my woman would recognize as ones I'd put on special. The only interruption of my new leaf was a phone call—and that apparently a wrong number, because the caller hung up when I said "Hello."

I was standing in my shorts scouring the sink hole when I heard someone open and close my office door. I grabbed at some clothes and was tucking my shirt in when I heard a low and lulling voice call, "Is anybody here?"

"Just a minute!" I couldn't find my left shoe so I settled for slippers.

A voluptuous redhead had settled in my client's chair. In slitted evening dress, pale green, with sequins. Lotsa slits.

I tried to find words to express my astonishment. But failed. I watched dumbly as she drew a cigarette holder from a tiny purse, delicately placed a long cigarette in the appropriate hole. Her fingernails were polished light orange; Mandarin. She said, "Do you have a light?"

"Just a minute." I slipped across the floorboards into the kitchen and brought back a whole box of kitchen matches. My natural conservatism. The first one might not light, or something. I opened the box, struck a match and lit her fag. She drew on it in short gaspy breaths. The excitement of it all, or maybe she just didn't like the taste of smoke.

"Do you do delicate work?" she asked. She pulled back a shoulder in a deliberate way, to show me . . . I began to feel distinctly uncomfortable. My natural conservatism.

"I do all kinds of work. What did you have in mind?" What can you do but take the horn by the bull? I tried to remember if I had turned my iron off.

"It's of a personal and delicate nature," she said, as if she were thinking of something else.

"Maybe you better tell me of the precise nature before it gets polluted away," I said remotely. My mind wasn't on things altogether.

She gave it another flounce. "Can you keep a secret?"

"Fifty cents an hour."

"My boy friend is a drug addict," she said. "Hard stuff, and I'm afraid for my life. I'm afraid one night he's going to do me an injury."

"Oh?"

She began to cry. "I can tell by your tone of voice you aren't going to help me."

I couldn't think of anything to say. I just watched her snuffling, began to remember I'm a hardhearted bastard, noticed that she wasn't wearing a coat, then spotted a furry pile on the floor beside the chair. "Is that mink?" I asked.

"Yes," she sobbed, "but just an old one." We sat quietly for a few minutes, contemplating our minks. I found her vastly more attractive quiet. Whoever she was; whatever she was.

"What can I do for you?" I said gently.

"I want you to protect me at night," she said. This time she was a little bit touching.

It turned out that her boy friend spent a lot of time hanging around her apartment evenings trying to get her to give him money. She wanted to give him up, she said, for real this time. She wanted to start a new life. She'd saved up some money from her modeling jobs and could pay me whatever I asked. Could I help protect her? Starting this evening?

"I'd like to help you," I said.

"I'd do *anything* if you would."

"But I'm already on a job."

"Oh no!" It sounded like a death rattle. Maybe she thought it was. "Can't you, kind of, shift it around? Make room? I'll only want you nights."

"Well, before we talk about that I really should ask you if you haven't given serious consideration to calling the police."

"You men!" She stood up like a shot. "You're all alike." She shrieked, then said, "A girl gets down and you all make sure to keep her there. I'm not going to lie still for it. I'm not!" She turned her back to me and bent deep from the waist to gather her coat in her arms. I didn't flinch. I'm not shy.

She jerked up and stomped to the door, which was ajar. "You know what you can do with it."

"If you'll only try and be reasonable," I called, and moved from behind my desk. But she was gone, the door slammed efficiently shut. I knew she'd be on the street before I could catch up with her.

But I went to the door anyway. Another satisfied customer. The problem with running an open-door business is people can come to you whether you are qualified to help them or not. Not that unusual people arrive very often.

Now Artie Bartholomew might have been able to help her, I thought, as I walked slowly back to my sink. Besides, I said to myself, it's not the money you make at this job that keeps you in it. It's your own hours. Choosing who you work for. The perquisites. I scoured away wondering what perquisites I'd passed up this time. It's enough to make a fellow feel insufficient.

But routine brings you back to earth. It was still a good day to take off. Maybe I could use the Christmas spirit ploy to slither back into the various good books I'd written myself out of. I would burst, joyful, on my woman's household. I would sweep them out for a delicious meal, say. Spare no expense. At my mother's, say. Refilling them all with that extra bit of life which my bon vivance induces.

And having decided to do just that, I reversed field long enough to give my notebook a perusal. To remind myself of such facts as I had, get them properly in mind so they could gel in my subconscious while my conscious was otherwise occupied.

Clearly I had a visit with Willson coming. Facts and dates.

What hadn't been clear when I'd gone to bed, though it stood out now like a twirly tassel, was that I must see Melanie. Let Kee ebb or flow, Melanie was the sailor with the chart to the secret passage. After Willson had made his lists, it would definitely be time for a shot at Melanie's prow.

And then? My crystal ball clouded.

Ah well. I had other things to do and all. While I gave Willson time to remember.

The rest of the day was a mixed success.

I did call Willson. To make an appointment for the next day to talk to him about chronologies. He wasn't at the shop.

"I'm tired. I stayed at home today."

"Your business been suffering recently?"

"Yes, but there are more important things in my life than the business. I feel like I'm about to be drowned in the past."

Whenever he was tired, he seemed uniquely concerned with himself. In fatigo veritas?

"I wanted to fix a time tomorrow to go over that information I asked you to look up."

"Tomorrow? I really don't feel much like starting on it. Is there a rush?"

"It's your limbo, friend."

"All right. I'll do it. When do you want to meet?"

"When will you be ready?"

"Why don't you come out here about two. I'll be back from church by then."

"Church?"

I didn't mean it to be an attack. But he defended. "Yes, church. I find it relaxing when I feel down. I feel terrible. How can I help it? I suppose the mistake was in Chicago, but when I found her again . . . It's like we spent five years building a life; now the first adversity, the first puff of wind and it's all washed away. It demoralizes, Mr. Samson. I hope it never happens to you."

How do you tell a man wallowing in his own mud that you've been neck high two or three times yourself? How many times had he been kicked out of college? How many marriages had he had decay under his feet of clay? Pray for me, Willetson, and save yourself.

It's remarkable how much more optimistic you are when it's not you that's depressed.

At last, free. A glorious winter afternoon.

My woman did not spurn my company. There was, I admit, a certain distance in her manner, but we'd been apart for quite a while. She had expected me, she said, either today or tomorrow. She'd planned dinner for me, something nice, and she said she was glad to see me again. I did my best by her. I didn't give her any lip. I was even fairly pleasant.

I should have suspected something. We don't talk business to each other, but there is no flagging when it comes to retribution for letting the other down. She was too nice to me. When I made my little speech about life being too short to fight with the people you care most about, she agreed too readily. I set myself up for the fall.

About five thirty we were making dinner. The phone rang. Lucy giggled.

"It's an old friend of mine," said my lady fair in earnest, when she came back. "She's just popped into town. I've invited her for dinner. I hope you don't mind."

Lucy giggled. I said, "Fine. There's plenty." Ten minutes later the doorbell rang. I was sent to answer it. The friend was female. Red of head. Full of figure. My erstwhile client of the morning. She ran in, threw her arms around me. "Help me!" she howled. "Please! My boy friend is after me and this time he means business."

My expression, they told me later, was all they could ever hope for. They emphasized the point, at length. It was humiliation evening for poor old Albert. Each mouthful was punctuated with a line like "I'd like to help you" or "If you'll only try to be reasonable" or "You men." It seems that on her person, I never did learn exactly where, she had carried a portable tape recorder. It was a very long dinner.

Lucy broke first. "You look so pitiful," she said. "Come on, let's give him a break."

"Fifty cents an hour," chirped my woman. So called.

30

I found Mars in chaos. Physical and spiritual. He hadn't slept, he said. He looked it.

"Excuse the mess."

"I'll try."

We dug for seats in the remains of the living room.

"I don't know what's wrong with me. I just can't get myself together. I was all right until you told me where she was. That she's getting some money. Going to leave me." He laughed. "Leave me, after all . . ."

"She's worth more than three days to you, isn't she?"

"She was," he said.

"So give her a chance before you write her off."

"But I keep thinking, two children. Two! And money! What else hasn't she told me about?"

Maybe he shouldn't ask. "Maybe she figured you already had enough on your mind."

"She was patronizing me. Condescending to me. How can I ever live again with someone who treated me like that?"

A point, of course; but he was a study in self-pity. Why is this fragile stuff, love, only to be given if it's given back?

"It depends whether what binds the two of you together is strong enough to survive a few mistakes."

"Whether blood is thicker than water, you might say." Bitter. "How long does someone get to decide he isn't loved anymore by the person he was giving his life for?"

Ho hum. I should know better than trying to reason against wallowing emotionalism. "Look, sport, I came out here to try to track down the past. To protect you, even if you're not interested in protecting Melanie anymore."

"I'll protect her," he said somberly. "I've committed myself to that. No one will fault *me* in this business."

The style was different, but Mars reminded me of nobody more than Kee himself.

"All right. Do you have the chronology I asked you for?"

"No," he said.

"Why not?"

"Sit down at a table?" he whined.

So I get to hold the pen and paper and ask you questions, right? So as not to tax your precious energies. Self-sorrow is never attractive. That's part of its nature, I suppose. Make yourself as unattractive as possible and then complain because nobody is attracted. "As close as we can get then," I reminded him, "I need dates, addresses, facts of what happened in Chicago."

"How do I know what really happened in Chicago?"

"All right. All right. Details of Chicago insofar as you were made aware of them. For instance, when did you first move there?"

"In the spring of 1963. Late April."

"How did it happen? Why did you go?"

"When Melanie didn't come back for Father's funeral, I knew she wasn't coming back. She was fond of him, you know. Her mother died, when she was eleven. Did you know?"

"Yes, I knew. So you went to Chicago. To do what?"

"To get a job in the furniture trade. I worked for a man in Kokomo for several years and I thought before long I'd make a go of it myself."

He'd got his job but chance had made a landlord of him instead of a furniture lord. He'd moved into a little apartment house, one room to himself. But then his landlady decamped, leaving nine tenants with no one to pay the rent to. Mars stepped in and took over the mortgage.

"I was lucky," he said. "I got the place at about half what it sold for three years later."

Fortune smiles on those with capital. "Where did the money come from to take the place over?"

"My mother. It was always understood there would be something for me to get started with one day."

"Did you know where the money had come from?"

"Oh yes," he said sarcastically. "From my 'father,' who was a wealthy I-don't-know-what and had gone off to the war and been killed before he had a chance to marry my mother." Mars shrugged like a victim.

"So Melanie isn't the first person to be less than candid with you." I was trying to make a point. Even *I'd* lied a bit to him. Maybe there was something about him which inspired deception.

"That was different," said Mars reverentially.

He'd moved his mother to the apartment building the summer of '65, to try Chicago for a year. Rented out her Kokomo house. Had no contact with Melanie, no information about her at all.

Then, in December of 1965, he came across Mels working in a department store.

"When exactly?" I asked him.

"Well, before Christmas, because I was in a lingerie department buying a present for my mother. Several days before Christmas, because I never wait until the last minute. But not too many days before, because I'm never organized enough to get it done well ahead."

"What happened?"

"She didn't recognize me at first. Then, well, there was a sort of magic." It was his first effort of fond remembrance.

"And you got back together?"

"I took her out to dinner and took her home."

"What was it like? I mean, did she open up to you, tell you all her troubles like a long-lost . . ." My big mouth. A long-lost brother.

"I was younger then," he said mysteriously. But being forced to go through it all again was doing wonders for his frame of mind. It was mobilizing him. "I sensed she had been through a lot of agony," he remembered. "I sensed if I was careful there was a chance I'd get her back. I felt it was the best Christmas I'd ever had."

People who never quite grow up have their good sides. I was

happy for him. For his "best Christmas." "So it took some time to get to know one another again?"

"A long time," he said. "She was very slow to talk about what she'd been through. What ate at me was why she had left Kokomo—and me—in the first place. She didn't tell me."

"Did you ask?"

He smiled briefly. "No. Neither would you," he said. Not knowing how elephantine, how like a whale in a tact shop I can be. "She seemed on a knife edge. No, she seemed over the edge with only her arms stretching back, to me. I was too happy to have her back."

"But did you live together?"

"Oh no. I had Mother at my place. And she never let me come to hers."

"Where was she staying?"

"She had an apartment. I would walk her to the corner."

"Did you see her very often?"

"Every day or two. I would make excuses to see her at the department store."

"But she could have had a private life you didn't know about?" I asked bluntly.

"So it seems," he said.

They went to movies. Talked about books. Met at corners, parted at corners. Furtive Kokomo kids, only older with less need, in my book, to be furtive. It went on like that for months.

"Then out of the blue her husband's detective found her at the store."

"How did she know he was a detective?" The Cosmic Detective Badge and the Secret Decoder Ring: I should have known.

"He asked people questions. One of the girls told her. So she quit the job."

"Just like that?"

"Yes," he said, rather proud.

"Let's go back a minute. You met Melanie in December 1965. How long had she been in Chicago before you came across her?"

"It was earlier that year, the spring. I don't know exactly."

"And when did the detective appear?"

Mars looked to the sky, a remembering motif. "It was before Memorial Day, 1966."

"You kept seeing her after the detective appeared?"

"Oh yes. More than ever." I could understand; he must have looked more and more like the only oasis in town.

"But you don't know where she lived then?"

"No."

"You never followed her when you left her on the corner?"

"No. We've *always* had this understanding. Trust . . ." He tailed off, back into the bleak reality of the present. A contrast with the rosy sufferings of the past. I did feel sorry for him. A little.

"What happened to the detective?"

"He must have found her address. Because her husband, Edmund Kee, came up to Chicago and made a big scene where she lived. She had to move."

"What . . . happened?"

"He showed up during breakfast time. She was home because of quitting the job. He came in and ranted and raved. He had a gun and he scared her half to death. I—I don't know what he thought he wanted. She got away from him. That night we went walking together. She was very upset. She told me why she had run away from me in Kokomo."

"She told you you had the same father?"

"That's right."

"And what did you do then?"

"We talked about it all night. Whether it mattered more than our being apart mattered. And we decided to take the plunge, consciously this time. It was dawn by the time we finally decided. Though I think she knew all the time. That day we, Melanie and I, flew to Miami for a couple of weeks, to figure out how to go about things."

"And when was that?"

"June first."

June Fools' Day. I know it well.

"And you made plans."

"It was a matter of picking a place my mother would accept, where I could make a living. We decided to live in isolation. To lay down false trails. I changed my business name."

"And established the homosexual cover?"

"That too. We went into things very thoroughly. Or so we thought."

"You didn't do badly," I said. I admired the energy and resolution of their design. It took guts.

"Except for details Melanie neglected to inform me about," said Willetson, trying, with some success, to re-create the depression he'd just clambered out of.

"Maybe she didn't want to scare you by hitting you with everything all at once. And maybe there just wasn't any decent chance to fill in the gaps later."

He cocked his head, let his eyelids droop.

"How long did you stay in Florida?" I said.

"Sixteen days."

"You remember precisely?"

"I remember precisely," he said. "Then Mels came here."

"She never went back to Chicago?"

"No. She said she'd left nothing there she wanted to bring along."

"No clothes? No rent to pay? Nobody to tell she was leaving?"

He shrugged a negative. Continued, "I stayed in Chicago to arrange things and break the news to Mother."

"How much of the news?"

"That I'd got a wonderful business opportunity in Indianapolis."

"So she went back to the same house where people in the street keep track of who goes in and how long they stay?"

"I don't think they care anymore."

"Did they ever?"

"Yes," he said, remembering. "They used to care, the bastards."

31

After talking to Willson I went to my woman's. About seven, barely in one piece, I left her in peace.

Which left me at home that evening. I decided to spend the time in meditative study. Having no constructive alternative. I had two projects to choose between. A direct shot at Melanie; or, if I wasn't feeling so bold, a trip to Chicago to reconstruct the critical period: after the child but before it vanished.

Willson's story helped satisfy my desire to believe Melanie was not a murderer. She had too many resources, was too capable of acting to solve her problems reasonably.

I twiddled all my knobs at home, playing for heat. I emptied my living room work surface—a flush door on boxes—and then filled it again with my notebook, other case documents and a small pile of papers. I put a pot of coffee on. I splashed my face with cold water.

It was then I called the service. "A Lieutenant Miller called you at three fifteen. No message."

He hadn't tried again. Not important enough for me to bother him at home then. The decks were clear. I sat down for the long haul. To scrutinize each of the interviews and pieces of information I had. To chart them. To plot emotional profiles. Ultimately to use my intuition and perception to divine what had really happened. Shrewd classical deduction. Why not? I was a detective, wasn't I?

It seemed like a good idea at the time. Why not? I'd stay up all night if necessary.

Only it wasn't. In less than half an hour I found a crack in the armor. Through which I glimpsed the promised land: an exonerating hypothesis.

I'd chosen to begin with the solidest facts I had, the documents Edmund Kee gave me. I studied them one by one.

Report of pregnancy. Prenatal examinations. Birth certificate, dated November 17, 1965. Attended by midwife A. I. Keough. She was someone I could look for in Chicago, I thought to myself. That was five minutes after I started.

It did strike me as curious that an expectant mother who made regular prenatal visits to a modern clinic—and it had to be at least modernized, because all the records were computer print-out—would then opt to have her baby at home, not in a hospital. But I couldn't think of anything it proved. I decided to ask Melanie about it. That was twelve minutes after I started.

I wrote down "Clephane Clinic" next to Mrs. Keough's name. I began to see Chicago's winter winds in my future. That was thirteen minutes after I started.

I got some coffee, rummaged abortively for cookies, then looked over the last document Kee had given me. Postnatal visits for the little babe. Same clinic as before, but different coding than on the prenatal computer record. Shots and stuff I guessed. Whatever they do these days to little babes.

It was hard to read, at first. Unfamiliarity. It took a few minutes to work out what was what. I was particularly interested in the dates of the visits. Because they were the last recorded observations of little Freeman's existence, alive and healthy.

The final date on the list, which I located twenty-five minutes after I sat down, was June 17, 1966.

I wrote it at the bottom of the list of dates I had been transcribing from the document. And then I wrinkled my face and looked at it.

I checked my notebook. Willson had said, decisively, that on June 1, 1966, he and Melanie Kee had flown to Miami and there they had continued in hotel residence, uninterrupted, for sixteen days. Whence Mels had gone directly to Indianapolis. It didn't add up.

Before the end of my thirtieth minute in the brainstorming seat I withdrew, second coffee and all, to my relaxing chair. You are an oaf, I told myself.

Willson had seen Mels every couple of days for months. And he had never seen the kid or gotten any hint of it. Was Mels so rich she had a nanny to take care of little Freeman? Or could she afford a baby sitter so many hours a week? Did she have a relative or close friend in town to care for the child all the time?

All negative.

And how had she, in one traumatic day, made arrangements for the kid which let her zip off to Miami, never to return?

I didn't think she had.

When Mars remet Mels over the Christmas lingerie, Mels was no longer in charge of the child.

You arrive friendless, moneyless in a new town. You have a child by a husband you've left. What do you do with it? Certainly you could give the kid away.

I wondered if Kee had thought to check official adoption records in his search for the child. He'd been quick enough to check death certificates.

This presumed Mels had given the kid away through some official adoption or fostering procedure. I couldn't think why she shouldn't have. Especially since the kid had been postnatally examined under his surname till he was seven months old. What happened then? Adoptive parents moved, something like that.

It was worth hypothesizing.

My coffee got cold. I slopped half of it down anyway, then dunked another thought.

If she gave the kid away—officially or otherwise—mightn't she have kept some record, some trace of the connection? In her private papers. An address. A name.

Find that and we might wrap up the ball game in a single swing of the bat.

It was too much for me to relax in my chair about. Only eight fifteen. The night was young. The exhilaration of possible physical evidence!

When I called, Willson didn't sound too bad. I just said I wanted to come out again. "Sure," he said gaily.

Problem with the drive from Indianapolis to Monrovia, it gives you time to think. Hypothesizing about other peoples' motives, deducing their secrets is low-return work. You rarely know enough to draw conclusions worth acting on. Why had Melanie bolted when I mentioned little Freeman? Residual unmollified guilt at having given him away? Possible. But the flaw with using generalizations is the people you actually meet are always specific cases.

Willson had done wonders since I'd left. He'd been cleaning house, staying busy. He was a different and more optimistic man. While I was more depressed.

"I have come up with some more questions."

"I see."

I told him about my notion that Melanie had placed the child after it was born, but before she'd remet him. "That would explain why she didn't tell you about it. It was a solved problem."

"Yes," he said, and I became aware he was glassy-eyed.

"Are you all right?" I asked.

"I took a pill," he said. "Two pills. To calm me and to put me to sleep."

"Fair enough. I won't keep you long." I asked him whether in Chicago, on their dates, Mels had ever had to be back by a certain time, or hadn't been able to come out. Or in any way seemed to have to allow for the schedule of some other person. A baby sitter.

Mars said, "No."

I asked him for the street names at the corner he used to leave Mels at.

"Grand and Remster," he said.

"The last thing is whether you're certain about the date you and Melanie went to Florida."

"Saturday, June first, 1966," he said slowly. While I'd check it from an independent source before I staked my life on it, his definitiveness was enough to proceed on. "And you stayed?"

"Sixteen days. The limit on the ticket was seventeen, but we only stayed sixteen."

"And Melanie went straight to Indianapolis?"

"Essentially. I mean, we flew back to Chicago together because of the excursion tickets, but she took a plane to Indianapolis straight from the airport."

"Did you see her onto the plane?"

"Yes."

"Did she make any phone calls or anything like that?"

"Christ," he said. "I don't remember."

He faded pretty fast. And whether it was the pills or what, he made no protests at all when I asked if I could look through Melanie's desk. Or wherever she was likely to keep private papers. "Sure," he said before I could explain.

He went to bed. I started with a room they'd set aside for Melanie's daytime endeavors. A whole room. Lots of places for secrets.

Only I hardly found any.

Melanie drew pictures, I learned that. Drew them well, if drawing things to look like what they look like is the measure. Animals, birds, flowers; nature's pick-me-ups. Some abstract patterns too, perhaps for fabrics or wallpapers. And some designs for jewelry.

There was a large number of drawings, taken together. What I found strange was that none were unfinished; there were no works in progress.

I saved my highest hopes for the contents of her desk, a lovely old rolltop. It was a hope buster. I got all set for minute examination of every scrap of paper in the half-dozen drawers and the dozen pigeonholes. But there wasn't much in it and the level of dust showed it had long been that way. There were no pieces of paper smaller than 4 by 5, and the only one Melanie appeared to have written on with her own hand bore a short poem.

I am so sigh and windweather weary.
Green ice sticks in my mind.
Red-nosed snowflakes rein into sight
And are slight.

Sleep until sunset
And regret no temptation.
Forgetting and giving are the good sides of love.

It was the only item in the room which hadn't been settled; written in pencil—the poem itself was printed in ink—just below the word "giving" was the word "getting" followed by a question mark.

As the kind of clue I was looking for, it left me cold. But as a hedge against future warmths, I took it with me.

That lovely desk, which I would have filled to the brim with personalia in three months flat, she had left half-empty for years. The two bottom drawers yielded one notebook which had yet to receive a note. It was pitiful.

Whatever secrets Mels kept, she carried them with her.

After a fruitless hour in her workroom I started wandering around the house. Where would a lady keep things that would interest an indolent private detective?

Kitchen? All I found there was a six-pack of Tuborg beer. Very tasty. I drank one on the spot and opened another for company. I walked around the rest of the house. I looked in every crevice I could find. I felt like a distant relation, the first back after a funeral. Looking for what was worth most that would bulge in my pockets least. It's not a very moral feeling.

And then I found it. What there was to find. In a drawer in a little table in the front hall. Where the phone was. What I found was Melanie's address book. Not exactly a personal diary of her life and times, but I cradled it in my hands as if it were. I didn't read it on the spot. I carried it into the living room, drank the dregs of a third beer, and tenderly opened to the first page. Not an old carried-through-life phone-number-and-address diary, but the kind you get when you've decided to recopy all those fading numbers in a new orderly little book.

Page by page I went through it. I admit despair. Most of the entries weren't names, but categories. Under "C" was the word "Clothes" and a list of seven stores. It wasn't till I got to "R," "Relatives," that I perked up a bit.

I copied names, addresses and phone numbers of two aunts and three unidentified relations. One in Kokomo. One in San Francisco, and three in small towns around north-central Indiana: Peru, Mount Etna and Camden. Fine towns all.

But the buried treasure was at the end. A phone number unidentified on the inside of the back cover. The sort of thing you can't be sure you're going to remember from your past, so you write it down. It brought immediate visions of the missing child and somehow made everything worthwhile.

I copied the number into my notebook: 262-4588. I replaced the address book in the drawer. I rinsed out the beer bottles. I went home.

When I went to bed, I hadn't decided what I wanted to do next. Go to Chicago to track down phone numbers? Or just bust up to Kokomo to ask Melanie once and for all what was going on?

But lying in bed early in the morning there seemed to be no choice. Here it was Monday morning, presumably the first day Melanie might make her move to wherever she had the mind to move to. And I wasn't there. She'd waited all weekend for me; a captive audience if I'd gone to talk to her. Captive because no matter how she disliked seeing me, she had to stay put in Kokomo to get what she'd gone there for.

I got out of bed. Why hadn't I gone to see her before? Knowing me, I must have had reasons. What were they?

I put on some water to make tea, new start to a new week. Then I browsed through my notebook. Nice thing about a notebook, you may note a lot of trash but anything worth noting stays there forever. You don't lose things, though you may forget them.

"Why not see Mels?" it read. "1. First find out all you can from Indianapolis sources. Mars. For the info to ask the right questions." Those were my notations on the subject, though they were an incomplete explanation of my delay in seeing Mels. The last time I'd visited her was a disaster. I'm delicate. She'd screamed at me and called me bad names. When someone violences me I'm twice shy. I don't jump back in the fire until I have survival equipment.

I reckoned I had it now. I'd not only whittled away some of the accusations against her, but I'd begun to build answers for her to escape the rest of the questions with. It's a service I provide for preferred customers.

It was settled as I spooned the loose tea into the pot. The direct line to Melanie in Kokomo.

Only I didn't take it.

The first detour was to look at the telephone exchanges in the Indianapolis phone book. 262 was not a Marion County number. I didn't expect it to be. I expected it to be the phone number of some adoptive parents in Chicago. But things have a way of backfiring when I want them too hard. I was playing it cool. The next question was whether it could be a Chicago exchange.

I dialed the Chicago area code, 312. The worst that could happen was I would be an eight-thirty A.M. wrong number.

It was answered almost immediately. A woman who said "Hi."

I said "Um," not having prepared what I was going to say —the trouble with impulses. "I'm sorry to trouble you at this hour, ma'am. But I am trying to trace a woman called Melanie Kee, or Melanie Baer, and I found this phone number in some documents relating to her. I wondered if you could tell me whether you know or have known anyone of that name, or anyone called Melanie who lived in Chicago about five or six years ago." Take the plunge: clear the convenience or flood the floor.

I expected her to say she'd never heard of any Melanie, but after a pause she said, "Oh well. I guess you better talk to Jack. Jack!"

I asked Jack the same question, but in a less nervous voice. It was easy as pie. "Sure, I knew Melanie. What about her?" Well, I did find the number in her telephone number collection. There's no reason for surprise when the people at the number know her.

What about her? "To be frank, her"—I nearly said "husband," but realized that would be a mistake if he'd known her just after she'd left Kee—". . . her brother has reported her missing and we are trying to track her down. Your number was in her address book. No name, no address, but we're calling because we thought it conceivable she might be there."

"She's not here," said Jack. "Not now."

"Would get a little crowded, eh?" I said, trying to be matey.

"Oh, she's welcome here whenever she wants. I guess she knows that. She was always free to come and go or to pick up and leave whenever she wanted to."

"Can you tell me when you saw her last?"

"More or less. Let me think. It was, uh, would have been kind of like spring '66."

"Do you think with some more time you might be able to pin the date down a little closer?"

"I suppose I might. Why?"

"Well, if we get stuck, it might help give us a lead. I'd sure appreciate it if in the next day or two you'd try to pin the date down. And one other thing now, did Melanie ever mention having a child? Or maybe had one when she lived with you?"

"No," he said definitely. The absoluteness startled me and I didn't know whether to press him or not. I decided not. Too easy to get hung up on.

I pressed for, and got, Jack's name and address instead. Pleasant fellow. Considering the hour, the day, and the rather private subject.

So now I'd made the phone call, and had had a little luck. It hadn't occurred to me before that Melanie picked up some masculine support when she packed herself off to Chicago, pregnant. A girl can do with some help and she'd done it before, in St. Louis. I worked it out; she was only about twenty-one when she hit Chicago. I was impressed again with how much struggle the lady had had in a compact little life.

Precocity is only useful when it helps you make better immediate use of the world. Most early blooming hurts in the long run. This kid had been hurt often and deep. When you are trying to predict what someone like that will do next, you cast your nets wider.

But still I didn't set off directly for Kokomo.

My second detour was to call police headquarters and ask for Miller.

It was eight forty-five but he wasn't there. I tried him at home; he wasn't there either.

I gathered belongings. Weather clothing. The book I was reading. The out-of-town kit.

I called again. Still not there. Damn. I hate loose ends.

I went downstairs to the panel truck. Loaded, bought a tank of gas with an oil chaser.

I still had Miller on my mind. If it was important he would have kept after me about it on Friday.

I drove by the City-County Building thinking I'd let fate

dangle me on one of its strings. If there was a parking place I'd stop to see Miller.

There wasn't. But I pulled into a lot.

Fourth Floor, murderers out, please. I wounded a man once, long ago. That's closer than a fella should come.

Miller was in, had been since eight, but at a briefing. The desk officer seemed loath to let me wait in Miller's office, so I sat out front and played at doing the morning crossword puzzle.

Miller spotted me as his meeting broke up, but turned his back. Maybe the chief had warned him about associating with known private detectives.

There was a buzz on the desk phone. The desk fuzz spoke a few lowly words, then said, "Hey, Samson. Lieutenant Miller wants to see you."

"I know the way," I said criminally.

"Thanks for coming in, Al. Probably not important, but I noticed a request came in that might interest you."

It was a business-before-pleasure day. O.K. by me. "Like?"

"Where the hell is it? Just a sec." He went out for a little walk, came back smartish. "Like a missing child, but what caught my eye was it was the same last name as that kid I got you cause of death on. Kee. Only from Chicago, not St. Louis. It was the name that caught my eye, and then I saw that the name of the mother is the same. Melanie Kee. Interested?"

"Yeah, as it happens."

"You know where she is?"

"Do you?"

"No. Now look, Al. Shoot straight with me. You know I'm not going to clobber you. We get a request from Chicago, right? They are looking for a missing child. Freeman Kee, born November 17, 1965. Making him, what, just six? The father has gone to court to try to get rights or something. They seem to think he might be around here. That's what I know. Now, do you know where the kid is?"

"No. I wish I did."

"Well, do you know where the woman is?"

Time to squirm. "Not precisely, no." Like I didn't know whether she was in the motel or at Goger's office, for instance.

"But you know her. You've talked to her?"

"Yes, but she's never mentioned the kid."

"She hasn't? Well, where is she? Where does she live?"

"She left the place she'd been living a few days ago," I said. It was time to introduce some diversionary action. "But about this kid. I can make a suggestion."

"Shoot." Dangerous figure of speech for a man in his profession.

"Tell Chicago to go through its adoption records."

He didn't look impressed.

"I'd sure like to know what they find," I said.

"Look, Al. They send me a request for information, some assistance. I can't tell them how to cover their own area. That's their business."

"A matter of delicacy. Can't you send something like 'Source here says child was put up for adoption in Chicago, 1965 or 1966. Please check. Reply.' "

"Oh well," he said.

I looked at my watch, obviously. I was a little too quick, a little too obvious. It suspicioned him. "Don't trust you, Al. Where you going? Off to take the kid sledding?"

He trapped me with that flattering bait. To think that I—*I* — would keep anything from our valiant constabulary. "I don't know where the kid is, Jerry. I really don't."

"So it's the mother you know where is," he said, having lured me.

I couldn't keep from grinning. "You do me an injustice, sir."

"I know better than to think you're going to tell me anything you don't want to. But I've got to warn you about keeping back information. It'll get you in trouble unless you come up smelling like roses."

Not much chance of that.

33

I drove a lot faster and a lot less relaxedly than I'd expected to. The roads have improved a lot since I first hitched to Kokomo in the 1800s. I made it from downtown Indy to the Apperson Motel in sixty-five minutes.

I didn't even think to turn on the radio. Kee going to the Chicago police opened up a whole new can of horse food.

I didn't filly around. I went straight to Melanie's room. I didn't remember the number but I remembered where in the motel it was. Turned out to be numbered 68. I knocked.

No response. Knock again. No response again. Again, again. Then I looked for her car. Not there.

I hotfooted it back to my vehicle and motored rapidly into town and the vicinity of Attorney Goger's office. Up and down, sideways. I couldn't find Melanie's car in all of central Kokomo.

I pulled up by a phone booth, sorted out a dime. Called the Apperson. Quite possible I'd passed her, I thought, that she'd left Goger's for the motel as I was making my way to Goger's. Just give us a row of doors and a couple of custard pies.

"Apperson Motel," said an Apperson voice. "May I serve you?"

"I'd like to speak to 68, please."

"He's out. May I take a message?"

"He?" I said, startled.

"That's what I said," said the voice.

I was getting excited. "But I thought a woman was staying there. I'm not sure what name she was using"—I felt my case slipping so—"but she was a friend of Mr. Goger's, Mr. Robert Goger."

"Look, friend, I don't care who you got her from. This ain't really that kind of place. Any lady friend of your friend must have checked out by Sunday morning, 'cause the guy we got in there now checked in last night for a week."

My stomach began to hurt. Melanie seemed to slip away.

I found two nickels and dialed Goger's office. Asked for the man himself.

"Who's calling, please?"

Gave the name.

"I'm sorry, but Mr. Goger isn't in this morning. If it's urgent I can put you through to Mr. Rule."

"Is he expected this afternoon?"

"Mr. Rule?"

"No, dear, Mr. Goger. It is extremely important that I see him, and the sooner the better."

"He may look in this afternoon. He often looks in on a Monday afternoon."

"If he does, slap him in leg irons and don't let him leave."

She giggled.

I wanted to call Goger's house but fishing in my pockets all I found was one nickel and five pennies. Not even a quarter. I jumped up and down with the frustration of it. The phone booth shook.

And like a miracle, *tiddly clack,* the phone regurgitated my previous two nickels. In a drier season I would have gone down on my knees in thanks. As it was, with each dialed digit I mumbled, "There is a God."

It occurred to me that instead maybe the phone had understood my problem and responded. As Goger's home phone rang, I kissed the phone in the booth. Cover all the possibilities. It rang a long time. Long enough for me to wonder whether maybe it was a boy phone.

Goger's housekeeper finally answered, and said "Hello." It was the high point in the conversation.

"He's out," she said abruptly after I'd identified myself and made my request.

"It is essential that I talk to him as soon as possible. It's really very important."

"He's out."

"But do you know where he is?"

"No," she said. I knew she lied. But what can you do?

"Will he be home for lunch?"

"No," she said. I didn't know what I'd done to deserve such spurning. I couldn't think of any question to ask that she couldn't dismiss with that too-brief negative. In the end I just hung up.

Melanie was slipping away and if we lost her it would be through my negligence. If I'd told Willson where she was, he could have gone to her, stayed with her. Or if I'd stayed in Kokomo. But who can tell.

It was cold. My hands were cold; I had left my gloves in the big city. I went and bought some. I felt too old to suffer physical hardships unnecessarily. I went back to the truck. I sat.

I should have called Goger from Indianapolis. I under-use the telephone manfully. I waste a lot of time.

Where would Goger be? Where would Melanie be? What to do? What to do?

Calm down, dolt. Calm down.

What can you do but wait? Your only decision is where.

After deep breathing and deep thinking I decided to do it by the clock. Wait outside Goger's house till one or one thirty on the chance that he'll come home for lunch. Plausible. Then shift to his office. Wait for him to check in for his Monday afternoon look-see.

And when he didn't show up? Back to the house, of course. I was feeling more resigned. Made a stop first. At Sears for some rubber insulation, wax, paint and a brush. Then to a fodder shop for midday edibles. Six-pack.

The best way to keep warm in a cold panel truck is to keep busy. I'd fix up the inside, make it homey. Insulation to ward off the winter winds, wax to shine the lusterless dashboard. Paint to redecorate the inside of the back. I got good quality, fast-drying gloss. If it dried fast enough, and I had to wait long enough, maybe I could give it all two coats. Wedgwood blue, I got. A bit brighter than the current rusty gray.

If I was still cold despite the lusty labors, I could drink myself into a stupor with the beer. I had it all worked out. After I awoke and was sensible that I needed relief, I'd be able to use the empty paint can.

There's nothing like fine detail.

It took me fifteen minutes too many to find the driveway to Goger's house. I didn't quite remember the way.

I planted myself outside it, where he'd have to turn around me. A quarter to twelve. I trimmed and screwed in the insulation strips for the two front doors. Cold work, that. You have to open them.

By ten past one I had done the ceiling and nearly finished the first wall. Through the back window I caught the blur of a car so I dropped the paintbrush into the can and crawled forward to look out the front window. A black Thunderbird veered sharply across my prow and into the driveway.

It was him. It was them. Two people in the car, a man and a woman. I knew it was Melanie. My heart raced.

I jumped into the driver's seat and started the truck. It took long enough to catch for me to consider jumping out and running after them. But it caught and we were off. Sharp left into the drive. I gunned it.

But the Thunderbird was pretty quick on its home driveway. By the time I skidded to a stop behind it, Goger and Melanie were out of the car at the foot of the steps of the house.

They turned as they heard me. Spoke a few words, then Melanie ran up the steps to be taken into the house, presumably by my friend the housekeeper. Goger waited behind.

I hopped out, and, notebook in hand, approached the lawyer. He smiled. Everything looked all right.

I said, "I've been trying to get to talk to you all day. And trying to locate Melanie as well. I was afraid she was gone."

"Nice to see you again, Samson," he said formally.

I said, "I'd like to come in to talk to Melanie now, please." I started for the steps.

He took my arm, and said, "Mrs. Kee is not available." It finally dawned that all was not well in the palace.

I thought we could at least go in and talk about it. "I'm cold," I said. "I don't understand what you're up to, but can't we at least go in and talk about it?"

"I don't think so," he said.

"I don't understand. What's happened?"

"Mrs. Kee has seen fit to engage me to represent her in further dealings on this subject."

"What the hell do you mean, 'this subject'? It's not as if I am the enemy."

"There seems to be a complicated legal position. Until Mrs. Kee's situation becomes clear, I'm afraid that I cannot allow you access to her. You are employed by Martin Willetson and it is not established that their interests overlap one hundred percent."

"You have a goddamn nerve," I said. "Everything you know about this goddamn case I told you."

"There has been a weekend since you were last here," he said snottily. "I think in that time I have learned a good deal."

"I have no intentions of doing that woman any harm. And you may just be stupid enough to turn me away without finding out what I've picked up over the weekend."

He was about to *coup* my *grâce* when I took a breath and told him something for nothing. "Do you know, my good man, that the Indianapolis police are looking for Mrs. Kee?"

"The police? What do they want to talk to her for?"

"I would be most happy to accept your invitation to lunch with you, Goger, my man. Hyperglycemia is catching up with me. Shall we go in?" I tripped lightly up the steps.

34

I never did get lunch. He led me through the corridors until we ended in his special study. The one he didn't let servants into.

I sat in a comfortable, overstuffed chair. He sat at a desk. I opened my notebook. He found a leather-bound note pad in a desk drawer and opened that. I drew my trusty ball point; he a desk-set fountain pen. On garde.

"What do the police want with Mrs. Kee?"

"Are you going to answer some questions for me? I'll be damned if I'm going to pour out my hard work for you just to be pushed out the door again."

He took a breath. Older than the last time I'd seen him in this room. Melanie disrupted people. I wondered where she had spent Sunday night. "For instance, where did Mrs. Kee spend last night? I know it wasn't at the motel you put her in. Do a little bringing up to date, please. Goger."

"Mrs. Kee," he said slowly, "spent last night in the guest room in this establishment. As I learned the nature of her circumstances it seemed prudent to both of us to make her less accessible."

"I don't understand what you're so afraid of. Who did she murder?"

"Nobody," he said stiffly. He added uneasily, "But I understand you are not the only person who has been concerned with Mrs. Kee."

"I see. You're worried about Bartholomew. No problem there. He's been recalled to Chicago."

"Bartholomew?"

"Kee's private detective. He's not around anymore. The town wasn't big enough for the two uh us."

He duly wrote down the crumb I'd thrown him.

"And the police," said Goger. "Are they really aware of Melanie?"

"I didn't make it up," I said. "The Indianapolis Police Department has received a request from the Chicago gendarmes with respect to a missing child, Freeman Kee, aged six. It was suggested that the mother, Melanie Kee, be located, if in the area, and interviewed."

"The police," he said, misty. "How could they . . ."

"I don't think it rash to suspect that Edmund Kee has gone to them with his documents and has convinced someone there the kid is missing. He may even have had his lawyer go to court to get some kind of order. I don't know how these things work, but Kee is the inspiration. There isn't any question about that."

"Documents?" asked Goger. "What documents?"

I explained their gist in exchange for the story Melanie had told her newly obtained legal adviser. She admitted going to Chicago, pregnant. It was the first confirmation of a second conception that I'd had from Mels. But in Chicago, she told Goger, she had a miscarriage. Not long after she got to town. Then she'd set about making a new life for herself.

There was quite an overlap with Mars's version. She'd run across Mars again in December. He helped her get away from Kee's earlier detective, and later from Kee himself. It was the first time I appreciated that Melanie had had a real period of freedom from Kee. The whole thing with Artie Bartholomew and me must have seemed pretty *déjà vu*. It would be easy for her to feel desperate.

She had elaborated to Goger the story of Kee's confrontation in Chicago. The one which led to her precipitate departure for Florida with Mars.

"She said Kee caught her at home one morning," said Goger, grave and looking more a spectator than a player. "He made a scene, obviously. He kept asking about the child. Apparently there is some history of preoccupation with having children. So she tells me." Goger looked at me for confirmation.

"So she told me too," I said.

"She told him she'd had a miscarriage. She says he threatened her with a gun."

"Oh?"

"She says he is vengeful and is perfectly capable of hiring private detectives to intimidate her, to make her life hell. She says all the trouble she's in, or appears to be in, has its origin with her husband."

"I'm sure you don't tell it as well as she can," I said. "I met Kee. He's not a nice type. But if he was just harassing her it seems unlikely he'd go to the police. Make himself too vulnerable."

"Yes," he said uneasily. "I don't know what to say. She is . . . the daughter of a good friend, of two good friends. She is my client."

"You can see why I want to talk to her."

"Do you have these documents with you? May I see them?"

"I don't have them on me," I said. They were in the truck in a pouch I've glued to one of the inner walls. "Oh my God," I said. "I was painting the truck."

"What?"

I swallowed. "I've had a good look at the documents and I see no reason to doubt them. But I'll check them out. I'm going to Chicago shortly." News to me. But not a bad idea.

"And I," he said with resolve, "I have no option but to ignore their existence until proved. I must accept my client's story until I have some concrete reason to do otherwise."

"So you aren't going to let me talk to Melanie?" The point of the exercise.

"When I spoke to her last she said she didn't want to talk to you."

"Can't you even go and ask her again?"

To my surprise he said, "Why not?" He got up and left the room without further words.

The key was this kid. If I could just find it. Going to Chicago was not a bad idea, I'd have bet it was still there. And I hadn't told Goger about Jack. Any more, apparently, than Melanie had.

Goger returned without warning. I rose, half-expectantly. But he was alone.

"She won't see you," he said firmly. She had inspired new strength.

"Why not?"

"She says you have sold out to her husband and you and he have caused her enough trouble. She says you can go back to Chicago."

"She knows which private detective I am? You're sure?"

"She knows," Goger said. "I think you'd better leave."

I sat down. "All right. I'll tell you what I'm going to do. The Indianapolis police want to talk to her, as I said. The request came to the attention of a friend of mine in the department who recognized the name and let me know. At present they don't know where Melanie is, or where she's been living. Whether they push depends on what pressure they get from Chicago."

The lawyer was not overly responsive.

I continued, "I was hired to protect Melanie from her husband's abuse so she and her boy friend can live together unharassed."

He sat up. "Her boy friend? What does that mean?"

"She hasn't told you about Mars?" It was too much.

"The man who took her away from Chicago, oh yes. What about him?"

"The man she'd been living with ever since. The man she ran away from to come here. What the hell's the matter with you? Don't you ask her any questions? Don't you have any idea what she's been doing, these last five years?"

"She said," he said, "that she's been working in an antique shop."

"Jesus." If she tells you it's Tuesday, look out for the Sunday paper.

"She said she's been living alone."

Shades of truth, if it came to that. I was wondering whether it was possible for Melanie née Baer to live anything but alone.

I was fed up. I made a speech. "I was employed to prevent Edmund Kee from being a Damoclean sword over her life and plans. I am in no sense in the employ of her husband. But I must find out the truth if any lasting structure is going to come out of all this. So . . . I'll leave now. And I'm going to Chicago to work on the last traces of those things which I can learn indirectly. I will not put the police onto Melanie, provided you will undertake to keep track of her. Do you understand? Because when I get back from Chicago, with or without this missing child, I intend to have a session with Melanie Kee— with you present if you like—to sort out just what the hell is the truth and what isn't. Then I'll compile what I know. Make my recommendations. Give a copy to you and her, a copy to her boy friend in Indianapolis and then I'm damn well going to wash my hands of the whole lot of you. I've never been lied to so much in my life. I don't like it, and when I've finished the job I've committed myself to, you and she and you all can go screw yourselves or each other or do anything you damn well please."

Goger's hands came apart when he realized I had finished. He looked pained.

I got up and left the room.

It took a lot longer to get out the front door than I remembered it taking on the way in. But I cooled off as I walked around. It occurred to me that I could wander, unchecked, around the house until I'd found Melanie's room. I'd have known it by the sobbing through the door, or the clink of ice cubes in the glass. Or the guileful mutterings, "Two and two is five."

I liked the idea of wandering childishly about a big house. The wandering. Passing suits of armor standing hollow in the hallowed halls. I felt fed up enough to do it. Devil-may-care, we calls it.

But I also realized I wouldn't have liked the end product, finding Melanie. I didn't want to find her. I didn't want to talk to her. I would rather wring her neck. I was fed up with her and the cyclone in a teacup which she seemed to be the center of.

It was cold on the doorstep. I took a few steps toward my truck.

A few fateful steps. Then I saw it. I would leave my mark on this place. Wedgwood blue paint was dripping out the back doors onto the driveway gravel.

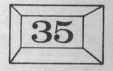

When I left Goger I was mad enough to take off for Chicago on the spot. But the paint turned my head. The idea of dripping for a hundred and fifty miles.

I opened the back door on the truck to have a look. Blue cushions. Blue polka-dotted mattress. I closed the door again. Walked to the driver's seat, got in, swung around and drove straight back to Indianapolis. Without looking back.

When I got home, I hit the phone.

Miller was out. It was late afternoon. Why wasn't he there when I wanted him?

I called the House of Antiquity. Willson wasn't there. Pity, I wanted to keep him up-to-date for a change.

Things had dragged on for so long—ten calendar days—that I felt some concern about Willson's mounting financial liability on this job. Not that ten days is very long, but with expenses it was getting up to the cost of having a baby.

I called my woman's. She wasn't there. I knew she wouldn't

be. But Lucy wasn't there either. All the zeroes were making me impatient.

I called airport information for the next plane to Chicago. There was one going just too soon. Then another an hour after that. I booked. Rummaged for some clothes that were reasonably clean. When I'm out of work I have more time to keep my clothes looking like I'm in work. I gathered my professional paraphernalia—notebook, writing instrument, head—and then threw in a few longer shots. Camera. Lock picks.

And I didn't forget my Chicago map.

I mobilized my dripping panel truck and drove to the airport. The cushions were one thing. When they dried I would turn them over and let it go at that. How do you turn a floor over?

At the airport I duplicated my earlier calls. The only person I got was Miller. I asked whether he was making progress on the Melanie Baer Kee inquiry. He made rude noises. He wasn't likely to get further with it until I helped him with trivia, like where Melanie was. I told him I was taking a couple of days off.

"Where are you going?"

"Hollywood," says I. "To be a star."

With the fifteen minutes I had before boarding I sat and worked with my map.

Plotting all the areas and addresses I knew. Kee's apartment building. The address of the Clephane Clinic, which the child was taken to both before and after it was born. Kee's work address. The department store Mels had worked in. Mars's home address when he lived in Chicago. The corner he'd left Mels at when he'd dropped her off after dates. Jack's address.

I plotted them, one after the next. Everything I could think of. Even the airport.

It's a good way to get grounded in an unfamiliar town. And I learned things from the exercise too. Jack's house was on a side street called Pry which crossed Remster near Grand. The corner Mars left Mels at. It had to mean Mels went back to

Jack's. Which explained why Mars never got invited in. It made me wonder what kind of setup Kee had burst in on that day he'd done his bursting.

They called my plane.

On the flight I considered whether to go to the Chicago police, see if I could find what their attitude was about the missing child. Whether they took it seriously, whether they were just going through the motions in response to an unbalanced citizen's complaint.

I could get the people making the request from Miller if I called him back, I thought. Worth a shot.

I wondered how the Chicago police would react to me asking about one of their cases. One hears things about the Chicago police. They'd lock me up. Throw away the key. Insulate the door. Paint it blue. No! No!

I also decided to look up Artie Bartholomew. Maybe his wife would invite me for dinner. Give me a kiss as I left. Get lipstick on my collar to make my woman jealous and passionate. Yes! Yes!

First thing at O'Hare I leased a phone. I called a hotel close to town center. Then I called Willson. To inform him of my present location with a thumbnail why. I also thought it fit to inform him gently that the police were taking an interest in things.

"Oh my God," he said. I could visualize the beginning of household decay.

"Look, it may be good. It may mean that Kee has overextended himself and we'll be able to cut him off." Didn't sound very convincing to me, I must admit.

"Oh my God!" repeated Mars. He wasn't listening to me so I hung up.

Next I called myself, my office, for messages left for me since I'd left. If the President calls, no matter who he is, you feel you oughtn't keep him waiting.

"Oh yes, Mr. Samson," gushed Dorrie, "the library called. They said the book you requested, um, *Sexual Patterns in a Midwestern Town,* is in and would you like to pick it up by next week. That's better than nothing, isn't it, Mr. Samson?"

Things were poised then, a busy day tomorrow.

To finish on a lighter tone I called Artie Bartholomew's home number. Given underneath the daytime digits on his business card. Couldn't hurt to learn whether Kee had had Arthur at work in Chicago. If so on what.

A lady answered and I asked for Arthur.

"Well I'll be fucked," he said cheerfully when I identified myself. "A voice from the past."

He invited me to dinner, despite the hour. I overcame my natural diffidence—"Yeah, great"—and asked for directions.

I followed them as soon as I had rented a car and checked in at my hotel. Bartholomew lived on a little development near a place called Homewood. He had a dog and a fence around the house. Mr. Average Guy. Looking at it I felt happy for him. The only thing that didn't seem right was Arthur's giant frame silhouetted in the doorway. But he was soon supported by not one, but two goodly blond ladies. I didn't ask embarrassing questions, but one turned out to be his wife, the other the wife's twin sister who was visiting for the holidays. From a university teaching job in Ottawa, no less. A divorced lady, she was.

Can a private detective lead an ordinary life in the big city? Yes, a thousand times yes. He even had a game room. That was the first thing that made me envious. I like games.

I considered, in a moment of distraction, moving my bed at home out of its cubbyhole into the living room. Then I could use the now-bedroom as a game room. The problem is that there aren't many games you can play in a tiny bedroom. When the bed's not there, I mean.

"Arthur *is* away a lot," said Penelope after the meal. "And I get pretty lonely."

"I'm sure he gets lonely too," I said. Trying to be all things to all people. Reassuring to Penelope. Tossing a sugary irony at Arthur. Looking forlorn and away-from-home for Doris, the sister. She was away from home too, right?

It was an extremely pleasant evening. Doris and I played footsie.

Just before I left, about two A.M. I said I'd come over to them the next night. Pending business.

I drove to the hotel so fast you would have thought I knew the way blindfolded or had friends in Traffic Division.

I was eager to get the last of my duties done. I still had to call my woman: not calling was a trap I wasn't going to fall into again.

But she wasn't pleased to hear from me.

"You know what time it is? Can you imagine what kind of day I've had?"

We don't routinely talk about work but Christmas is a rough season for people who deal with people. I can count to two, but I have trouble enough putting one and one together.

That's the problem with people who are unlike. When things are good they make a bigger whole than other couples, but when they are gliding on separate winds, the gap between them is a chasm.

It brought me back to earth. Just as well.

The story made late editions of the Monday evening papers, but was still unexploited enough to be given a pretty big play on Tuesday morning. Front-page play: LOCAL CHILD SOUGHT. Fear of Foul Play. There was a picture of a baby. I choked on my flapjack and syrup.

I was up early. I had things to do. But I'd decided on a proper breakfast, a good look through the papers. Give the spring a good wind, and then let it make the toy detective go for all he's worth.

The picture, the story knocked the wind out.

It made pulp reading. The abandoned father-to-be who kept searching for the child he'd never seen. Who'd saved up money to follow his runaway wife to Chicago. Who'd stayed in town looking for her, managed to get an important job as a programming administrator with the census committee in the city government. Who with great personal effort had compiled a dossier on the missing child. Who had gone as far with the job as he could go alone and had finally come to the police.

"At first," a Detective Inspector Dowdell was quoted, "we didn't take Mr. Kee's problem very seriously. But the evidence he gathered was impossible to ignore. He's traced the clinic his wife went to before the boy was born. The midwife who was present at the birth. The child's clinic visits after the birth, up to the date when it would seem that the child vanished. There is no trace of the boy after the age of seven months. A series of vaccinations was left incomplete. He hasn't been registered at any local school. The father has shown us circumstances which are certainly suspicious."

Dowdell was not publicity-shy, whatever else he was. Some cops like publicity more than others. "I fear for the child," he'd said. "We have reason to believe that his mother is not a very responsible person."

He promised to release a picture of Melanie later. He said she was "sought for questioning."

Beside the story was the baby picture. "Last Known Picture of Freeman Kee: at age 5 months."

The story unsprung my plans for the day.

It took me some time and coffee to figure out what I should do. I considered returning to Indianapolis. But the work I could do there, mostly defensive, I could do by phone. There were people to see here. Dowdell, for one.

I cleaned my plate, paid my bill and went back to my room. I called Indianapolis homicide; Miller hadn't put in his appearance yet. So I called Willson.

Who I caught. "Was just leaving for the store," he said. He didn't sound any too steady, for a Tuesday A.M. But I passed on news of the story.

"I guess she's really in for it now," he said, as distant as if he'd just heard that Marie Antoinette's cakes were stale.

"You may be in for it too."

"Me?"

"Kee's made his move. Putting his version of the story in public hands. They're going to retrace all the steps and that means they're going to be coming to you."

"Me?" he said again. "But what do I do?"

"That depends on what you want to do. What you feel for Melanie."

"Depends what she feels for me, doesn't it?"

Does it? This could go on forever. "Do you think she killed that second child?"

"I . . . I don't know anything much anymore."

"You did live with the lady for five years."

"It seems . . . Hell. No, I don't think she killed any child. She would be . . . capable of doing . . . things, but only . . . No."

"Good. Then we're agreed. And when it's settled you two ought to come out all right."

"I don't think it wise to group us anymore."

"Individually, together, part of a circus. I don't care. What do you think *you* should do?"

"I . . . I don't know. What should I do?"

"I would advise a little vacation."

"What? A what?"

"Pack a suitcase with your favorite books. Put on some clothes you would be ashamed to be seen in. Drive to your bank and get a wad of money. Go to the airport and leave your car in the long-term parking lot. Like a vacation, see? Then take a bus back to town and check in at a second-class hotel. Tonight call me with the number I can reach you at. My number is . . ." I looked up Artie's home number and gave it. "And if I'm not there, don't leave your name, just the number and I'll call you back tonight or tomorrow morning."

"You mean I'm to avoid being talked to by the police?"

"I mean that you should take a little vacation to relax."

"But," he said sadly, "what if Melanie should try to call me at home?"

Second time lucky, I got Miller. I asked him if there had been any hot-up of the Melanie Baer Kee stuff.

"Dunno," he said. "Just got here. Desk told me you called, would call back soon."

I told him about the excitement I'd suffered at breakfast.

"I just don't know," he said. "But it sounds like we'll be hearing from them. I'll keep an eye out."

"Thought I'd go downtown to talk to them. If I do, will you cover me?"

"What does *that* mean?"

"Well, you hear these stories about Chicago police."

"I suggest you put on your Sunday suit and remember to say please."

"Did you get any word on that adoption stuff I asked you about?"

"Like I say, I just got here."

"You're a big help."

"What do you want me to do? Make up answers? The kid was adopted three times, but each time he killed his new parents."

I found Dowdell at ten forty-five. That is, I found the branch he was supposed to be at.

"I'm looking for Inspector Dowdell," I told a hollow-eyed young deskman.

He looked at me. Then my notebook. "You missed the general press call. Last night at seven."

"So I read. But he's not hiding today, is he?"

"No. He's doing TV interviews now. Next call is seven tonight."

"When does he work on the case?"

He didn't bat a deep-set eyelash. "I think you better let him worry about that."

And then, from some recess not too distant, I heard a scream. Honest. But it couldn't have been routine. The kid looked up. Then he smiled. "Just some of the fellas fooling around," he said. "Honest."

He pointed me to the corridor up which Dowdell was being interviewed, and through the second set of swinging doors I spotted the action. The bright lights.

The good inspector stood, one hand on hip, chest puffed out. Looking for all the world like an English country gentleman crossed with a pouter pigeon. He was a smoothie all right. Glib and lightly local; I saw immediately what was going on. This was a human-interest case which had been picked out for the force to emphasize its humanity with. Dowdell was their hearts-and-flowers man. He was saying, "I'm worried about this child, I really am." I didn't believe him. Thousands would.

As I approached, my arm was lightly taken by one of Dowdell's plainclothed shepherds. He held me back and at the same time put a finger on my lips to show me I should keep quiet. No one had ever done that to me before. It wasn't a situation I knew how to handle. While the finger was poised in front of my face, I bit it.

The guy took a deep breath and grunted but not loud. Someone else turned around and looked daggers at him. I nearly sealed his lips with my finger. But I didn't risk it. If he did unto me, I would have cried. I lack self-control.

The interview went on another four or five minutes, and by the end Dowdell had everybody in the room crying for poor little Freeman Kee. On TV they'd condense the interview like onion soup and there wouldn't be a dry eye in town tonight.

Dowdell, looking smaller as he released himself from the TV stance, said, "Right. Now who's next?"

The man who'd daggered my finger-man said, "Not here yet, Chief." Honorary title, no doubt. "But there's somebody else. Came in in the middle."

"What's he want?"

"What do you want?" the dagger man asked me.

"I'd like to talk to Inspector Dowdell," I said. "I've just come up from Indianapolis."

"He's come up from Indianapolis, Chief."

Dowdell squinted. Indianapolis hadn't been mentioned in the paper. "All right," said Dowdell. "You send him to Interview 3. I'll talk to him there. I'll go wash this makeup off and be there in a minute.

"You might leave it on, Chief. You've got one more to do."

"Well, they're not here on time, are they? When they do show up we'll just have to put it on again, won't we? But suppose they don't show up for an hour. I'm not going to walk around all day looking like Tony the fucking Tiger."

He disappeared then. I got led around to a waiting room. I waited. Dowdell called me from one of four available doors.

"This way, son," he said. We walked through one Spartan room into another. I felt like I was in a maze. And since I didn't know my way around, I must be the rat.

We sat on opposite sides of a table. I realized, at long last, that this was not a press interview room. It was an interrogation room.

"May I see your credentials, please, son?"

"What?"

"Your credentials, please."

It caught me flat. I dug for my wallet and had to decide whether to give him a press card I have. It was a year out of date; that was the problem. I get them from a friend at the *Star*, but she charges me exorbitantly. I had decided to make this one last and hadn't had trouble about it yet. I figured I'd have trouble with it now. I gave him my PI I.D.

He chuckled. "I didn't think you were really press."

"I never said I was."

"We've already had the *Star-News* stringer here. And this ain't the kind of story any of your ethnics would be interested in."

"No," I agreed. A cop experienced with the Midwest press.

"Samson," he said. "Samson," savoring it. "You must be the PI that Willetson hired."

"So you are really in charge of the case investigation? Not just the public relations on it."

"I'm a cop," he said. "I investigate. I have a mandate from the public to investigate crime. Which is more than you do. What's your interest, son?"

"I want to find out just how seriously you really take this stuff. That's my interest."

"Murdered kid? We take it pretty seriously."

"That kid's no more murdered than I am," I said, committing myself.

"You know where he is?" he asked sharply.

"No, not yet," I said. And I wondered, for an instant, if I might just be wrong.

Dowdell didn't go for my lead-in. He didn't ask about my ideas on the kid. He was a sharp cop and kept his mind on his own work. He said, "Do you know where this Kee woman is?"

I hesitated, just a moment. Then said, "No."

"Don't believe you," he said swiftly. Daggers for me.

I knew I would be in desperate trouble if I let him get me on the defensive.

"I don't know where she is," I said, mustering forcefulness. To get him off the seat of my trousers I tossed out a bone. "I did meet her once."

"Where?"

"In Indianapolis. In a diner on the corner of Alabama and Ohio streets." An old breakfast haunt.

"When?"

I made another mistake, just a fraction, but too much. I glanced at my notebook, then said, "December fourth."

He gave it a momentary rest. Gathering cavalry on the flank for an aggressive action. I drew my wagons in a circle.

"Where did she live then?"

"Don't know."

"What did she say about the kid?"

"Nothing."

"When did she see him last?"

"Don't know."

"When did she kill him?"

"She didn't say a word about that or any other kid, Chief."

"Suppose I had you thrown in jail overnight. How would that affect your memory."

"Not at all," I said. "They never told me where she lived."

He made his thrust at the vulnerable point I had shown him. "Suppose I use the day you're waiting in our cozy cell to peruse that notebook you keep such close rein on."

I tossed the notebook over to him, though it hurt. "Read away. I keep dates and facts in there. And there's nothing in there that I wouldn't tell you here and now. Except the phone number of a blonde named Doris I met last night."

He flipped the notebook open. Looked at the disorderly scrawl I was, for once, thankful for. He flipped it back to me. I had weathered his attack and would hold my own. "So what do you want?" he asked, and sat back. At long last.

"I want to know how seriously you're taking this guy Kee. Whether you really believe what you're telling them out there. Whether you believe half of what he told you."

"He's got pretty convincing stuff. You seen it?"

"He gave me copies."

"I get the impression, Mr. Samson, that you came here more to tell me some things than to ask me questions. So get to it. What's your message?"

"Just that I am surprised to see you making such a big play on nothing more than Kee's so-called evidence. I think you have a lot of work to do before you can get away with accusing Melanie Kee of murder."

He smiled. "I haven't, yet."

"Climb down. We both know the way it's being set up."

He said sharply, "She had the kid. So where is it now?"

"I don't know, yet."

"But you think you're going to be finding out soon, is that it?"

"From the way you guys are chasing shadows I'd bet I'll find it before you do."

"Sheet," he said. Honest.

"All right," I said. "Let me tell you a couple of things. You're going half-cocked about Melanie Kee being a dangerous person, and my guess is you've been listening to her husband's stories about what happened to their first kid. Well, check it out. You get the cause of death from St. Louis and then you find yourself a doctor to tell you what it means. That's the first thing. Then you think about this. Melanie Kee was in Miami —that's in Florida—from June first to June sixteenth, 1966. From there she went to Indianapolis. That's a fact. You look at the kid's records which say he got vaccinated on the seventeenth here in Chicago. Now you tell me the odds that he was in the care of Melanie Kee at that time. Or that he was ever in her care again after then."

He pulled on his left ear lobe with his right hand. "That all?" As if that detail could be explained away a hundred different ways. Which it could.

But I said, "It's enough to kick what you've been telling the papers in the balls. That's all PR, of course. But if you're interested in finding the kid, I think you're a lot better off looking for him. Instead of assuming he's dead and playing hunt-the-witch-his-mother. The odds are she gave him away legally or otherwise, and he's been brought up from the beginning by somebody else. Maybe somebody who moved in June 1966. Maybe somebody who realized then that the kid was hers for keeps and she shouldn't use his mother's name anymore."

"That's what you think?"

"That's what I think."

"And what is it that you would have me do, son?"

"Check adoption records. Check abandonment records for kids of the right age. And failing that, get the whole city started on tracking down women who have a kid of the right age. Who maybe have come to a new neighborhood without bringing along the medical records which include details of the pregnancy. Use some of these fine relations you seem to have with the press to spur on a little useful inquiry. That's what I would do."

"Catch your breath, son," Dowdell said then. Mused. "I see you have friends in the Indianapolis Police Department. You're the one that got them to ask us to check adoption records, isn't that right?"

I nodded.

"Well, son. Let me tell you some things. I don't assume anybody is dead until I smell the body rotting. I haven't buried this kid yet and I haven't decided who killed him if he is dead. You can believe that, son. But the other thing I want to tell you is this. You are gonna have to trust me to get the most out of the people of Chicago in this investigation. I'm not going to explain it all to you. But it's a fact that by tonight just about everyone in this damn city is going to know about this little boy and is going to be thinking about him. It's called human interest, son. And when we have a case that's got some we use it for all it's worth because it opens doors. Without it we knock on a door and they see a cop. With it we go to the same door and first thing they think of is this murdered kid. I don't have to tell you which way we get more help. Now I'll keep what you say in mind, son. Don't worry about that. The only other thing I want to tell you is this. We checked the adoption records in this city and we drew a blank. There now. That gives you a little something extra to think about."

37

Prejudice is a funny thing. Everybody has it; it's essential to balanced mental function, because you can't go around thinking out every move you make. You know ahead of time that you "like" banana mocha almond fudge ice cream with strawberry sprinkles. The reasons you used to establish the fact may or may not have been good, but you are now prejudiced in flavor's favor; it frees your mind to work on whether the countergirl is making eyes at you or is just nearsighted.

Prejudices are the mental habits which parallel learned physical reflexes. And they get you in trouble only when your original judgment was made without enough information, or when you apply a prejudice to a situation it doesn't suit.

Now I am prejudiced against a lot of police function and style. I don't like their guns and their self-righteousness. But on my home ground, Indianapolis, I know I'm prejudiced and can allow for it. Letting it pleasure me in private with snappy witticisms, but not necessarily letting it affect the way I deal with the real people I meet from time to time who happen to be dressed in blue.

I got in trouble in Chicago because, without adjusting for it, I was extra prejudiced against Chicago police and I let it affect the way I went into my conversation with Dowdell.

It hadn't occurred to me that I didn't know everything there was to know at the moment, and more than him. It hadn't occurred to me that he might be better able to judge how to function as a policeman than I was. It hadn't occurred to me that he might be reasonably intelligent, reasonably sensitive, and reasonably professional.

Live and learn, to coin a phrase.

Which left us with the little matter of finding Freeman Kee, The Unadopted.

Somewhere. Blissfully daydreaming about Santa Claus. Not yet old enough to be aware of the commercial world of Santa Callous, purveyor of presents.

I tried to want something for Christmas.

Couldn't think of anything. The world is too barbarous even to hope for important goodnesses, and the days when things I wanted sprang to mind have been left behind. When I was younger, say, thirty, I wanted things. A new scarf. Some mousetraps. But not today. Not anything besides finding out what had happened to this kid, this erstwhile kid. This never seen but ne'er forgotten six-year-old chocolate-smeared urchin. Somewhere out there.

Put him in my stocking, Santa.

Put him in your own fucking stocking, Albert.

What'd I tell ya? Santa Callous.

I got out the map of Chicago. I would do things in an orderly way. Start at the southernmost point I'd plotted and work north.

Or should it be north to south?

I started in the south. On the off chance it would be warmer there.

My first call was the Clephane Clinic, 6500 South.

The University area in Chicago isn't exactly the fanciest part of town. I suppose students aren't as fancy as they used to be either. The Clinic, however, was a bastion of the relatively new. A plaque next to the main entrance bore the date 1964 like a challenge to the elements.

I shuffled through the draft-excluding double doors and found a big sign staring me in the face. It read "Information" and pointed, not rudely. Just what the doctor ordered.

A squat brunette with puffy cheeks and premature frown lines sat behind a hole in a glass wall, waiting to inform me. I stood mute before her window no longer than ten seconds before she looked up and said "Yes?" She forced her mouth into a professional smile, but the configuration strained her muscles so she quit.

"Sorry to bother you, but I wondered if you could tell me a little about the clinic's history."

I had done her an injustice. No negativism for me. She said, "Sure," and said it cheerfully. She smiled even. I guess the initial chilliness was because I'd looked like a patient.

Before long I'd gathered she thought I was press and not the first of the day. I didn't disabuse her; you take what you're given.

Not surprising there'd been reporters there ahead of me. Dowdell had released the name of the clinic though he'd held back most other names. Already the information girl had a set routine. I learned how many patients they got through on an average day; when the Chief Administrator for Cook County's health services had first broken ground; how to spell the Director's name. It was seven letters long and very hard.

"They seem to get it wrong a lot," she said. "So I spell it."

"Do you have a particularly large pre- and postnatal clinic?" I asked.

"Well, not especially large," she said. "I mean not large. We handle most of the area here."

"But you wouldn't call it a specialty?"

"Not especially, no. We have quite a good emergency service, though. I think if we had a specialty, that would be it. But we're really not very special here." Giggle. "One of the new neighborhood clinics. To deal with the chronic outpatient conditions of the neighborhood and to provide emergency services."

"So you said before." She had. "But another question. Do you keep medical records on a computer?"

"Oh yes. We're very modern. Mind you, they had a lot of trouble with that computer."

"Oh?"

"Yeah."

"What sort of trouble was it?"

"Well, I wasn't here then myself. All we use it for is records, which is very useful for chronic types of patients. But it did print up some funny stuff, recordwise. Those first few years."

"Doesn't it make mistakes anymore, then?"

"Oh no. There was some screw-up, pardon my French, with its insides and they finally had it fixed. Some bigwig came out and changed the whole whatchacallit. Took weeks and then all the other information had to be put back into it. Really a mess."

"Were you here when they did the reprogramming?"

"No. I only been here two and a half years. We have quite a high turnover rate, as a matter of fact. I'm third in seniority in the office department already."

"Is there anybody around who was here during the reprogramming?"

"Just Lorraine." It sounded like Low Rein, which turned out to be appropriate because Lorraine was a pretty horsy type. My information girl let me behind the glass wall and brought Lorraine to me. I said, "How d'ya do?"

She said, "Hi."

I asked her about the computer troubles and tried to get her to date when they got straightened out. She measured time by how much she was earning. "So when that guy was here fixing the computer I was getting $1.82 an hour so that will be the spring of 1968."

I didn't ask what lofty heights her wages had risen to. I'd get jealous. I did ask, "You don't remember the guy's name, do you?"

She smiled. "I never knew it. The whole time he never talked to hardly anyone. But he sure worked hard." Lorraine and my information girl burst into giggles together.

"He really sweated over his work," stammered Lorraine through a gale of insufficiently suppressed titter. The comment not only reinforced their own amusement but made the other three girls working in the office within earshot stop for a laugh.

Turns out the unfortunate man had two qualities: being too snooty to talk to anyone; and coming up from behind the machine with his face absolutely pouring with sweat. Every office has its legendary characters. They had never met him but everyone knew the story. They had me starting to laugh. Ha.

I only had a couple of questions left. Whether the high turnover rate in the office staff was matched in the gynecological section. Whether there would be anybody there who might remember a patient from 1965–1966.

They didn't know, but my information girl tried to give me directions.

"I'll find it," I said. "No sweat."

When I finally found a room of pregnant women I asked a nurse for someone who might remember back that far. She thought, but finally said there wasn't anybody. Then I got a bright idea and looked at the copy I had of Melanie's clinic records. They bore a doctor's code. I decoded it with assistance. But no luck. My special doctor wouldn't remember poor old Mels and her poor old child. He was dead. He'd died of a heart attack just under four years before on the steps as he'd been coming out of church. 1967. One of the other doctors on duty seemed to have made a study of coronaries in the medical profession. He gave me a very full account.

38

First stop north of the clinic was the residence of Mrs. A. I. Keough. At least her residence as of November 17, 1965, the date of Freeman Kee's birth. She'd been on the scene. The midwife.

It was quite a way to Mrs. Keough's. Across the river and almost to Cicero. Not an elegant place. The apartment building was four stories high and red with brick.

Apartment 3A. Knock. Knock.

"Who's there?" someone asked quickly from inside. A woman.

"You don't know me, but I'd like to speak to Mrs. Keough, please."

"Who?"

"Mrs. Keough."

The door opened far enough for me to see a nose, a rouged mouth and choice of eyes. "Who?"

"Mrs. A. I. Keough," I read. "The midwife."

"This some kind of joke?"

I earnestly hoped it wasn't. "I don't think so. She was the midwife at the birth of a little boy six years ago. I was hoping she would remember something about it."

"Not likely."

"Why not?"

"'Cause she died, that's why not. What's this all about anyway?"

"I'm trying to locate the little boy. Nobody seems to know what happened to him." And give Dowdell a chance: "Maybe you read about it in the papers today, or heard about it on TV?"

"You mean that little kid that his mother killed him?"

"We don't know whether he's dead or not. That's what I was hoping Mrs. Keough could help me with."

"Oh, he's dead all right," she said.

I said, "The police haven't been here yet then."

"Here? Why would they come here?"

"Because Mrs. Keough's name is on the kid's birth certificate."

"Does that mean they're going to come here?"

"I would think so. I'm surprised they haven't already." No I wasn't; for all Dowdell's protestations it was obvious they were working on the presumption the kid was dead.

"Christ," said my hostess through the gap, "I better clean up the joint."

"Did you know Mrs. Keough?"

"Yeah," she said. "I knew the old lady."

"She was old?"

"Yeah. About a hundred it seemed like. Vic and I waited eleven years downstairs till she died and we could move up here. It's the biggest apartment in the whole building and she hung on to it all alone. Years and years. We thought she was never going to die. Mrs. Methuselah is what Vic called her." Mrs. Vic was getting friendly, but we were still talking through a crack.

"But she was a midwife, wasn't she?"

"Oh yeah. Whatever that is. I mean, I know what it is. And she was one. She had a certificate to prove it too, on the wall."

"A certificate?"

"Yup. On the wall. Registered Midwife for the City of Chicago. I took it down and threw it out myself. After she died, of course."

"Do you remember when she died?"

"July 18, 1968. No, she died on the seventeenth. We moved up here the eighteenth. But she was pretty old, you know, I mean in the end. I kind of would have been surprised to know that she had done any work, midwifing. She was pretty old. Say, this is kind of rude for me to be talking to you through the door like this. The place is a mess but if you want to you can come in."

"No, thanks." There was nothing left to talk about. A little rudeness, all part of life's rich pageant.

Before I pushed on I sat for a few minutes in the rented car. Sulking, I guess. Depressing myself. Nothing was breaking. Nobody was popping up, kid in hand. If I wasn't such a disciplined individual, I thought to myself, I'd . . . But I didn't know what I'd do. I am such a disciplined individual. I decided to go shopping.

I like to walk around department stores. They're warm in the winter and cool in the summer. I remember spending a whole day in Block's once as a kid. I was reading some Russian novel and read as I walked, read as I rode the escalators, read as I sat on the chairs put out for patient husbands. Those were my hoity-toity days, my ill-spent youth. I remember I was going to do Strauss's, Ayres's and Wasson's in sequence until I finished the book. Never did though. Something came up.

It wasn't the best time of year to arrive with questions at a department store personnel section. Too chaotic with the temporary Christmas staff, trying to train a little common sense into them and give them the most rudimentary idea of "how we do things here." Nevertheless, I cut a young man from the personnel herd and flashed my identification. I was about to tell him he could call Indianapolis to check me if he wanted to but he had already left to call his department manager.

The manager turned out to be a decent sort. When I hit him with the Indianapolis call idea—which was meant to frighten him off, see, because of having to justify the long-distance call to his superiors—he shrugged it off. "C'mon," he said. "You'll make a nice break in the boredom of the Christmas excitement."

He took me to a small office and quickly laid bare the history of Melanie Kee's employment with them. It read like a scout report: honest, trustworthy, brave. And reliable, it seemed. She had been employed June 29, 1965, had quit abruptly on

May 11, 1966, and in the whole time she hadn't missed a work-day.

The personnel man saw me write it all down in my notebook and follow it with an exclamation mark. He said, "Yeah, well, when she came to us for a job she needed one pretty bad, but we weren't hiring. Only I hired her."

"You remember her, then?"

"Oh yes. Personal personnel is m'trademark, suh. I remember her, all right. I had the feeling she would be pretty good and I have just enough clout here to follow up the occasional feeling. She was an asset to the store, suh. Promotion potential, only I figured she might not be around long enough to cash in on her abilities. One of the cases I was right about." He scored one for himself.

"Do you remember whether she was pregnant?"

"Excuse me, suh!"

"I mean during her time here did she ever say she was pregnant or did she look pregnant?"

"I caught your question; I'm just surprised."

"That means she didn't?"

"I never had a whisper. Not, mind, that that means she wasn't. I've known sales staff who carried it off without anybody knowing until they quit, at least twice, I remember, in the eighth month. And I've heard of one woman in a supervisory post who used a truss and nobody knew till she took a week off when she actually had it. That was a matter of staying in line for a promotion which she didn't get anyway. If she'd only come to me I'd have told her from the beginning it was never on, saved her a lot of trouble."

"Is the store closed any day during the week?"

"Every Monday."

I didn't know the days of the week, offhand, for 1965. "Could I have a copy of her hours through November '65? Could you make me a copy?"

"Long as you don't flaunt where you got it from," he said, and took the file to another room. Came back with a copy.

"You couldn't see your way clear to being Santa Claus for a couple of weeks, could you? Pay's not very good but there'd be a little present for you at the end."

"Sorry," I said. But it reminded me of a little Santa-Clausing I needed to do. The kind that was getting too late. Santa-Clausing for my own kid and her Christmas with her mother in the Caribbean. "But thanks."

"No thanks needed."

"Have the police been around here yet?"

"Yet?"

"I guess you don't read the papers much, do you?"

He laughed. "Not this time of year, no."

"Well, when you get around to it, or hear it on the TV, don't believe it all, will you?"

"Never do," he said.

Salt of the hearth.

When I left personnel, I took the escalator up, to toys. But I didn't have my hearth in it. Looking at the crush of shoppers, and, more oppressive, the enormous piles of each kind of product. It didn't feed my fatherly fires. I love my daughter, but I couldn't help but decide the best service I could give her was to plod on without trying to inspire myself to a distraction on her behalf.

So I plodded on.

The next spot on my map was Kee's office. I decided to give it a miss. It was a gut decision, but my mind was not far behind. I wasn't ready for him, that's all. To be ready I wanted a unique alternative theory strong enough to hit him over the head with. At the moment I was working with feathers, and the range of choice was increasing, not decreasing.

So I drove off to have a look at Willetson-Willson's old apartment building. To get to which I had to cross yet another river.

Or was it just a branch of the same one? Where's that map?

It didn't look very interesting. Maybe because I was hungry.

It was just short of one o'clock. I figured I had just a chance of catching some local news, if there was any, on the box. I blew into the nearest gin mill, ordered a beer and asked the barman if there was any TV news, if he'd mind turning it on. "Sure, sport."

Only it was national, the lunchtime respite-from-soap-opera five minutes.

"No local news?" I asked him.

He smiled, "You do something newsworthy, sport?"

I didn't deny it. He turned the box off and pulled an old radio out from under the gin. Blab-blah-dee-blah, bloop! Your 25-hour-a-day news station!

We waited through a feature on a breakthrough in the scientific battle to find the revolutionary pill, the one you take once a day, in the morning, and it deodorizes your whole body, all over, completely, all day long without sprays, roll-ons, creams, mists or powders externally applied. What they'd found, occasioning the story, was a poison which, taken in massive quantities, deodorized sweaty rats for six-hour periods. Before it killed them. "It's a limited advance," drawled the aged scientist, "but it is a step forward in principle." Rat sniffers, rejoice.

I had time to order and receive two westerns before they got through the weather, the time and sponsors. To the news that interested me.

"The search continues for six-year-old Freeman Kee. . . ."

It was a rehash of the foul-play fears. But they had a clip from an interview with the daddy, my own Edmund Kee. "All I want," he said, voice nervous but purposeful, "is to get my son back. I don't wish her any ill will." "Are you not afraid it may be too late, that your son may have come to some harm?" "I can only hope, pray, that he's all right." "Why did you wait so long before bringing your story to the police? It's been several years now, hasn't it?" "I didn't wait," Kee snapped. "As soon as I realized she'd run away I went to the police. I told them I was afraid of what she might do to the boy. But they didn't take me seriously. So I've been gathering evidence which they can't help but take seriously." Self-righteous, triumphant. But without doubt a sympathetic, hard-won-respect type character. Mels wouldn't be winning any elections in Chicago.

They followed Kee with asking Dowdell why the police hadn't looked for Melanie and the child five years ago. Dowdell was smooth, natch. The unfortunate fact was that in Chicago they got 110 million reports of missing people every day, for many of whom relatives fear violence. "You get us the manpower," said Dowdell, "we would be only too pleased to follow up every report just to put the people's minds at rest if nothing else. It's not that we don't want to take reports of this kind seriously. We just don't have enough officers to do it. I can report a little progress in this case now, however," he continued. "I received a report this morning that the child's mother, after leaving Chicago, moved to Indianapolis, where she is either living now or has been living until very recently. We have dispatched men to Indianapolis to assist the local police in their investigation."

It took me half an egg and a gulp of beer to realize the report he had received had come from me.

That sort of thing is a shock. I nearly brought the egg up. I realized the barman was watching me closely. Because, I began to realize, I was behaving more than interestingly. I was behaving suspiciously. If I'd been listening hard to news of a robbery he wouldn't have batted an eyelid. But my attention to this gave him thoughts.

Gave me thoughts too. What did it mean? What conclusions were to be drawn from what I'd heard? What, damn it! Think!

I thought I'd have another beer. Regain my cool. Received it with professional detachment. Dispatchment?

Dispatching men to Indianapolis? Nothing Miller was going to like better than outsiders looking over his shoulder. He couldn't sit on things now. He couldn't sit on me. It was not

too far-fetched to think that the Indianapolis police were looking for me. Me.

Dowdell was a crafty S.O.B. How do you distract people
from the unpleasant detail that you turned the guy away a few
years ago and now you regret it? You give them something
that looks current. Dowdell had known from the first there
were Indianapolis links with Melanie Kee.

The questions were: how close they were to Mels; whether
they had caught up with Mars. I forgot I'd told Mars to hide.
Then I remembered and was glad. It gave us, what, a day or
so before they found him. A day or so extra before they got out
of him that Mels was in Kokomo, before they ran her down.
Chasing her from room to room in Goger's big house. She'd be
screaming, remembering days of horror she'd lived through
before. They'd shoot . . .

I desperately wished I knew what Mels had to say. What the
facts, all-powerful, elusive, were. Everything I'd learned was
a jumble. Contradictory messes. Colors of the rainbow mushed
up. I needed a prism. It occurred to me it was possible I'd end
up in prison.

Why was I so preoccupied with the need to keep the police
away from Mels? Wouldn't they get the facts out of her in a
way I would never, probably, be able to do?

Because I felt protective of the lady. Another gut reaction.
My mind wasn't quick behind my gut this time. That's what
I'd been trying to do, get my mind up with the gut feeling
which told me: Mels good, Kee bad. And to move the mind you
need facts.

I downed the last of my beer and tried to decide whether
I should call Jack's to see if he was home. But if he was home
I felt like maybe it would be good to surprise him. If he wasn't,
it wouldn't matter. Sometimes the gut helps you make good
decisions, sometimes less good.

But the idea of the phone wasn't bad. The observant barman
made change. I dialed direct, the number for the Indianapolis
police.

I asked for Miller at the switchboard, and they rang his office. "Gartland," said the answering voice. I tried to place the name.

"Where's Miller?" I asked.

"Not right here," he said. "Who's calling, please?"

"Tell him Al called," I said.

"Is that Samson?" said the voice. "Al Samson?"

"Yeah," I said. "Do I know you?"

"Miller said you might call. I think he'd like you to come in for a chat, he said," he said.

The guy was making me nervous. "Can't make it just now," I said. "I'll call him back."

"It's more than a request, Samson," said Gartland. "He wouldn't like to have you picked up. Quite a nuisance all round."

"Save your bully-boy bluff . . ." And then I got stuck over the name to call him at the end of the sentence. By the time I worked out the best one, someone had hung up. It was me. Whitey!

I drew myself together. Talking to Gartland had sobered me. Gartland. That was Captain Gartland! Of course I remembered him. I'd met him when he was pretending to be a plainly clothed bear. How could I forget?

By trying, that's how. Not one of my favorite buddies.

Things were on the move in Indianapolis, of that I could be sure. Not often a captain covers a lieutenant's phone.

I got the dial tone back and called Goger's home number in Kokomo. The housekeeper answered. Another favorite buddy. But I played the heavy; asked straight for Goger.

"He's not here," she said. To keep her record clean.

"I'll leave a message," I said. "Do you have a pencil?"

"Go ahead."

"This is Samson. I'm calling from Chicago. Tell him not to read the papers. Not to watch television news. Not to listen to the radio. So that he won't know whether anybody is looking for his client. But tell him not to tell anybody where his client is. Do you have all that?"

"I have it, Mr. Samson," said the housekeeper. And I heard what I'd never thought I'd hear—her voice without malice as punctuation. I wondered what I'd ever done to her in the first place.

"Thank you," I said heartily. "And tell him I'll call back later. When I can."

"I'll tell him," she said. "They've gone on a picnic."

"A picnic?" In this weather? It must be love.

That's all I need, I thought. Goger and Mels in, gasp, love.

For an easy come, easy go kind of guy, Jack had a pretty classy house. A big one.

One bell saved my decision-making faculties, such as they were. I rang it. Waited a minute. Rang it again. Repeat dosage as required. I was on my best patience. Even so, I was about to leave when I finally heard footsteps inside. Jack may have been nimble but today he wasn't quick.

Only it wasn't Jack. It was a stubby raven-haired female person. She opened the door, looked at me, and smiled. "Hi," she said.

I gave my name and asked for Jack.

"My name's Delia. Will I do?" Friendly city, Chicago. I followed her into the house for a chat. She gave me a cup of coffee, and chat. A gentle girl, in comfortable circumstances. She gave me home-made bread with the coffee.

Jack, it turned out, was a wood carver and had a workshop in easy walking distance. After twenty minutes I pushed off for Jack's.

Setting aside the disclaimer Jack made on the phone, I was looking for the kid. The only person I knew Mels had had friendly contact with in Chicago was Jack. So odds were on friends of Jack's for little Freeman; friends who might not worry about formal adoption procedures. And if Delia was a sample of what Jack's friends were like . . .

I felt pretty good about things. For a change.

There was no sign over the workshop, but when I found a display window filled by a man carving wood I took a wild guess and walked in. Homey place. Wood, wood shavings, gouges, carvings complete and half-extracted. And a couple of teen-age boys watching the master. I stood in the doorway. Nothing much happened. I closed the door behind me.

"So I guess she kind of learned her lesson," said Jack, trying to pick up the conversational flow I'd broken. One of the kids glared at me hard.

"Sorry if I've interrupted," I said lamely. I wasn't nearly the tough, concise guy of my internal dialogues during the walk over.

Jack winked at me and said, "Well, if it had been real private stuff we'd have locked the door, drawn the blinds and been in the back room." Then he winked, other eye, to the lads. The nonglarer smiled. The glarer glared, still at me. "What can we do for you?" Jack asked me finally. And went back to work on what looked like a piece of ornate molding. It was a piece of ornate molding.

"I called you yesterday morning," I said. "Early, about Melanie Kee."

"Ahhhhh," said Jack. He had a bushy beard and muscular arms. He didn't say anything for a moment, gouged gently on. Then put down the tool, stood up, dug into a pocket and came up with some change. "I have to talk to this guy," he said to the kids. "You do me a favor, will you?" He gave the nonglarer a handful of change and said confidingly, of the glarer, "He's not in a mood to do favors for anyone, but you take this and get two dozen oranges and take them to his mother for me.

And you get two grapefruits and you give one to him and keep one yourself. Then you guys come back here later this afternoon, O.K.?"

The nonglarer took the money and the duties eagerly and pulled the glarer by the coat sleeve out of the door. "C'mon, Claude," he urged. Claude finally complied.

"Well then," said Jack, "should we draw the blinds and move to the back room? I wouldn't advise it. The only heater is here."

"I've got no secrets," I lied.

"I was wondering when you'd show up," he said. "After I read the paper this morning. But I kind of figured you were a cop. You don't look like a cop to me."

"I'm from Indianapolis," I said. "I called you before I knew Melanie's husband had started things rolling like this."

"What's it about then? What I read sounds like she killed some kid."

"It's the kid that I'm trying to find. Her brother hired me to track him down, but I haven't been able to do it in time to avoid all this trouble."

He squinted. "Brother?"

"He's her half-brother," I said. "She's been staying with him and he wants to help her."

Jack just nodded without taking his eyes off me. "I think I remember now," he said. And kept nodding. "You wanted to know when I last saw her. Years. She left suddenly. Some guy came around waving a pistol when I was out one morning. He made a lot of noise but didn't actually hurt anyone. Then Melanie packed her bags and left. Someone from the house came to tell me as soon as the guy left, but by the time I got back she was gone. Never heard from her since. She left a note, but it wasn't dated. It was sometime around Memorial Day, 1966. I remember it was close to the 500. Big day for you folks in Indianapolis, Memorial Day."

"What did the note say?" I asked. "Do you remember?"

"I do, because I kept it and looked it up after you called. It didn't say much. Thanked me for what I'd done for her. Wished me luck."

"No . . . ?"

"Nothing that couldn't have been written at a hundred other times. But that's the way she is, isn't it?" He shrugged, as with wisdom.

"How long did you know her?"

"About a year. She kind of found me. She needed a place to stay, heard somewhere I have some room and a generous disposition. She'd been living pretty rough. Hadn't been in town very long. I did what I could, you know. Clean sheets. Hot meal. But she didn't have much to say. Not for a couple of weeks, used to just sit and listen to the rest of us. We didn't push. Then she started looking for a job. Got one, and kind of began to come out. Troubled girl, you know. You must know. What with one thing and another."

"Well, she is certainly in trouble now."

He smiled. "She was in trouble then too." Wryly.

I cocked my snook.

"Pregnant," he said. "I mean pregnant. Which wouldn't ordinarily mean trouble for a married girl, only she didn't have the best marriage, did she?"

"It's about this kid that I need to know," I said. "I gather from the kind of setup, from the kind of guy you are, that you helped her with it."

"People. My weakness," he said, shrugging again.

"You helped her find a place for it, am I right? Some folks who would take it unofficially. Bring it up." He frowned, but I tried to anticipate his trouble. "Problem is that no matter what arrangement you made with them about covering up where the kid came from, we are going to have to know who they are and what happened to the kid, because otherwise Melanie's going to be in all kinds of trouble."

He shook his head. "I . . . I can't really tell you somebody who has the kid."

"You have to," I said. "You must."

"Because," he continued, "she never had it."

"What?"

"She had it aborted."

"What?"

"Aborted. Abortion. Termination of pregnancy."

My mind whirled about; my understanding diminished. "Are you sure?"

"I should be," he said.

"You did it?" Involuntarily I glanced at his wood gouges.

"Christ no. But I arranged it for her."

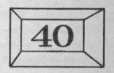

It's what I deserved, I guess, for committing myself to a theory before I had facts which demanded the theory. But when you're faced with a variety of lies it's not surprising that you spend more time picking and choosing among them than you do thinking about throwing them all out.

The essence of my business is checking purported fact. Crosschecking purported fact. And triple-checking if you can find a third slant on it. Genius lies in the ability to find ways of checking facts; it's a beginner's blunder to take anything at face value. *Anything.* Much less to draw unsupported conclusions from those unchecked facts.

The purity of this approach is diluted, of course, by what one is willing to accept as a check. I take my intuition, my gut. Recognizing its failibility, perhaps, but trusting it for the area truth is most likely to be found in. When Jack told me he had arranged Mels's abortion, I believed him.

"When?" I asked.

"Let me see. She was pretty far gone, so we had to do it pretty fast. End of June. Well before the All-Star game."

Oh. "I'm not much of a moralist, but what kind of . . . person did the work?"

Smile. "I've got a doctor friend," said Jack. "Nice friend to have. A moral service. Not for profit."

"Any chance of my having a word with this friend of yours?"

"A snowball's chance," said Jack.

I believed that too and didn't push. I had work elsewhere. I left him to wait for the grapefruit twins.

I can't claim that I had everything clear in my mind right away, but I knew, guts again maybe, that I had shot my bolt in Chicago, that I was due home. I drove back to my hotel.

One thing occurred to me on the drive and before I packed. I checked it. Freeman Kee's birth certificate: weight seven pounds and nine ounces. Let's see. Mels terminated by July. At the most a conception after the abortion would make the middle of November a four-and-a-half-month fetus. Very rare to get to seven and a half pounds by then . . .

Home, baby, home. I didn't even argue when they charged me for two days in the room. The cost of convenience. I sped to the airport and with a burst of unlikely luck I ran, literally, onto a plane about to take off for Indianapolis. ETA 5:45.

It wasn't until I was over Lafayette that I remembered I was supposed to be going to Artie's that night. Dear Doris, Sorry about tonight, but there was this abortion in 1965 . . .

I felt surprisingly little regret. I guess I'm a worker at heart. Rounding off a job . . . more satisfaction than a social occasion. Or maybe I am shy.

I called Penelope Bartholomew from Weir Cook and apologetically let her know I wouldn't be coming to dinner.

"I should have guessed," she said. "It wouldn't have been much of a party anyway. Arthur has been down at the police all day. Something about the case he was on down your way."

I assured her how sorry I was and to show my good faith I asked after Doris.

"She'll be disappointed, Albert," said Penelope pointedly.

To show my good faith I asked for her address and phone number in Ottawa.

"Just a minute, I'll get her to come and give it to you herself."

I did my best to convince Doris of my good faith and considered catching the next plane back to Chicago.

After we hung up I remembered Willson was supposed to be calling there tonight to leave me his phone number. I tried to decide whether he would have called already and whether I should call back. But he wouldn't have, so I didn't. Save it for later, when Artie might have made his idle way back as well.

I found my truck, stowed my gear and bought it out of its parking place.

"Hey, buddy," the attendant said lazily. "Y'know you got a big blue spot there on the backside of yore v-hickle?"

I was well aware of my backside and burned rubber as I left him. Insofar as my v-hickle was able.

Five minutes later I turned on the radio. I caught only the headline repeats. I learned the reported merger between Stark Wetzel and Indiana Bell was off, that the police were making progress in their search for Melanie Kee, mother of the missing Chicago child.

Hearing that made me drop back to the speed limit. Maybe they'd picked up Willson. Or maybe the elusive and dangerous private detective had been cornered and then captured whimpering like a puppy. I would definitely whimper.

Which gave me pause. I wondered if they had a pickup out on me. Or whether they had little friends waiting in my office. I had things at home I wanted to get for the trip to Kokomo, but they were just personal things, comfort things.

I stopped at a phone booth which was, my luck holding, working.

First I called the police. Using a silly voice I said, "I have a person-to-person call from Chicago for Lieutenant Miller. Is he there, please?"

Desk said, "I'll put you through." I recognized the voice of the desk officer, Sergeant Mabel. Back from maternity leave.

"Gartland."

"I have a person-to-person call for Lieutenant Miller from Chicago. Are you Lieutenant Miller?"

"Who's calling?" asked Gartland.

"Who may I tell Indianapolis is calling, Chicago?"

"Albert Samson," I said, as distantly as I could.

"Albert Samson is calling, Indianapolis. From Chicago."

"I'm Miller," said Gartland.

"No, he's not Miller," I said.

"My party says that you are not Lieutenant Miller. When will Lieutenant Miller be available to take a call, do you know?"

"I'm Miller. Put him on."

I flipped the receiver lever quickly. "I'm afraid Chicago has terminated his connection, Indianapolis. Good night." Bleep.

Miller being out didn't relax me any, no matter how hard I'd worked on the message that good old A.S. was in Chicago.

So I called myself. No answer until at the end of the fourth ring the call was intercepted by my very own Dorrie.

"I'm going to call back again in a minute, Dorrie, and I'd like you to let the phone keep ringing in my office this time. I want to see if anybody's there to answer it."

"Oh I got you, Mr. Samson. Do you want your calls? I mean since you called?"

"Sure."

"Well, a Mr. Miller has called twice today and wants to see you, that was his message. And a Mr. Willson called about fifteen minutes ago."

"Did he leave a number?"

"No. No message."

I called my office again and let it ring twenty times. Nobody answered.

I drove near home, parked on Pearl Street, a zig and a zag away. Walked cautiously. I got an idea. How about going up to the roof of the neighboring building and then across to the roof of mine. They are the same height. I crossed the Maryland and Kentucky intersection and had a look. There was a gap of about five feet between the two buildings.

Nothing. Piffle. Any fool could jump five feet. I could fall five feet.

I could fall fifty feet too. I got another idea. Crossed Capital to look at my building from across the street. Suppose I could get the fire escape ladder down, then manage to get myself up. But I didn't know just what the gain would be. I keep the window locked. Ah yes, I would be able to examine my living room to see if I had visitors. Was it worth the trouble?

It wasn't. I crossed the street, walked in the front door and went upstairs.

Nobody. I was being nobody's fool.

I got some fresh clothes and a little cassette recorder I bought last time I got paid. In case Goger didn't have one. Speaking of whom, I made a call. To Goger's in Kokomo. The housekeeper, my good friend, answered. I told her who it was. "I'm not going to ask you if he's there. But I'm driving up to see him this evening and I have some important news. If you do happen to see him, please tell him that."

She said she would, and from her tone I knew he was in the house. Presumably they were in the house.

I put on two extra sweaters and an extra pair of socks and walked slowly back to the panel truck. It was getting to be a delicate time. And I wondered if I was going to be delicate enough to handle it.

Two things happened on the way to Kokomo. First, I stopped at the library to pick up that book. Then a little later it started to snow. Wet, slushy snow.

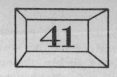

Mels, Goger and I had a long, long talk. We closeted ourselves in Goger's study and I told them truths. All the truths which would have saved so much time had Mels come forth with them in the first place.

Melanie simply is not capable of trusting people to help her. Even the people she asks for help. She never tells the whole story. Navajo sand painters do it too: when outsiders ask them to do a traditional painting, they leave it just a little bit unfinished. With Mels it's some kind of defense; always keeping something back helps her feel she still has some control over her own destiny. The type of person private detectives and lawyers should avoid like the plague.

She was disturbed when I told her things she'd lied about. It really upset her. But there are situations when nothing less than the entire painting will do.

She recovered though, once she understood the people sticking fingers in her pie were not just tourists looking for plums to take home. She felt guilty about some of the things; she doesn't approve of abortions, for instance. Though she had one. She cried on my shoulder.

I helped her feel better when I moved us past recapitulation. When I started talking about what was happening in the present. What I thought we ought to try for in the immediate future.

The question that took longest was what it would take to get Kee to move.

Other things were easier. Like what to do about Miller. I called him at home and puppet-mastered the strings of our friendship enough to get him to promise to drive to Kokomo in the morning. For a party. To come alone.

And the housekeeper. Willing to do anything for Goger, she didn't press for detail when we asked her cooperation in certain respects. I'm sure she loves him. That she was nasty to me at first because I was associated with Melanie Baer and it wasn't clear that Mels wasn't a threat. That's my theory; but I didn't press for detail there either.

But Kee . . . Goger and I had difficulty agreeing what Kee was likely to do in response to various stimuli. But Melanie was in the swing by then. Chicago to Kokomo is a long way to come for a party; she knew him best of us all and suggested: "Talk to him as if you've got him in the wrong. Just a hint. He can't stand seeming to be in the wrong."

We took the advice.

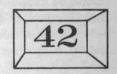

"Who the hell is this? Do you know what time it is? Nearly one A.M.!"

"Mr. Kee?"

"Yeah. What do you want? If this is another reporter you'll have to wait for the press conference in the morning. It's timed so you'll make your deadlines."

"This is Albert Samson."

"Who?"

"Albert Samson. I have some information for you that couldn't wait."

"Samson?" He remembered.

I said, "I've found your son, Mr. Kee. I've located your boy. He's alive and well. I thought you'd want to know at the earliest possible moment."

He didn't talk then, but I could hear him breathing. I checked to make sure the suction cup on Goger's microphone was secure. I'd planned to hold my cassette's microphone up to the earpiece but Goger, it turned out, was fully kitted for this sort of thing.

Kee came back. "I . . . I find it hard to believe that you have the right boy, Mr. Samson. After all this time, I mean."

"Children have been known to live even more than six years, Mr. Kee. Frankly, I'm surprised at your reaction to the news. I thought you'd be pleased. I called you first because when I met you I was deeply impressed with your desire to have your child back. I haven't even called my client yet. Or the police."

I gave him a chance, but he didn't say anything.

I said, "In fact I've come across something a little peculiar. It must be some mistake, but your boy seems to have been born on a different day than you thought. He seems to have arrived about a month, well let me figure it, three weeks and two days earlier than the birth certificate you gave me says."

"Then it can't be my child," said Kee bravely.

"But it is your boy, Mr. Kee. There just isn't any question about that."

"Where are you, Samson? Chicago?"

"No. I'm in Kokomo. Your wife left the child in the care of one of her relatives here."

"Is my wife there?"

"No. Just me and the woman who's been taking care of the child. I only just found him tonight. I haven't had any time to do anything but call you. Mrs. Seale is housekeeper to a rich local man. She doesn't get off duty until eleven when the guy goes to bed. She couldn't dig out the birth certificate until she was off duty and that's why I haven't called till now."

Kee was not at his most chatty. But then he broke my heart. "What's he like?" he asked. "The boy?"

What could I say? "I've only seen him asleep, but he has your coloring."

He didn't talk right away, again. I almost believed I could hear the churning inside his head. When he spoke he said, "I don't know whether to believe you or not."

I got offended. "Well, that's up to you. I considered it my moral responsibility to let you know first. Melanie has obviously abandoned the child. Mrs. Seale says that she will give him up to you if you really want him. It's up to you. But I've satisfied my conscience. I'm not going to run up a bigger phone bill for this good woman because you have strange doubts. I have other calls to make, you know. My client and the police."

"All right. All right," said Kee. "Just where are you in Kokomo?"

I gave him the address.

"And you and Mrs. Seale are the only ones who know about this?"

"At the moment."

"And the only ones who've seen that birth certificate?"

"That's right."

"Well," he said, and his voice drew itself up two or three inches, "don't tell anybody else about it. I'll tell you what I'll do. I'll drive down to Kokomo tomorrow and have a look. If it does turn out to be a mistake of some sort, which seems likely, there's no point in involving anybody else. I'll come down and check it out tomorrow, how's that?"

Swallow the vomit. "That's very good of you, Mr. Kee."

"And you *will* wait, and not tell anybody else about your 'discovery,' won't you, Samson? I'll pay any expenses you might incur, up to, say, fifty dollars. And tell Mrs. Seale I'll be more than happy to pay for this long-distance call."

"We'll be waiting for you, Mr. Kee."

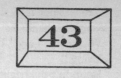

It was just that, the waiting, which was hard. It was a matter of what time he got here next day. If it was too early we wouldn't be ready. We wouldn't have a kid to show him, though Mrs. Seale, the housekeeper, assured us she could borrow one by late morning. Her eight-year-old grandson, but small for his age. We wouldn't have a birth certificate either; that was Goger's assignment. But before we went to bed we moved all the cars out of sight. Melanie's and mine to the street; Goger's garaged. We didn't want the man thinking we'd held a convention. And I declined a bedroom in favor of a couch downstairs nearer the front door. Who knows?

We got to bed by two, more or less. But I couldn't sleep very well. I kept trying to remember what I had said to Willson when I'd called him. Whether I was to call him back tonight. It bothered me; and kept me from relaxing and from sleep.

There was nothing for it. About two thirty I phoned Chicago, Artie Bartholomew's number. My name would be mud forever, calling in the middle of the night. But probably my name was already Moist Dirt.

To my great surprise Arthur answered the phone on the first ring.

"This is Samson," I said. "I was afraid I was going to wake you up."

"What do you mean? You think I get somebody to tell you to call me and then go to sleep?"

"Tell me to call you?" I asked humbly.

"Yeah. I've been trying to get to you for an hour. You mean that guy who left his number didn't tell you to call me?"

"I'm on my own recognizance."

"Well if that doesn't take the cake."

"I was calling to get the number that was left."

"After I tried your office, I called the number to see if the guy knew anything."

"You don't know who the guy is?" I asked.

"No. Didn't ask."

"Your good friend. Martin Willson ne Willetson."

"No shit. Midnight conversations with a fairy and I didn't even know. Must be getting old."

"Remind me to tell you a bitter truth someday," I said. "What were you calling me about?"

"Because I got another call, about an hour and a quarter ago. I thought you'd be interested in it."

"What?"

"The call," said Artie, "was from *your* good friend Eddie Kee."

"What?"

"Yeah. He mentioned your name in vain, that's how I know you're good friends."

"Well, what did he want?"

"That I should leave a comfortable, warm, friendly bed and go out in the snow. There's a blizzard here. I don't know what it's like where you are."

"Come on, man, don't drag your tongue; what's it about?"

"Well, it seems there's this private detective working for his wife who's trying to trap him."

"He said that?" I wished I had the recorder on.

"Sure did. Wanted me to go to Kokomo. Is that where you are?"

"Yeah."

"Go down and check it out. Find out what kind of trap you think you have in store for him."

"Why does he think it's a trap?" I asked.

"Well, you told him you have his kid, right?"

"Yeah."

"Well, do you?"

"What does he think?"

"He says you can't have his kid."

"Why not?"

"His same old song. He knows, I mean *knows*, the kid is dead. He sounded as sure as if he'd killed it himself."

"So what does he think I do have?"

"That, my dear Albert, is what he wanted me to find out."

"So why don't you?"

His voice took a graver tone. "Among other things because the Chicago police have seen fit to restrict my movements for a few days, because of what they think I know about their current hot case. That's why. And, unlike some people, I have a family to support and a license to protect. So I'm grounded. But I'll tell you this, Al. He's afraid of you."

"He should be," I said with feeling.

"I mean physically afraid, Al. Before I told him I couldn't go, he was pretty emphatic that I should be ready to use my *pistole.*"

"What?"

"He talked like he figured you were setting him up to do him some harm."

"That's crazy," I said, again with feeling.

"Well, in my reports I kind of emphasized the physical side of your functions for your client."

"Thanks a lot, buddy."

"Just to contrast with the high-minded delicacy and intelligence with which I'd been pursuing his side of things."

If he'd made himself look delicate, I must have been painted as a steamroller. "So what is he going to do, since you can't come?"

"Well, Al," said Bartholomew seriously, "he wanted to come out and pick up my gun for himself."

"And you let him, I suppose."

"Of course not," he said.

"Which leaves us with the big one, Artie. What's he going to do?"

"Well, he sounded like he was going to do it himself."

" 'Do it'? Shoot it out with me? That's going to be a little hard, isn't it, considering that neither of us have guns."

"But I think he does, Al."

"Oh great."

"I think he had one all along, but he just felt that all the money he's paid me gave him the right to use mine. I think he was looking for an extra way to hedge himself. No, I'm sure he has his own gun, but was mad that I wouldn't go down and do the dirty work for him."

"When do you think he's coming?"

"Sounded like tonight. You can see why I wanted to warn you, Al. I don't know what you've got on him, or what he thinks you've got on him. But I wouldn't go taking long walks in dark alleys."

My sleep it didn't help. I stayed up trying to figure things out. How far it was between Chicago and Kokomo; a good three hours as the crow drives. But in snow? And how would it fit with Miller's arrival?

I regretted having rushed into things. It seemed like such a nice idea at the time; prod Kee tonight, then while he was driving down in the morning use the precious hours to acquire the props. One child, suitable size and shape; a birth certificate to match. And then ask Kee why they couldn't be genuine. How can you be so damn sure, I would have asked. Miller, Mels and Goger secreted in a closet. "How can you be so damn sure?" I actually said it out loud, then looked around the living room, embarrassed. But no need. Just me and the candelabrum.

I'll tell you why you can be so damn sure this kid isn't your kid, I'd say, shaking the rent-a-child by the shoulders. Because you know as well as I do you don't have a kid. You don't have this child, you don't have *any* child, do you, Edmund Kee!

I cannot tell a lie, he would say. I did it all with my own little computer.

Enter eavesdroppers; my foot rises to take its place on Kee's chest: tableau of triumph. Willetson—no more need for an alias—parachutes in to join his amour at the moment of freedom from harassment. Fanfares, trumpets.

Only the dirty little coward had to go and get me thinking about guns.

But what can you do about it, I asked myself.

I strolled through a few front rooms. Checking the windows. They were locked. Mildly reassuring to know it for sure.

And then?

I spent a long time looking out the window in the room I was going to sleep in. It was snowing like blazes now. I urged it, willed it, to snow like double blazes. The deeper the snow, the slower the Kee. With it coming down like this—and hadn't Artie said it was blizzardy in Chicago too?—there wasn't a chance Kee would be able to make it here before a decent time in the morning.

Well, maybe only a little chance. And the longer it took, the better chance we all had.

Snow, snow, come today. Inches of it! Feet of it! Sleet! Ice!

I decided to lie down. I wouldn't sleep, I knew, but I could lie down.

I turned the couch so that nobody would see me from any of the windows in the room. I decided to read a little bit.

Sexual Patterns in a Midwestern Town was not the most fascinating tome I'd ever thumbed. Not every private detective's idea of titillation; most of us prefer something a little more direct to fire the fantasies. But I wasn't bored while I read it. I already knew about some of the people, which helps make nonfiction more novelly.

At one point I even got my notebook off the end table I'd left it on. I leafed back to the beginning of my notes on the case. Goger had told me about Melanie's father in our first interview. Freeman Baer and the earful he'd decided to give the sex scientists. "Nobody had more bastards than Freeman," Goger had told me. Six.

It wasn't hard to find the section which detailed Freeman's contribution. And it wasn't surprising that Melanie had come across a young man who turned out to be her half-brother. All six bastards were boys, every one. "Then I got married," said Mr. X. "A mistake from the first. We went to Niagara Falls on our honeymoon and on the train I started feeling bad. I spent a whole two-week honeymoon with mumps. And that made my balls swell up something awful. And were they tender! All I could do was rest. I don't think she ever forgave me for that. Never. She only gave me the one child, and that one a girl. Before I got married every time I turned around I was having a boy. But that's what marriage will do. In eighteen years she never forgave me."

And he obviously never forgave her. The book was my first direct contact with Melanie's father. It was the first time it had occurred to me his marriage had not been smooth before his wife died. Not even a blissful childhood for our Melanie. I made a note to ask some questions, if I ever got a chance, about that childhood.

I read about an hour, a little more. Then I turned out the light and fell asleep. It must have been a little after four.

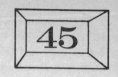

It was seven thirty when I first heard noises. I was awake in an instant. Still pretty dark. I rolled to the floor, scrambled for clothes to cover my underwear, and listened.

Someone was in the house. And downstairs.

The door to the living room—the door which led to the hall and the front door—was open. I didn't remember leaving it open. I was pretty sure I hadn't left it open. On all fours I scrambled toward it, peeped around it.

Nothing.

The sounds were not coming from my end of the house. They were wood and metal sounds and they came from inner reaches. Where I had no logistical knowledge. I hadn't checked windows and doors back that far. They were so firmly and regularly locked up front that I'd felt it foolish to intrude into rooms where I hadn't been invited. I felt foolish again now, but for different reasons.

It's a terrible situation to be in. To know there is danger nearby that you have initiated, virtually asked for, and then to have to decide what to do about it. Sensible thing, of course, is to run.

But faced with the actual situation I chose to stay. It's not the sensible decision, but what I'd never realized before, when I would flaunt my abstract cowardice, is that a dangerous situation I've created is different. Specific. To be sensible and run would make all past efforts and pain worth nothing. I had too much invested.

You can learn things about yourself, even at seven thirty in the morning. I moved down the hall toward the sound, as quietly as I could. I looked for a weapon. The only thing I found was an umbrella. I waved it menacingly a couple of times to figure out the best thing to do with it. To hit with the hook. Or use the point and plunge.

The notion of hurting someone made my stomach turn.

I got too close to a door. It opened suddenly and without warning. In retrospect I realized there was thick carpet on both sides of the door so I couldn't hear footsteps from the other side. It was so sudden, so surprising, all I could do was jump back as the umbrella was hit by the door. It turned out to be a push-button umbrella. I know. I pushed the button. Up the nylon flew, kind of filled the hall.

Nearly knocked Mrs. Seale's tray out of her hands. "Oh goodness!" she said.

"Good morning, Mrs. Seale," I said peering over the umbrella. I didn't really want to come out from behind it. But I did, finally.

"Mr. Samson! Heavens! Mr. Goger's umbrella!"

"Yes," I said.

"I don't think you'll need that this morning. It's stopped snowing. It's so very beautiful I'm not surprised you thought about going out for a look."

"Oh, I'll put it back then and go out now for a short walk," I said feebly. Fumbled. Finally folded it fully.

"I had a little look in the living room when I came down this morning," she said. "I didn't know whether you'd want to be getting up but I thought probably you would. So when I made breakfast for Mrs. Goger—that's Mr. Goger's mother, who's bedridden upstairs—I thought I would take the opportunity to make some breakfast for you as well." She gestured to the tray she was carrying. A silver tray with silver plate and silver cup. "If you'd like it?"

"Yes," I said. "Thank you. In the living room, please. Here, let me carry it for you."

"I am perfectly capable of carrying a tray of food to the living room, Mr. Samson."

Which she proceeded to establish beyond doubt. I followed behind her dumbly. We turned the corner into the living room and she said, "Shall I put it here on the table? Next to your shoes?"

I sorely regretted my shoes. Why had I put them there? I

couldn't remember. Probably to keep all my possessions to-gether in one pile so they could defend themselves against the luxury they were surrounded by. But I was brazen with it. "Yes, by the shoes, please, Mrs. Seale." Then, "Is anyone else awake?"

"Only Mrs. Goger. She always awakes early. I'm about to take her breakfast up now."

"Fine," I said.

"If you want that walk I'll take your tray back to the kitchen to keep the food warm."

"Don't bother. I will have a look outside, but I like my eggs cool."

"As you please," she said, and left.

I took a deep breath, then a toast half. Real butter. I put my shoes on. Took two more toasts and went to the hall for my coat.

A little look from the front porch just to be consistent. I even left the door open.

I wasn't three steps outside when I had an arm around my throat and the dark gray barrel of an automatic pistol staring at my left cheek up close. "If you make a sound, Samson, so help me I'll blow your foul head off."

"All right, all right," I hissed. "Whatever you say." He pulled me aside, roughly. Leaned me against the house.

The day was just beginning to make itself felt in the sky and on the pristine snow.

"You are a bad man," Kee was whispering in my ear. "Why do you call me in the night to tell me you have my boy here?"

I didn't get a chance to answer. From inside the house Mrs. Seale's upstairs tray banged against the open door. "Mr. Sam-son! Mr. Samson, can you hear me?"

I prayed that she wouldn't put her head out.

The cold barrel pinched against the flesh over my cheek-bone. "Answer her," Kee whispered.

"Yes, Mrs. Seale. I can hear you."

"I won't come out," she said. "But I want to know what time

that horrible man is coming. I'll have to explain to my daughter why I want my grandson, you see. And I want to know whether I should go as soon as I take Mrs. Goger's breakfast up or whether I'll have time to make breakfast for Mr. Goger and Mrs. Kee."

"You'll have plenty of time, Mrs. Seale," I said, all too truly. "You stay and make them their breakfasts."

"All right," she said, and pointedly closed the door. On all my plans.

Kee was neither slow nor stupid. "I should kill you, Samson," he said, savoring the words. He pressed me harder against the wall of the house and enjoyed it. He moved his gun to press my adam's apple. It hurt. But he wasn't pressing too hard. He was controlling himself, so I didn't fight it. Besides, my hands were full of toast.

"Don't do anything foolish," I squeaked hopelessly.

"If I needed to kill people," he hissed, "believe me, I'd kill you. Her grandson was the boy you were going to say was my child. I'm not crazy, you know. What do you take me for? Why is my wife here? I don't understand any of you people. You lured me down here. You were going to kill me, I suppose, to shut me up. You're scum, Samson. And my wife is scum. And if I needed to kill people I'd kill you both." I didn't need convincing.

Then he stepped back a pace and with his left hand he pushed the side of my head. Underneath the powdery top snow there was a layer of ice. In my everyday shoes I didn't have a chance for balance. A kid could have pushed me over.

When I was groveling he relaxed his self-control enough to give me a kick in the midsection. He had to take power out of it to keep his own balance, and my coat absorbed a lot. If he hadn't been lucky and got me just where you knock the wind out it wouldn't have hurt at all.

I lay gasping. I didn't know what in hell's name he was going to do next.

What he did was run. Carefully down the porch steps, first.

Then less carefully down the driveway. The icy undercoat wasn't thick enough to make gravel difficult to run on. It was the snow, nearly up to his knees, that kept his speed down to slow motion. I just watched him. I couldn't believe it.

All the way down here from Chicago in weather like this just to brandish his automatic, deliver a little speech and give me a kick. Lord knew how long he had been lurking outside the house until I had happened into his parlor. And when he decided that I had lured him to Kokomo to kill him, he just ran away.

It was insulting. If I had a gun I could hardly miss with the snow isolating him as a dark and lonely target. He hadn't even checked me for a weapon. It was really absurd.

Except for the fact that I was gasping in the snow and there he was, enticed more than a hundred and fifty miles, just running away to go home. All my plans kaput.

Well, screw that.

I took out after him.

It wasn't until I was halfway along the driveway and panting that I began to wonder whether I was doing the right thing. It was the gun that worried me. Of course if he shot me he'd really be on the hook. There was, however, one minor complication.

But I ran after him anyway and to my great surprise I gained on him. The going was slow, but five miles an hour is still faster than four miles an hour and Kee, like a lot of the horses I have

bet on in my time, looked fit but just didn't seem to be able
to run. If only he hadn't had such a big head start.

When he turned left at the end of the driveway I was only
about fifty yards behind him. Twenty seconds later I emerged.
In time to see his Dodge push through some snow and glide
onto the roadway.

The snowplows had been at work, as they are all night in a
heavy snow. Two lanes were reasonably clear. I was desperate.
He was getting away. Ten miles an hour and coming straight
toward me, but he was getting away.

I fumed with a need to respond to his intimidations. But I
didn't know what to do. I couldn't let him go, not just flit into
the sunrise. I'd worked too hard for too many days. I began to
realize how heroes are made. How men feel situations crumb-
ling and grow desperate to keep everything they've worked
for from slipping away.

So as he drove toward me, I walked toward him.

I don't think he understood what was going on. What I
intended. A matter of reducing the distance between us.

He got closer and closer. I couldn't see the expression on his
face. But I could imagine it. Red-eyed pleasure. About fifteen
yards away he turned on his lights, then his high beam.

I wasn't prepared. I stood rubbing my eyes. How long could
it have been for? Longer than most stunned rabbits get. I had
that advantage, the car was slower than a bullet.

When it was about ten feet in front of me I began to back
up. Carefully, no risk to my balance. A matter of reducing the
difference between our speeds.

When he was six inches away I stepped on his bumper and
jumped on his hood. My turn to give him a little surprise.

It did. As he saw me half scramble, half roll across the hood
toward him, he instinctively turned the steering wheel to
avoid me. I bounced flat-backed off the windshield. I grabbed
whatever I could as I felt the car go into a slide. I got a couple
of fingers into a water drain, and managed to hook a foot on
the aerial.

The problem for Kee, of course, was that I was lying over almost the whole windshield. They haven't yet made the car windshield I can't cover.

He sideswiped a parked car and stopped. For a moment. Just a moment.

I let go my holds and turned over to face him.

And his friend. I watched him take off a glove and transfer the gun to his bare hand. I saw his thumb cock it. I don't know if there is a thing to cock on guns like his, but that's what I saw.

He raised it. I saw the glint of the third eye, reflecting dashboard lights.

It was certainly my chance to get him into trouble. I could cross my fingers over my heart to give him a good target. Then he'd be in deeper trouble than he'd ever be in for inventing babies which never existed.

But I decided to pass the chance. I went easy on the guy. Instead of letting him shoot me I climbed up on the car roof.

Crazy, I suppose. Car roofs can't help showing where a full-growed man is kneeling. If he had really intended to shoot me, he could have done it then. Though it didn't occur to me at the time.

And perhaps it didn't occur to him.

Out of sight, out of mind. He backed the car out of the dent he'd made in an otherwise impeccable '71 Merc convertible and he started his slow journey along the street.

How jockeys sit on top of horses I will never know. I clung with tentacles I grew special.

He picked up speed. I began to realize how cold a roof is to ride on. And that from the roof the only way to go was down.

I seemed to have been cold half my life.

I nearly lost it at the first turn he made. Except he had to slow down to keep control. The street must have been very slippery indeed.

I think the very weakness of the roof saved me. It bowed to make a hollow for me to lie in. To sleep in. To freeze in.

Making it around the first curve brought us onto a street running out of town. I remember looking around. Not seeing anyone to shout to. I remember my eyelashes seemed to be freezing. I knew then if we ever got to open highway where he could get speed up, I was a goner.

He had an idea after that first corner. He got firm control in the middle of the straight street, then smacked the brakes to try to toss me off. It nearly worked. My right hand slipped and I slid feet first back onto the hood. I made a lovely dent. If his brakes had been out of alignment, if the sudden jerk had turned the car to one side as well, I would have been off. Instead I was roughly back where I had started, crouched upright in front of the windshield, instead of lying on it. If he had hit the brakes right away again I would have gone off the front and under the car. But he didn't.

I didn't wait for him to get around to it. I got my balance and lunged back to the roof. I half stood on the hood, my toes under the passenger side windshield wiper, half lay across the roof. The cold wind came straight up my coat; I felt like a trophy deer. The only thing it was good for was seeing where we'd been.

We rounded a second corner. I couldn't tell where we were going. It didn't look like a main road, but even at slow speeds I knew it wouldn't be long till we were into the country.

At the same time I was using every frigid muscle to hang on. I was trying to work out what I should do and when. I almost made a desperate move, when Kee hit the brakes sharply. It caught me by surprise yet again. But I didn't fall off. And as I tottered on the hood before hugging the roof again as affectionately as ever, I realized my foothold was more secure than it had been. As the motor warmed up residual snow had melted off and left the footing rather good, as footing on the hood of a moving car goes.

Then I spotted a man walking his dog.

"Help!" I called twice. I saw the dog turn a head briefly. But not the man.

And then I saw a sign which said, "Welcome to Kokomo." It got smaller. Our speed was picking up.

It was time to do something.

I spread my feet wider, using the new traction. If only we were going toward Indianapolis. Miller would undoubtedly be winging toward me at this very moment. He'd spot me. He'd save me.

Only the Indianapolis road is a divided highway. When I twisted gingerly to look in the direction we were going, I saw only two narrow lanes coming to a bend to the left. And two signs. One said "Young America 10"; the other said "Limit 65."

I made up my mind, measured my distance. When I figured we were half a dozen car lengths from entering the bend I kicked at the windshield as hard as I could. I kicked and kicked. I had visions of a billion tiny glass fragments blinding Kee, killing him. I wasn't in the best of moods.

I kicked with the right foot. Then the left foot. I put all the passionate violence I own into those kicks. I spread them around. If the glass was only cobwebbing with cracks, at least I would give him a spider's worth. I'd gone into his parlor; it was time for him to come to mine.

I felt the car losing its certainty long before I stopped kicking ribs, head . . .

He wobbled, then tried to take the turn. Only his vision must have been impaired because he oversteered and we went off the road on the left. He had started braking but he didn't have a chance. Under the drifted snow was a ditch. Deep enough to catch a car. I tried to brace myself on the hood but the sudden stop heaved me into the air. I twisted and cavorted, trying to see where I was going. I wasn't in the air long enough to hope I didn't land on any big rocks or logs. But I lay in the snow long enough after I'd landed to be thankful I hadn't.

My ride on the 247-horse open sleigh was over.

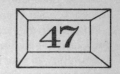

47

I didn't lose consciousness but I wasn't up by the count of ten either. I lay shivering. After a while I got to my feet and struggled to keep the shivering from affecting my vision. It was hard. I was pretty cold.

What I saw was Kee's Dodge stuck irretrievably. I saw a figure, must be Kee, standing on the other side of it. Must be checking if he could get it out. Then he came around the back of the car toward me. Must be going to ask me to help him move it. A weary traveler. Soliciting my Hoosier hospitality.

I saw, in a bare hand, a dark thing which improved my vision. That gun again.

He waved it. "I know what you want, Samson," Kee told me. "I know what you want." He may have said it several times before I began to hear, before it began to register. I knew what I wanted. One thousand heaters.

"I know what you want, Samson," he said as he clambered over the ditch line. Got too close.

"I know what you want. You want me to kill you, that's what you want."

I took a couple of steps backward; tripped.

"You would like nothing better than for me to lose my control and kill you."

My mind cleared. I tried to get up. Succeeded.

"But I'm not going to do it!" He was screaming. "You can torture me if you want but I'm not going to do it! I am not going to lose control for one moment and ruin my life. I don't have to do that, Samson. But when I get finished with Melanie I swear I'm going to ruin your life. I'll make it a misery for you. I don't have to use this!" He waved that all-too-familiar gun. But he shut up.

He had done a lot to warm me up. We stood for a moment in silence while I came to a boil. It was my turn to talk.

I took a step forward, then another. "You do what you want. But I came along on that ride for one reason. I have some things to say to you. I didn't get the chance while you were shoving me around on Goger's porch." We moved like a dance team. Through the ditch; I backed him against the car. I waved my weapon, the finger of accusation, in his face. A good feeling. A great feeling.

"You try to threaten me? Let me tell you something. You're not ruining anybody's life. Not mine, not Melanie's. Because I *know*, Kee. I *know* what you did and how you did it. I *know* why a kid in Kokomo couldn't be your son. You don't have a son, that's why. You caught up with your wife in Chicago and she told you she had that baby aborted. That's fact. All this missing-baby stuff you made up to get back at her. You created a child by punching some buttons. The birth certificate is phony. You put records of the kid in the Clephane Clinic's computer. You found a midwife you knew had died since then and placed her on the scene of the supposed birth. Every goddamn thing was phony! And you took it to the police and now you have them trying to pin the kid's murder on her. Now just how the hell is she supposed to have killed a kid who never was?"

He leaned against the car, quite calm. He said, "She did kill him."

"Now I know why people think computers are inhuman," I said. "It's the people in charge of them."

"She killed my child. *My* child. I didn't want her. I didn't want her back. Just the child. My son. Or daughter. It didn't really matter."

What can you say?

"She deserves everything she is going to get," he said, as the aggressive side of his coin spun back into view.

It wasn't the time to explain there were other ways to get children than to demand that a desperate woman bear one and turn it over to you.

After all that. Everything. I felt kind of sorry for the guy. The harsh Kee asked me, "Who else knows what you know?"

I laughed. "It's all in my notebook back at that house we left. The Indianapolis police should be there now. But you can go ahead and kill me now if you want to. You're the man with the gun." I put my hands up in mock surrender, but I got cold again and started to shiver.

"I can't shoot you," he said almost apologetically. "I didn't trust my self-control. So . . ." He stuck his left glove in his mouth and pulled it off with his teeth. The right hand was still filled with hardware. He stuck his left hand into his coat pocket and pulled out a magazine of shells. "So I took the clip out before I got out of the car"—shyly—"so I wouldn't be able to kill you even if I really felt like it. Look," he said, and he put the gun up to his jawbone. "It's completely harmless." He squeezed the trigger and blew his head off.

48

A few cars passed me as I walked back. Just another winter day in Kokomo.

I didn't leave as soon as it happened. Sometimes you watch things—maybe on the news—and you can't believe they've happened. Things too quirky or too unjust to be true. I just stood.

I never thought about where I was walking. I had crossed the railroad tracks and was at the site where the Hotel Frances used to be, when Miller's car pulled up within a snowpile of the sidewalk. The poor old Frances. Kokomo's finest till it burned down earlier this year.

Guns are like computers in a way. There's nothing necessarily evil about them, but they both attract a lot of flawed people.

I made my way to Miller's car and got in like it was the most natural thing in the world. I'd been thinking about my own little girl and Christmas. Wondering if there was still time to buy her a present and get it to the Bahamas by the big day. She spends every other winter in the Bahamas. Now.

The first thing Miller said was, "Are you O.K.? How are you?"

I said, "Do you know what the last mailing day to the Bahamas is?"

When you talk you talk to people; when you think you think alone.

I'm no expert on automatic pistols. Miller was the one who told me about shells getting into the chamber, but he also says you can't fire an automatic with the clip out. He says anyone who knew enough to modify the pistol must have known there was a bullet in the chamber. So Miller thinks Kee committed suicide.

I don't; but I'm only the person who was there.

Someone else said a lot of the cheap .32 automatics don't work right; I never read through the full reconstruction. I can only recall it the way I saw it. Left-hand glove clenched tight between his teeth; pieces of face separating.

That's when I got splattered with blood. It froze, red, on my coat and chin though I didn't realize it till later. I was pretty when I climbed over the snow to Miller's car. I've mixed in an unnatural amount of blood the last couple of years. I've had a run on the rougher side of life and I don't know whether I'm cut out for it.

Still, you take what you get.

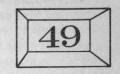

49

Everyone in the house was oblivious to what had been going on outside. Mrs. Seale hadn't missed me; I don't know what she figured I was doing in the snow. Maybe she thinks down south in Indianapolis we never see snow like they get in Kokomo.

When Miller had rolled up at the front of the house and walked up the impassable driveway he'd found Goger and Melanie having breakfast. Before too long they discovered I was not in the house.

Miller had suspicions anyway. On the way in he'd noticed the footprints in the snow. He'd looked at them, compared them to his own track and deduced that they were the trail of two people running toward the road.

"Must be my Indian blood," he said.

When he found I wasn't in the house he went back to the road. Found my panel truck under some snow and realized I was either on foot or with my running mate. He was never worried about me. Knowing how fit I keep. "Did you know," he said, "somebody's smeared a lot of blue paint over the back of your truck?"

Miller didn't know much about mailing dates. I showed him how to get to Kee's car. It took some thinking to work out which road it must have been. Roads look different from inside a car.

When we got to Kee, Miller was mercifully quiet until the arrangements for photographing and collecting the body had been made. I didn't realize quite what was happening; the whole thing had left me in some shock. I'm still amazed all that horrible, curling cold didn't do anything permanent. The doctor Goger brought in was amazed too, but I think he thinks I exaggerated what happened.

They put me to bed and didn't ask many questions. But by then I wasn't so far gone. While I had the doctor available I asked him some questions about mumps. He was very nice about it, a fine old bedside manner. I never did get his name. But he was very kind; he let me ask questions and then said, "Is there anything else I can tell you?" Before he left me to go do the post-mortem on Kee. I wouldn't let him give me a shot to make me sleep. Miller, my shepherd, promised to let him know if I got any more delirious.

The bed was in one of Goger's rooms. I slept on my own steam until about six that night. I was all alone in the dark when I woke up. I spent quite a while working on where I was. And then I wondered if the doctor knew when the last mailing day to the Bahamas was. He seemed to know everything else I wanted to know.

Finally I realized there was a light I could turn on, and when I did I found a note directing me to a button which, if pushed, was supposed to bring Mrs. Seale on the trot. I didn't know whether I wanted Mrs. Seale to trot or whether I wanted to get up myself. In the end I pushed the button. It brought a whole collection of people. Mrs. Seale, Mels and Goger. Miller and two uniformed Kokomo policemen. A plainclothed Kokomo policeman. And two other cops. One whose face was familiar but which I couldn't place. The doctor wasn't there, but they said he would be coming.

When I saw Mels, I sat up because I wanted to talk to her. But they pushed me down and took her out. "No!" I said, but it didn't seem to carry much authority. People always seemed to be keeping me from talking to Mels when I wanted to.

After a day or two, however, I couldn't talk enough for them. I spent most of my two weeks' recuperation going over and over the story, giving them things to check. They finally came around when they tracked down the family of the late Mrs. A. I. Keough, midwife. The old lady had been paralyzed on her left side for the last four years of her life. That's when they finally accepted that Kee had actually created the child in the memories of various computers he had access to, and had intended, from the beginning, to use his creation to harass his wife. Cops are resistant to that kind of thing; it's not their kind of human behavior.

Whether Kee ever believed he could get Mels convicted of murder we'd never know. But she'd have lived in hell wherever the story was public. Which he could make sure was everywhere she went.

The paralyzed midwife was the turning point. The familiar-face Indianapolis plainclothed cop, who turned out to be Captain Gartland, topped us all in the end. "Shit," he said. "A midwife. You should have spotted that a mile away, Samson. That stinks to high heaven. Nobody has midwives anymore. Where you been this last medical revolution?"

Overstating it of course. Some places are coming back to midwives. But don't ask me, friend, ask Kee. One presumes he would have given little Freeman Kee a hospital birth complete with footprints if he'd been called in to revamp some Chicago hospital's computer system at the right time.

Mels and Mars got back together when I managed to remember to have someone call Mars at his hotel. I didn't talk to them again for weeks. I was resting.

But I thought about them a lot. There was some unfinished business, but I thought about them in personal ways too. Mels more, of course, because she was the more elusive personality to grasp and was the class of the duo. But even Mars; I'd never seen him at his best. I wished I'd seen Mels more, not just to simplify the case, but because I liked her, the fighting qualities. There are a lot of things in life which give you trouble. You only have the energy to fight a few of them effectively. They had picked the fight that was important for them and had committed themselves to the battle. It was, in retrospect, a credit on their sheets which none of their other failings could take off.

On the Monday after Christmas I called Mars at the store and asked him if I could come out to the house that night.

"Anything special?" Mars had asked.

I wanted it to be a surprise so I said, "Just a chat. And I thought I'd give you my bill."

"I'd forgotten all about that," he said tiredly. But we decided it would be O.K. for me to come out that evening after dinner. He would call Mels.

By seven thirty, on the way out, I was in rare good humor. Relief-of-Christmas-being-over spirit and the excitement of the anticipation of doing something nice for someone else. So Mars was tired. I'd seen too much of Mars tired and not enough of Mels. With any luck I would correct that in time to come. I thought they might make friends for me and my woman. I figured they were just about due for some friends.

It felt like old home week when I turned off Indiana 42 toward their house. They had decorated the front of the house with Christmas lights and it looked positively friendly. Out in the country, I wondered who they could be intending all that electric cheer for. Immodestly I thought me, maybe.

Mels met me at the door. A little weary, from the look of her; you'd still never guess she was only twenty-seven.

She just said, "Hello."

Mars was relaxing in the living room. Mels ushered me in,

filled my hand with a drink. A hot wine and fruit concoction which matched my mood. Mulled, she called it.

"Cheers," I said, and thought about my present.

"You said you were coming about your bill," said Mars a little testily after I'd sat down and we'd all endured a few moments of silence.

"Yeah," I said. "We all have to live, and, much as I hate to admit it, that even includes me." I handed the accounting I'd typed up, the modest labor charge of $550 plus $250 expenses, over to him. He didn't even look at it. He passed it to Mels.

Who forced a smile. I thought it meant not to worry about it.

"It was work done on her behalf," Mars said defensively. "And she's the one with the money." Which I took to mean that her father's money had come through and was now spendable. I had a mercenary thought: a fleeting wish I'd doubled all the figures on the account. We all have to live.

"I hope you've had a reasonably pleasant Christmas, under the circumstances," I said, hoping to be chatty.

Mars just snorted. He acted like he'd never come out of the slide Mels's leaving had put him in. He raised his glass. I saw he was drinking whiskey.

I took the initiative then. "I haven't come out just to give you a bill. I could have done that by mail. I have a present, some news I thought you might be interested in."

"Oh yes?" said Mels, and she sat down. Mars didn't move or make any sound. I guessed that, in the circumstances, that meant he was listening.

"It's about your father," I said to Mels. Then I knew everybody was listening. "I don't think he was your father."

"We know," snorted Mars.

"What?" I said.

"Mr. Goger suggested the same thing while I was in Kokomo," said Melanie gently. "He showed me a book my father was in. Daddy had mumps on his honeymoon; that's what you were going to tell me, wasn't it?"

"Yes," I said. "It was."

"So mumps sterilized old Freeman before he got a good crack at Elvira," slobbered Mars on the last of my good mood. "What the hell difference does it make, does it really make? Melanie still made it into the world. He still brought her up and left her loads of lovely loot. I wax poetic. That's what I should be. A poet, a playwright."

"I would think," I said, "with Freeman's fertility record before his marriage . . ."

"Sounds like documentation of a stud bull," interjected Mars. He was not at his most charming.

". . . that there is a pretty good suggestion Melanie is not her father's child."

"That's what Mr. Goger said," Melanie said quietly.

It didn't go at all like I'd imagined. Maybe it was a bit much to expect them to go goggle-eyed and hurtle into each other's arms. But they could have acted like it was pleasant news. Even if they already knew it. It ought to mean a lot to them. No more need to hide, to live different.

I'd even half expected Melanie to ask me to find out who her biological father was. Though I'm an old hand in that racket, I'd decided not to do it for her, though if I did take it the best place to start was surely a now-elderly attorney residing in Kokomo.

But my news had not been a surprise; things weren't going as I had expected.

Melanie continued, "Mr. Goger said that when he was executor he found some letters in my father's desk which he thinks my father had just found. He thinks that when I left home my father waited a while and then decided to leave the house. He'd been cleaning out my mother's things and—"

"And found some letters and killed himself. Ho hum," said Mars. "People kill themselves every day in Kokomo."

It wasn't till then I remembered we were talking about his father too.

But, damn it, all this sourness is out of place. You'll be able to get married now, if you want to, and have your own kids.

I almost said it out loud. Instead we all sat and breathed audibly; I finished my glass of wine.

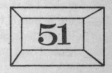

51

Things must have gotten better, because a month later I received an announcement that Mars and Mels had married. I remember considering whether I ought to buy them a present. But I didn't. They hadn't paid my bill; I sent a note of congratulation. Bought my woman a present instead.

By the end of March 1972, I was getting worried about the money. I'd heard nothing more from the Willetsons. By then my life was much as it is when it isn't going badly. I'd attended to those social fences I'd let fall into disrepair. Most things are reversible in life.

And work muddled on. A little here, a little there.

I considered calling Mels at home. But decided to leave the crass subject another week.

And the way it happens so often, the next day I got a letter.

Dear Mr. Samson,

I am very sorry to have taken so long paying you. It's only on remembering that I realized how much you have done for me. In consideration of that I have taken the liberty of adding a little present to the amount I owe you. Belated holiday greetings!

Being a detective, you have already noticed the postmark that will be on this letter. No, Mars and I are not on vacation. To come to it quick, I have left Mars.

Please! Please! Do not tell him about this letter, what city I have gone to. He will just follow and make a scene. I sure do pick them, Mr. Samson.

There are lots of reasons. The money that went to me was only part of it. My father loved me, that is all I can say about that, even if he wasn't my father. I just cannot seem to be what a man wants me to be, Mr. Samson. Are all men the same? I hope not.

But he was just never the same after all the trouble. I think he made me marry him because he thought he had to. He didn't, but he didn't know it.

I guess I shouldn't say all this, but I think you understand, I hope.

I can't think of anything else to say.

> With best wishes,
> MELANIE BAER

The postmark was Louisville, not every detective's idea of a March vacation.

I put the letter down with a sigh. Mars and Mels had stayed together with apparently firm adhesion because of a guilt, a common enemy. Now the source of the guilt was gone—how could things possibly have stayed the same for them? Now the enemies were within.

Of the two of them Mels was the realist. Mars undoubtedly would have squandered their lives, pissed and bitching. Whatever Mels's weaknesses, she had always been the sort of person to look for better ways to spend a life.

I looked at the checks she enclosed. They would have made

me happier if I'd had any reason to think she would ever be happy.

One for the $800 of my bill. The other, the gift, for $2000.

Not as much as I might have given me, maybe. But a lump of bread. Something toward a nest egg. Meaning that now all I needed was a nest.

MORE MYSTERIOUS PLEASURES

Order #	Titles	Price
	HAROLD ADAMS	*The Carl Wilcox series*
501	MURDER	$3.95
601	PAINT THE TOWN RED	$3.95
602	THE MISSING MOON	$3.95
420	THE NAKED LIAR	$3.95
502	THE FOURTH WIDOW	$3.50
603	THE BARBED WIRE NOOSE	$3.95
901	THE MAN WHO MISSED THE PARTY	$4.95
	THOMAS ADCOCK	
902	SEA OF GREEN	$4.95
	TED ALLBEURY	
604	THE SEEDS OF TREASON	$3.95
802	THE JUDAS FACTOR	$4.50
903	THE LANTERN NETWORK	$4.95
904	ALL OUR TOMORROWS	$4.95
	ERIC AMBLER	
701	HERE LIES: AN AUTOBIOGRAPHY	$8.95
	KINGSLEY AMIS	
905	THE CRIME OF THE CENTURY	$4.95
	ROBERT BARNARD	
702	A TALENT TO DECEIVE: AN APPRECIATION OF AGATHA CHRISTIE	$8.95

Order #	Titles	Price
	EARL DERR BIGGERS	*The Charlie Chan series*
421	THE HOUSE WITHOUT A KEY	$3.95
503	THE CHINESE PARROT	$3.95
504	BEHIND THAT CURTAIN	$3.95
	ROBERT CAMPBELL	
508	IN LA–LA LAND WE TRUST	$3.95
	RAYMOND CHANDLER	
703	RAYMOND CHANDLER'S UNKNOWN THRILLER: THE SCREENPLAY OF "PLAYBACK"	$9.95
	JEROME CHARYN	
906	MARILYN THE WILD	$4.95
	GEORGE C. CHESBRO	
907	BONE	$4.95
		The Veil Kendry series
509	VEIL	$3.95
606	JUNGLE OF STEEL AND STONE	$3.95
		The Mongo series
908	SECOND HORSEMAN OUT OF EDEN	$4.95
	DICK CLARK (WITH PAUL FRANCIS)	
909	MURDER ON TOUR: A ROCK 'N' ROLL MYSTERY	$4.50
	EDWARD CLINE	
804	FIRST PRIZE	$4.95
	K.C. CONSTANTINE	
805	JOEY'S CASE	$4.50
	MATTHEW HEALD COOPER	
607	DOG EATS DOG	$4.95
	CARROLL JOHN DALY	
704	THE ADVENTURES OF SATAN HALL	$8.95
723	THE ADVENTURES OF RACE WILLIAMS	$9.95

Order #	Titles	Price

ERLE STANLEY GARDNER

| 913 | THE ADVENTURES OF PAUL PRY | $9.95 |

JOHN GARDNER

| 103 | THE GARDEN OF WEAPONS | $4.50 |

BRIAN GARFIELD

301	DEATH WISH	$3.95
302	DEATH SENTENCE	$3.95
303	TRIPWIRE	$3.95
304	FEAR IN A HANDFUL OF DUST	$3.95
914	MANIFEST DESTINY	$5.95

THOMAS GODFREY, ED.

614	MURDER FOR CHRISTMAS, VOL. I	$3.95
615	MURDER FOR CHRISTMAS, VOL. II	$3.95
915	ENGLISH COUNTRY HOUSE MURDERS	$4.95

JOE GORES

| 518 | COME MORNING | $3.95 |

JOSEPH HANSEN *The Dave Brandstetter series*

| 647 | EARLY GRAVES | $3.95 |
| 809 | OBEDIENCE | $4.95 |

PATRICIA HIGHSMITH

706	THE ANIMAL-LOVER'S BOOK OF BEASTLY MURDER	$8.95
707	LITTLE TALES OF MISOGYNY	$8.95
708	SLOWLY, SLOWLY IN THE WIND	$8.95
724	THE BLACK HOUSE	$9.95

DOUG HORNIG

| 616 | WATERMAN | $3.95 |

The Loren Swift series

| 519 | THE DARK SIDE | $3.95 |
| 810 | DEEP DIVE | $4.50 |

JANE HORNING

| 709 | THE MYSTERY LOVERS' BOOK OF QUOTATIONS | $12.95 |

Order #	Titles	Price
	ED McBAIN	
524	ANOTHER PART OF THE CITY	$4.50
815	McBAIN'S LADIES: THE WOMEN OF THE 87TH PRECINCT	$4.95
926	McBAIN'S LADIES TOO: MORE WOMEN OF THE 87TH PRECINCT	$4.95

The Matthew Hope series

414	SNOW WHITE AND ROSE RED	$3.95
525	CINDERELLA	$4.50
629	PUSS IN BOOTS	$3.95
816	THE HOUSE THAT JACK BUILT	$3.95

GREGORY MCDONALD, ED.

711	LAST LAUGHS: THE 1986 MYSTERY WRITERS OF AMERICA ANTHOLOGY	$8.95

JAMES McCLURE

817	IMAGO	$4.50

CHARLOTTE MacLEOD   *The Professor Peter Shandy series*

627	THE CORPSE IN OOZAK'S POND	$3.95
927	VANE PURSUIT	$4.50

The Sarah Kelling series

818	THE RECYCLED CITIZEN	$3.95
819	THE SILVER GHOST	$4.50

CHARLOTTE MacLEOD, ED.

928	MISTLETOE MYSTERIES	$4.50

WILLIAM MARSHALL

929	THE NEW YORK DETECTIVE	$4.95

The Yellowthread Street series

619	YELLOWTHREAD STREET	$3.50
620	THE HATCHET MAN	$3.50
621	GELIGNITE	$3.50
622	THIN AIR	$3.95
623	THE FAR AWAY MAN	$3.95
624	ROADSHOW	$3.95
625	HEAD FIRST	$3.50
626	FROGMOUTH	$3.50
820	WAR MACHINE	$3.95
821	OUT OF NOWHERE	$3.95

Order #	Titles	Price

THOMAS MAXWELL

523	KISS ME ONCE	$4.95
822	KISS ME TWICE	$4.95
628	THE SABERDENE VARIATIONS	$4.95

RIC MEYERS

725	MURDER ON THE AIR: TELEVISION'S GREAT MYSTERY SERIES	$12.95

MARCIA MULLER   *The Sharon McCone series*

930	EDWIN OF THE IRON SHOES	$3.95
931	ASK THE CARDS A QUESTION	$3.95
932	THE CHESHIRE CAT'S EYE	$3.95
933	GAMES TO KEEP THE DARK AWAY	$3.95
934	LEAVE A MESSAGE FOR WILLIE	$4.95
935	THERE'S NOTHING TO BE AFRAID OF	$4.95
823	EYE OF THE STORM	$3.95
936	THERE'S SOMETHING IN A SUNDAY	$3.95
937	THE SHAPE OF DREAD	$4.95

FREDERICK NEBEL

712	THE ADVENTURES OF CARDIGAN	$9.95

SUSAN OLEKSIW

728	A READER'S GUIDE TO THE CLASSIC BRITISH MYSTERY	$19.95

ELIZABETH PETERS   *The Amelia Peabody series*

209	CROCODILE ON THE SANDBANK	$3.95
210	THE CURSE OF THE PHARAOHS	$3.95

The Jacqueline Kirby series

411	THE SEVENTH SINNER	$3.95
412	THE MURDERS OF RICHARD III	$3.95

ELLIS PETERS   *The Brother Cadfael series*

824	THE HERMIT OF EYTON FOREST	$4.50
808	THE CONFESSION OF BROTHER HALUIN	$3.95

Order #	Titles	Price

DAVID WILLIAMS   *The Mark Treasure series*

112	UNHOLY WRIT	$3.95
113	TREASURE BY DEGREES	$3.95

GAHAN WILSON

843	EVERYBODY'S FAVORITE DUCK	$4.95

CORNELL WOOLRICH/LAWRENCE BLOCK

646	INTO THE NIGHT	$3.95

- -

AVAILABLE AT YOUR BOOKSTORE OR DIRECT FROM THE PUBLISHER

Mysterious Press Mail Order
129 West 56th Street
New York, NY 10019

Please send me the MYSTERIOUS PRESS paperback titles below:

Order #	Title	Price

Please add another page for additional titles.

                                              Shipping

CREDIT CARD # _____

Circle One: AM EX, VISA, MC   Exp. Date   TOTAL

I am enclosing $_____ (please add $3.00 postage and handling for the first book, and 50¢ for each additional book.) Send check, money order or credit card only—no cash or COD please. Allow 4 weeks for delivery.

NAME _____

ADDRESS _____

CITY _____ STATE _____ ZIP CODE _____

New York State residents please add appropriate sales tax.